LOYALTY

A SCI-FI ALIEN ACADEMY ROMANCE

WARRIORS OF THE DREXIAN ACADEMY
BOOK TWO

TANA STONE

BROADMOOR BOOKS

This book is for all the nerdy girls who, like me, spent their childhoods happily buried in books.

CHAPTER
ONE

Torq

I hissed in a breath as I buttoned up my shirt and the fabric brushed one of the small burns on my chest, a painful reminder of the final challenge within the maze. It could have been worse, I told myself. Considerably worse.

I glanced at the empty bed across from mine, the bed neatly made with the gray blanket tucked mercilessly tight. My roommate wouldn't be returning, although I didn't know if he'd been a victim of an alien beast or one of the other deadly challenges. So far, no one could tell me, and I wasn't sure if I truly wanted to know.

We hadn't been close, but he had been one of the only other high-born Drexians in our cadet class, so we'd had a baseline understanding of each other, even if he had talked too much for his own good. Now he was gone, and the room felt unnervingly quiet.

At least I'd survived. At least I hadn't been eaten by one of the vicious alien beasts that had been roaming the maze. At least I'd made it out.

"Barely." Even now, I shuddered as I thought about the trials and how close I'd come to dying. No doubt about it, I would have died if it hadn't been for the other cadets in the maze with me and the two instructors.

I pushed this thought roughly from my mind. I hadn't been raised to be grateful to those who were beneath me, and every one of the cadets and instructors who'd gotten me through the trials were what my high-born family would consider beneath them.

Now my mind stirred with thoughts of my family, something I wanted to dwell on even less than almost perishing during the trials. But it was impossible to banish them from my mind forever, since it seemed like I was haunted by their influence even when I wasn't with them. Even when I was at the academy and far from their grasp.

I smoothed my hands down the front of my dark shirt, glad that my family hadn't been at the trials, glad that they hadn't witnessed me emerging from a ship filled with humans, glad they wouldn't know that I hadn't made it out solo.

But they would know. They always knew. It was one of the curses of being from a well-known clan. Their power and influence meant that they had friends—well, informants—everywhere.

I wondered if they had known some of the High Commanders who'd been dragged off the dais. Then I remembered that those Drexians had intended for me to die along with every other cadet, and I hoped that my family didn't have a connection to them. My parents wouldn't have allowed me to come to the academy if they'd known, would they?

That should have been an automatic no, but with my

parents, I genuinely did not know. If they'd been told that sacrificing their son would gain them favor with even more elite Drexians, would they have refused such an offer? The idea that they might not have rejected the idea outright made my stomach harden into a rock and familiar pain seize my heart. This was not the first time I had felt torn between the fear that I was nothing without my clan and the fear that trusting my clan to save me would be my end.

"You are not nothing without them," I told myself, even though the whispered words felt traitorous as they left my lips. As much as I'd relied on my clan's name to bolster my confidence in the first term, my status had done nothing for me when I'd faced down a monster. It had not been House Swoll that had gotten me through the maze. The deadly tests in the trials did not care about clan, and I was starting to think I should not either.

I pivoted toward the narrow slit of a window that let in hazy afternoon light and drew in a long breath, wishing that I could catch a hint of salt in the air from the sea. I imagined I could, and that I was standing on the cliff overlooking the Restless Sea sucking in breath after breath of crisp sea air that purged my body of all the anger and fear that had welled up in my chest.

A loud knock on the door brought me back to my dorm room and back to reality. My pulse jangled, not because the knock was unexpected but because I'd been waiting for it.

Making it through the maze had only been one part of the trials. Being selected by a school because of your actions in the maze was the part that mattered.

Of course, there was no part of me that thought I'd wash out of the academy, even though it wasn't uncommon. My own brother hadn't made it far enough to be placed into a school, a stain that still marred my family's legacy and had made them even more insistent that I join the academy and become a pilot, like so many of my forefathers.

My heart pounded as I placed my hand to the panel beside the door and it slid open. My chest was already puffing out in anticipation of greeting the representative from the School of Flight. But one of the Wings wasn't standing outside my door holding a sealed invitation.

It was an instructor from the School of Battle, the one who hung around Lieutenant Volten, and the envelope he held wasn't imperial blue, it was purple.

I fought the urge to shake my head. This couldn't be right. I'd been chosen to be a Blade? I was supposed to be a Wing. Every male who'd made it through the academy in my clan had been a Wing. Blades were grunts who were on the front lines of every battle, the first ones to be slaughtered, the ones who sacrificed the most blood and sweat in every war.

"Torq of House Swoll?"

I nodded mutely, my protests stuck somewhere deep in my belly, along with a primal scream.

"I am Kann of House Lannis. As an envoy from the Blades, I invite you to be initiated to our ranks." He extended the shimmery, purple envelope that was sealed with the gold emblem of two curved blades.

I managed to take the envelope, still without speaking, as Kann stood smiling at me.

"Your bravery and blade skills in the maze were admirable, as was your dedication to your team." Kann thumped a hand to my arm. "We need more brave and loyal Drexians like you in the School of Battle."

I almost laughed out loud at this. I'd never once thought of myself as brave or loyal. Even though the Drexian Empire prided itself on these traits, they'd never been championed within my clan. Personal glory had been something to strive for, perhaps even courage to fly into battle, but loyalty? The only things that had ever commanded my clan's loyalty was their own status and anything that could elevate it.

Even so, I liked the sound of it, and I liked the way Kann looked at me. Not like everyone else at the academy, who either wanted to gain favor with me or avoid me. The avoidance had come from the humans, and I'd brought that on myself. But what would it be like if everyone believed I was the Drexian Kann thought I was? What would my life be like if I was brave? If I was loyal?

As we stood facing each other in silence, Kann's smile faltered. "Do you not wish to be a Blade?"

I cleared my throat and found my voice. "No, I mean, yes. I would like to be a Blade. The honor of the invitation startled me, that is all."

If I was going to be a Blade, I would need to stop lying. Bravery, loyalty, and strength did not go well with deception. But for the moment, I did not want Kann to know that it had been shock and horror that had left me unable to speak. Especially since the disappointment was quickly fading.

Another glance at the empty bed reminded me that I was lucky to have survived and lucky to have been chosen by a school. Considering that no cadets were intended to make it out alive, I should have been dancing in circles that I was a Blade.

Kann's smile stretched across his face again. "I cannot promise you that the work of becoming a Blade will be easy, but I can promise you that you will emerge one of the fiercest fighters in the entire Drexian military." He slapped the side of my arm again. "Most of the Inferno Force ships are filled with Blades."

Inferno Force. I liked the idea of joining the elite Drexian fighting force. Not even my family could scoff at that.

Kann dropped his gaze to the envelope in my hand. "I will see you at our initiation. For the first time in the history of the school, we will be adding human cadets to our ranks."

Humans? My pride soured. Although I had worked side by side with humans in the maze and even proclaimed that I would go into battle with any of them, the thought of a female in the School of Battle made all my long-held beliefs about humans rush to the surface. "Female Blades?"

Kann wrinkled his nose. "Not females. Two human males were chosen for Blades."

I let out a loud breath, to Kann's amusement.

"No desire to spar with a female, cadet?"

I wouldn't mind sparring between the sheets with one particular female cadet, but that would hardly be allowed at the academy. I tried to stammer out an intelligible answer, but my mind went immediately to one female in particular, the one who'd intrigued me since I'd first met her, the last female I should ever have desired, the one who haunted my thoughts.

CHAPTER
TWO

Jess

T held the umber-bronze envelope in my hands, brushing
my fingertips over the iridescent paper. My name was
written on the front in darker ink, and it was a thrill to
see it lettered so elegantly.

The color of the envelope told me which school had chosen
me, even if I hadn't already known from the Drexian who'd
delivered it and extended a formal invitation to become an
Assassin. I'd been so shellshocked from surviving the maze
that I'd barely spoken when the tall warrior had stood outside
my door with the envelope in his extended hand. He'd said
something about the intelligence and skills I'd displayed in the
maze, but I'd only been able to nod along.

Now that he'd gone, and I was alone with the shock and
satisfaction, I blew out a breath and allowed my shoulders to

sag. Since I'd first heard about the academy and its four schools, the School of Strategy had been the one I'd desired. Planning and strategizing were what I loved to do, and I was thrilled at the thought of an entire division of the academy devoted to just that.

I carefully opened the envelope that contained the official invitation to the Assassin initiation and withdrew the ecru card inside. More scrolling text covered the paper, and I smiled as I realized that the invitation was a riddle.

Day is up and night is down,
But when it falls you know,
Go to where the words are kept,
And knowledge overflows.

That was easy. I was to go to the Stacks at sundown. My pulse quickened at this. What better place to initiate those cadets who loved research and reveled in wisdom?

A knock on my door drew my gaze from the invitation, and I pressed my hand to the panel to open it.

"Well?" Morgan hurried inside waving an envelope the same color as mine. "Did you get one too?"

I held up my invitation and envelope. "Strategy."

Her face broke into a wide smile. "I knew it." She wrapped me in a bear hug. "I had a feeling we'd both get in. How could we not? We're clearly the best cadets when it comes to Assassin type of stuff."

I laughed at her assessment of the skills needed to be successful in the School of Strategy. "Assassin stuff?"

"You know what I mean." She pulled back, her expression

still elated. "Maps, plans, strategy, patterns. I cannot wait to drop all the sparring nonsense and go deep into battle theory."

I didn't disagree with her. The Drexian Academy was heavy on physical challenges, especially during the first term when every cadet had to prepare to be tested in the trials and chosen for a school. Now that we'd survived that, I hoped my time in a sparring ring would be limited.

"You figured out the riddle, right?" Morgan ran her fingers through her blonde hair, which I noticed she'd styled since we'd emerged sweaty and slightly singed from the maze.

"Sundown at the Stacks."

She nodded. "A little simple, but maybe they're being kind after the trials."

"Kind would be good."

Morgan laughed, a hint of bitterness in the sound. "After almost being killed many times over, I won't argue with that." She gave me a brief up and down glance. "You ready? It's almost time."

I pulled my hair back and looped it into a low ponytail, which was my version of styling it, and nodded. "Let's do this."

We left my room side by side and walked briskly down the tower stairs, across a high stone bridge, down more stairs, and across the large, main hall. Other cadets passed us heading in different directions, and I wondered where the other schools were holding their initiation ceremonies. I noticed a few cadets walking with heads down and remembered that not everyone was chosen for a school. Even worse, not every cadet had made it through the trials.

When we reached the tall, wooden doors of the Stacks, Morgan and I paused outside them. Unlike the modernized doors throughout most of the ancient school, these doors did not slide open at the touch of a hand. They had been left heavy and looming, only to be parted when you leaned against them. The bottoms scraped against the stone floor and the hinges protested and creaked, more evidence that they were as ancient as some of the rolls of parchment held within.

Now that we'd reached the place, my heart thumped, and my pulse skittered. Familiar nerves teased me, telling me that this was a mistake, I wasn't good enough, I wouldn't succeed as an Assassin. I brushed aside the dark doubts that plagued me, just as I had every time before. I'd earned my place at the academy and in the School of Strategy. I deserved to be standing in front of the terrifying doors.

"Do we knock or go in?" I whispered to Morgan, already adopting the hush tones I did inside the Stacks.

Before she could answer, there was a resounding boom from inside that made us both jump. Then the doors slowly opened, both sides being pulled from inside at once.

I cast a glance at Morgan, who reached for my hand and gave it a squeeze. Once the doors stood fully open, we walked inside, our boots tapping softly on the stone floors.

The long tables had been pushed back so there was an open space surrounded by the towering bookshelves, and inside the open area was a circle of figures wearing Drexian dress uniforms. They held daggers to their chests, and glittering, gold masks covered their faces, an echo of the school's emblem. The light from the overhead chandeliers glowed faintly and cast shadows around the Assassins, making them look even more sinister.

Another boom of the gong sounded from deep within the Stacks as more cadets walked in behind us. When we were all inside, the doors were pushed shut.

A masked Drexian that I was almost certain was Admiral Zoran stepped forward to the center of the circle. I hadn't noticed the figures that had come up behind us until a blind-fold was wrapped around my eyes and given a tight pull so I could see nothing.

Then the admiral's deep voice echoed off the walls and the books. "Welcome to the Assassins."

CHAPTER
THREE

Torq

I'd never been in the atrium of the School of Battle, even though it sat in the middle of the building. The main corridor leading into the school fed cadets to the sparring rings, holo-chambers, and climbing walls that surrounded the atrium, but the central space was kept closed. Except for special occasions. Except for now.

I stood between two cadets I knew from first term as we walked slowly into the round room with weapons strapped to the walls: glinting, curved blades; long swords with ornate handles, shields with the School of Battle crest embossed on the metal. Shadows stretched long fingers across the stone floor from the only light in the space, a tall, bronze brazier in the middle with a blue flame dancing high in the air.

"The eternal flame," one of the cadets, Kort, said under his breath, as much to himself as to anyone else.

I shot him a quizzical look. "How do you know that?"

"My father was a Blade," he said in a reverent hush. "He told me about the eternal flame that honors the fallen Blades. We're the only school to have anything like this. As long as Blades fight for freedom and honor throughout the empire, the flame will burn."

I'd never heard about this, which made sense. My ancestors had been Wings, and I knew that the School of Flight had no such flame. Even though the ancient fire was not part of my personal heritage, I felt my heart swell with pride as I imagined generations of Blades defending Drexian honor all over the galaxy.

This now represented me and my Blade brothers. This eternal flame was part of my story, my pride.

"They say that the flame is cool to the touch," the other cadet said, leaning closer to me so he didn't have to raise his voice.

I glanced at Zenen, who had been with me in introduction to engineering class but had evaded much of my notice because he was not high born. Now that we'd both survived the trials and been chosen as Blades, that did not matter so much.

"How many cadets have tested that theory?" I asked.

He grinned. "I did not say it did not burn, only that it would feel cool as it melted your skin from your bones."

I shivered at this, wondering if the blue flame was part of the old magic that was rumored to be part of our planet's history but had been replaced by technology and advanced science.

More cadets filed in around us, and soon we were surrounding the saucer-like brazier that rose high over our heads but would not relinquish our gazes. No heat emanated from the fire, which gave credence to Zenen's story that the flame was cool to the touch, although I would not be the one to test this myself.

Shuffling sounds behind me made me turn my head to see older Blades assembling against the walls. When they had encircled us, they thumped their fists across their chests in unison. The thump made everyone pivot to face them.

"The School of Battle welcomes the newest Blades to our ranks," one of the elder Blades intoned, his voice booming and filling every space in the circular room. "You have been chosen for your bravery and your valor. You are now part of an elite fighting force that has led our people into battle for centuries. Blades are brave, strong, fierce, and loyal. There are none that come between us and our honor."

He strode from his place along the wall, parting the circle of first-years around the flame. Then he ascended steps on the other side of the brazier that I hadn't seen, and he stood at the level of the fire. He drew a curved blade from either side of his waist and held the gleaming metal over the twisting, blue flame.

Drawing them out, he pressed the sharp, curved edges together. Sparks flew from where they touched, spitting and hissing and making all the first-years take a step back. "The Blades are not to be crossed or to be defeated, not from without, and not from within."

He descended the stairs and walked purposefully around the cadets, leveling a hard look at each of us as he passed. "Do not cross the Blades."

The upperclassmen and instructors lining the walls repeated him in a thundering reprise. "Do not cross the Blades."

He said it again, this time barking the words with so much force that I felt them in my bones. "Do not cross the Blades."

Now all the first-years joined in, our voices rising as one

and bouncing off the domed ceiling and making the eternal flame flicker. "Do not cross the Blades."

My heart raced and my pulse jackknifed as the deep voices of my fellow Blades reverberated through me. All thoughts of the Wings, my family's expectations, and my misguided belief that I belonged somewhere else, anywhere else but in the School of Battle were purged from me like poison being sucked from a wound. I clenched my hands in fists by my side as pride pulsed through me, a sensation I'd never experienced in such a pure form.

I was a Blade. I was a proud Blade. I was a proud Blade who was part of a long line of brave Blade brothers. And I should not be crossed.

CHAPTER
FOUR

Jess

My steps were uneven as I made my way through the long tables toward the back of the hall. I'd had too much Drexian wine, and my vision was blurred as I made my way toward fresh air and quiet. More cheers went up around me as cadets celebrated making it through the maze, or older cadets celebrated inducting new cadets into their school.

I didn't begrudge anyone their celebration. I was thrilled to have made it into the Assassins, which had been the school I'd always wanted. After the treacherous maze, I would have been happy with anything, although I didn't give myself great odds for lasting long in Blades.

I lifted a hand to tap the new emblem pinned to the collar of my dress uniform, my fingers tracing over the shape of the long sword and the mask on top of it. Part of me still couldn't believe that I was at the alien academy, that I'd survived the trials, that I'd been selected to be in the School of Strategy.

I was just a girl from a small town in middle America, and whatever was the opposite of being born with a silver spoon in your mouth, that was me. Being an Assassin was lightyears—literally—from where I'd started, and part of me couldn't believe it was real and that it was happening to me.

The initiation had been everything I'd imagined from an induction into a school known as the Assassins. Standing blindfolded with upper class cadets and instructors encircling me had made me question my life decisions a few times before I'd successfully repeated an oath, had my blindfold pulled off, and the black cords wound around my wrists untied.

I touched my wrists and could almost feel the silky cords again. I could imagine that the loud din in the hall was the cheer that went up once the Assassins had taken off their masks and stepped forward to welcome me and the other new members into their ranks. It had been one of the proudest moments in my life, which explained why I'd felt the need to reward myself with way too much Drexian wine.

"Bad idea," I scolded myself aloud. "Awful."

I should have known better. People in my family were not famous for holding their liquor. Thinking of my mother's slurred speech and weaving gait that had been as much a part of my childhood as Barbies and coloring books made me regret even more that I had allowed myself to get drunk.

Once I'd reached the end of the tables and emerged from the long hall and into the cooler and less raucous foyer, I took a greedy gulp of breath. I walked to the stone banister and leaned against it as I focused on inhaling and exhaling until the dizziness—and urge to vomit all over my polished boots—passed.

"You okay, hon?"

I lifted my head to see long, skinny legs encased in shiny, orange pants. Pushing myself up, I took in the rest of Reina's colorful outfit, a multicolored, sequined tunic that would have looked at home in a nightclub. I managed to smile at her. "Just getting some fresh air."

"I don't blame you." She let out a high, chirpy laugh. "It's warm with all those celebrating Drexians." She glanced at the insignia on my uniform. "Congratulations on making it through, cadet."

My weak smile broadened. "Thanks. I'm excited for what comes next, although I think what comes next for me might be bed."

Reina patted my arm. "Why don't I get you some cold water before you decide?" She backed away from me and toward the open doors. "I get the feeling that celebrations here are few and far between, so you might want to savor this one."

I watched her return to the hall, pivoting away and breathing in deeply. The Vexling might be right. The academy did seem heavy on the danger and light on the parties.

I took another few breaths and leaned against the banister again. I did feel better. Maybe I could return and raise a glass with my fellow female cadets one more time before turning in.

"Leaving so soon?"

I pivoted to the voice, startled that it didn't belong to Reina, but relaxing as Torq sauntered from the hall. "Not leaving, just taking a break."

Before we'd made it through the maze together, I would have been nervous to be alone with him. The Drexian was big, strong, and handsome and had always emanated a dangerous sort of privilege, like he believed anything he desired was for the taking—including me.

He nodded as he joined me at the banister, stretching his

legs long in front of him and crossing one over the other. "Congratulations on becoming an Assassin."

"Thanks." Now that I wasn't surrounded by the heat of the candles and bodies and the swell of cheering and laughing, my head had cleared. I noticed the gold emblem on his dress jacket. "And to you for becoming a Blade."

He gave a half shrug. "I'm the first one in my family to go through the academy and not be a Wing, but since my brother didn't even make it past the first term and some Drexians didn't make it out of the maze, I guess it isn't so bad."

"Are you kidding? I could never be a Blade. They're way too tough and scary."

He grinned. "Tough and scary isn't bad." He leaned closer to me. "You aren't scared of me, are you, Jess?"

His question surprised me, but it wasn't unwarranted. He was at least a head taller than me and had always struck me as a predator slowly stalking his prey. Not to mention the fact that I'd caught him watching me more than a few times, and he'd cornered me in the female tower the night before the trials. Still, I didn't think that meant much. A guy as handsome and built as him wouldn't be into a nerdy girl like me. Hot guys never were. "Should I be?"

His smile was so silky that I almost didn't catch the narrow of his eyes. "Not if you give me what I want."

My brain was sluggish, but it wasn't mush. Growing up in a small town in Arkansas where there was nothing to do but hang out in the Dairy Queen parking lot or make out in the back of pick-up trucks had taught me how to spot a guy who wanted more than I was willing to give. "What?"

He moved quickly, his hands going to either side of me and pinning me in although his smile hadn't faltered. "I heard what you said in the maze about coaching. I know that you and the other humans got extra help."

I opened my mouth to spin a lie, but he cut me off.

"I have no plans on telling anyone. Who knows? If you hadn't been coached, you all might not have gotten us through those challenges."

"Is that a thank you?"

He laughed. "I don't mind admitting that I wouldn't have made it through myself, so I guess that is a thank you."

I didn't believe that he was going to hold his tongue for nothing, and I sensed that he hadn't followed me from the celebration banquet for idle chit-chat. "What do you want?"

He let his gaze roam lazily up and down my body before locking it onto mine. I forgot to breathe for a moment as I allowed myself to sink into the heat of his gaze, realizing only vaguely that he had striking, green eyes. Before I fell completely under his spell and released a sappy sigh, echoes of my mother's voice snapped me out of it.

It's a good thing you're so smart, Jessie, 'cause you aren't winning any beauty pageants.

I straightened, sobering even more at the memory of her backhanded compliments. I'd never cared about beauty pageants—or being pretty—the way she'd wanted me to, and being smart was what had gotten me an ROTC scholarship to college and away from that going-nowhere-fast-as-lightning-bugs town. But it reminded me that Torq wasn't leaning in close because he wanted me. He wanted something else.

"Kronock lessons."

I gave my head a shake, not sure I'd heard him right. "You want—?"

"You said you're good at languages. I'm not, but even Blades have to pass basic Kronock tests to advance. You tutor me after hours in Kronock, and I won't breathe a word of your other after-hours meetings."

My mind had come up with a heap of things he might

demand me to do for him, so being asked to tutor the guy in the alien language was a relief. "That's all?"

He leaned so close that his lips feathered my earlobe and sent a shiver of unwanted desire dancing down my spine. "For now." He took a deep breath, as if he was memorizing my scent, before he pulled back, his gaze dark and dangerous. "Then we'll see what else."

CHAPTER
FIVE

Torq

As I leaned close enough to Jess to breathe in the scent of her—floral and slightly sweet, as if she'd been dusted with sugar—my heart hammered recklessly in my chest. I was flirting with danger by even talking to her. I should back up, back away, and leave her alone. The last thing I should do, the worst possible thing I could do, would be to ask her to tutor me, which was exactly what I'd done.

Even worse? She'd said yes. She could have said no, kicked me in the shins, and told me to *grek* off. It was what she should have done, especially when I'd told her that we'd see what else I'd require of her.

Why had I said that? Why had I given her the faintest hint that I wanted her for more than her easy understanding of Kronock?

I bit my bottom lip as I backed away from her. Jess was the last female who should be occupying my thoughts. She was a human, whom I'd always been taught were an inferior species. Not only that, but she also was not one of the sweet and biddable tribute brides. She was a member of Earth's military who was tough enough—and smart enough—to make it into the Assassins. She was far from the type of female I was expected to take as a mate. She wasn't even the type of female I usually pursued for a fun fling.

Then why was I fighting the urge to nibble on her ear, kiss my way up her neck, and then capture her lips and see if her mouth tasted as sweet as she smelled?

Her eyes were wide, and strands of her dark hair had unspooled from her neat topknot, reminding me that she was quite pretty when her face wasn't buried in a book, and her nose wasn't scrunched as she peered at holographic diagrams during class.

You've spent too long watching her during class, I told myself.

"Have a nice night, Jess," I managed to say without my voice croaking. "I'll see you soon."

Once I'd backed a few steps away, she darted for the doors of the banquet without glancing back or responding.

I groaned and pivoted away from her. That had not gone well. I might have gotten what I wanted—more time with the human—but it was not what I needed. I needed to be focused on my upcoming work as a Blade. I did not need to distract myself with a female who could never be anything more than a diversion.

"Not that she wants to be your diversion."

I couldn't explain why she had captured my attention. It made no sense. There were more beautiful females. There were even more beautiful females at the academy now, but none of them drew me to them like the female who nibbled her lip when she concentrated.

Maybe it was because she was so different from me and from females I'd known that she fascinated me. She relied on her brains, while I'd always relied on a combination of physical strength and status. From what I could tell, she possessed neither, which made her the most tempting kind of forbidden fruit.

Instead of returning to the party, I headed down the stairs. There was nothing more for me in the banquet hall aside from a headache and even more regret. Blades might not be known for temperance, but I did not trust myself to be in the same place as Jess. A few more glasses of Drexian wine and I might tell her all the things I secretly wished to do to her, and all the places I wanted to take her to do them.

I slowed on the last two steps as my swollen cock strained the confines of my pants, and I paused at the bottom of the sweeping staircase, trying to think of anything I could to take my mind off the human. "A three-headed lizard, sour chidi berry juice, my brother's smelly socks..."

"Interesting mantra, cadet."

I almost yelped as my gaze focused on Kann standing in the shadow of the curving staircase banister. "What are you—?"

"Waiting for Volten." Kann straightened and joined me. "Tivek told me he and Ariana were speaking to the admiral, and then he escorted her to her quarters. I thought I'd catch him here."

"If he went to her quarters, do you really think he will return to the party?"

Kann frowned. "You make a good point. The odd thing is that neither of them have joined the celebration at all. It isn't like Volt to skip something like this."

I remembered how the flight instructors had looked at each other like no one else existed in the universe. "If I had a female who looked like the lieutenant..."

Kann barked out a laugh and threw a hand around my shoulders. "Another solid point, Torq. You're starting to sound as logical as an Iron."

"I assure you, I am no Iron."

"Neither am I." Kann walked us both across the wide foyer. "I would say we are both Blades through and through."

I thought his statement would make me flinch, but it didn't. After being initiated into the School of Battle around the eternal flame, I'd felt that I truly was a Blade. It hadn't hurt that all the upper-class Blades had welcomed me warmly, making me feel like I'd been inducted into a family. A family that embraced me more than my own ever had.

We reached the far stairwell that led to staff quarters and cadet dormitory towers but hadn't started up it before Volten bounded from it and almost knocked us over.

"I was starting to think you had abandoned the party," Kann said, his grin faltering as he noticed Volten's heavy breathing. "Wait, are you okay? Where is Ariana?"

Volten scraped a hand through his hair. "Packing up to leave."

"Leave?" The word shot from my mouth before I could stop it.

"Why would she leave?" Kann's question was calmer than mine. "I thought you two had worked things out."

"We did." Volten groaned as he sank to the floor. "I am not why she is leaving. Her sister is."

"Her dead sister?" Again, I hadn't thought before I'd blurted out the question.

"Her sister is not dead." Volten seemed almost dazed.

"Apparently, she is being held by the Kronock, and Ariana is determined to find her."

Kann drew himself up to his full height, his jaw tight. "When do we leave?"

CHAPTER
SIX

Ariana

My heart raced and my palms were damp as I wiped them down the front of my pants over and over and paced the length of my compact room. Sasha was alive? It wasn't possible, was it?

Volten had left me so he could get our ship prepared, although I was distantly aware that two flight instructors couldn't commandeer a Drexian ship and leave the academy without a solid plan. Right now, I didn't have the capacity to plan more than how many steps I could pace before turning and heading in the other direction.

My mind had been a messy tangle of dark thoughts and anguished scenarios since Admiral Zoran had revealed that my sister hadn't been shot down by the Kronock. She'd somehow been taken by the enemy, and only now did the Drexians and Earth Planetary Defense realize this fact. How could that be true? How could the aliens have held my sister all this time without anyone knowing? How had I not felt it?

That was what ate me up inside. Sasha had been out there this entire time, and I hadn't known. I hadn't been tormented by the sense that she was alive. I hadn't been convinced she had survived. I hadn't held out any hope that she hadn't blown up, like the reports had claimed.

What kind of sister did that make me?

"One who hadn't spoken to her sister in too long." I sank onto my bed and put my head in my hands. Now that I knew Sasha was alive, our petty differences seemed even less important. So what if we'd always competed for our father's attention? So what if we'd always fought to beat each other in everything? It had made us both achieve great things.

I didn't even care about our father's attention anymore. I was long past caring about his approval. But I did care about Sasha. She was the one other person in the universe who had been there with me, who understood my past, who knew me like only a sister could.

My heart twisted in my chest as I thought of her alone in some crude alien prison. Did she believe that she was forgotten? Did she think I knew she'd been taken and didn't care? Did she think she'd been abandoned by her fellow fighters? The idea made bile tease the back of my throat, and I jerked to my feet.

I couldn't waste any more time. Not when Sasha was out there alone and suffering. I strode to my dresser, opened the drawers, and started pulling out clothes and tossing them onto my bed. I didn't know how to pack for a rescue mission, or how long I'd be gone. From what the admiral had said, they had no idea where the Kronock were keeping Sasha. How long would it take to search Kronock space?

I turned to appraise the pile of clothes when my door beeped. I barely glanced at it. "It's open."

The door slid aside, and Fiona walked in beaming. "You're

missing the par—" She smile faded as she shifted her gaze from me to the pile of clothes. "What's going on here?"

"I'm packing."

Fiona nodded slowly. "Why are you packing?"

I released an exasperated breath. "Because I'm leaving, of course."

Fiona gave a brief shake of her head, as if trying to dislodge the confusion evident in her eyes. "Why are you leaving? Is this because of the mess with the trials?"

A sob welled up in my throat. "No, I would never be scared off by something like that."

My friend eyed me. "Good, then why—?"

"It's Sasha," I blurted, my voice cracking.

"Your sister?" Fiona's tone softened as she sat on the corner of the bed.

I nodded. "She's not dead. They thought she was, but they just discovered that she was taken captive by the Kronock."

Fiona put a hand over her mouth. "Holy shit." She reached her other hand to me and rested it on my arm. "I'm so sorry."

Her touch made my knees wobble, and I sank onto the bed next to her. "Thanks, but I don't have time to be sad. Not when Sasha is stuck in some alien prison. I have to go find her."

"You're going to go after her?"

"Who else?"

"Maybe the Drexian forces or the Earth Planetary Defense or some kind of specialized strike team that knows something about the Kronock?"

I stood quickly, my grief quickly replaced by the hot flush of anger. "She's my sister. I have to go after her. I can't wait for military bureaucracy."

Fiona glanced at the pile of shirts. "Your grand plan to run off by yourself tonight?"

"Not by myself," I snapped. "Volten is coming with me."

She rolled her eyes. "That's it? Two pilots against the might of the Kronock? That's insane."

"No, it's not. Insane is what I'll be if I don't go after her."

Fiona scraped a hand through her hair. "You can't just fly out of here!"

I hated fighting with the woman who'd become closer to me than anyone since my sister, but she was very wrong. I could just fly away from the academy. I could if it meant saving Sasha.

CHAPTER

SEVEN

Jess

"I had no idea the Drexians knew how to have fun like that." Morgan swept her blonde hair from her mascara-rimmed eyes as we walked up the spiraling steps of the female tower. The softest glow of sunlight was bouncing off the surprisingly placid surface of the Restless Sea and seeping into one of the slivers of window, as if confirming my friend's words.

"I don't think they do it often." I glanced over my shoulder to ensure that no one was following us. The only reason I hadn't come back to my quarters earlier was because I didn't want to leave myself open to being cornered by Torq again. It wasn't that I was afraid of the fellow cadet. After working with him to survive the maze, I knew he wasn't as bad as he wanted everyone to think he was.

I was afraid of myself when I was with him.

My heart tripped in my chest as I thought about his eyes resting on my mouth and how much I'd wanted him to kiss me. For a moment, I'd been sure he would. Then he pulled away.

Because he's not into you. Guys that hot do not go for nerdy girls.

Not that I cared. Not really. I was used to being overlooked while the pretty girls got the guys. It had been the story of my life, so why would the Drexian Academy be any different?

"Do you think we'll have a massive party after the battle between the schools at the end of the year?"

I looked at Morgan, trying to forget thoughts of Torq and concentrate on her question. "Battle between the schools?"

"Kind of like the trials, but it's schools fighting it out, and it doesn't take place in a maze." She cast her eyes toward the ceiling. "Thank you, whichever Drexian god finessed that."

I almost tripped on the next step, catching myself before I slammed my knee onto the stone. "There are more trials?"

"I said they're kind of like the trials, but not really. From what Fiona said, they should be less deadly, and they take place outside the academy."

"I guess that's good." How had I missed the discussion about this new competition? And why did there need to be more competitions at all? We'd already made it through the trials and into schools. Wasn't that enough?

"It's not until the end of the year, so we have plenty of time before we need to worry about it, although Fiona did say she wanted the Assassins to win." Morgan spun toward me when we reached the landing with our rooms. "Apparently, the Blades have won twice in a row."

Torq would be pleased to know that. Maybe it would make him happier with his school. Why was I thinking about Torq again, and why did I care about his feelings? If I thought about him at all, it should be to be outraged that he'd blackmailed me into tutoring, and implied that he might want more than that.

But instead of being flooded with anger at him, my heart pounded at the idea of what more he might want from me.

Oh, for fuck's sake, Jess. Get it together, girl. Stop obsessing over the Drexian hottie. He only wants you for what you can teach him.

"You can't just fly out of here!"

The sharp words brought Morgan and me to a standstill. That was Fiona's voice, but it was coming from Ariana's room. We exchanged a look as we stepped closer to the open door.

"What would you do, Fi? Sit around and let your sister be tortured by the Kronock?"

Whoa. Whose sister was being tortured by the Kronock?

"I'm not suggesting you do nothing, but you don't know where she's being held. All you know is that they have your sister. What are you going to do if you leave? Fly around hoping to run into a Kronock prison?"

Holy shit, Morgan mouthed to me.

Holy shit was right. I'd known that Ariana's sister had been killed defending Earth from the Kronock—everyone had known that, even though the lieutenant hadn't been the type to talk about it—but had that been wrong? It sounded like it, and from Ariana's frantic voice, it seemed like she'd just found out.

"I don't know what I'm going to do." Ariana's tone softened. "All I know is that I have to do something. I can't let her waste away…" Her voice cracked and bed springs creaked.

"Listen," Fiona's voice had also softened. "I know you feel compelled to do something. You're a pilot. Action is your answer."

"Actually, flying is my answer."

Fiona let out a low laugh. "Well, my answer to any problem

is planning. What your sister's rescue mission needs is a solid strategy."

"My sister's rescue mission?"

"Yeah, your sister's rescue mission. What? Did you think I'd let my new best friend fly off without a plan—or without me? And no way will I let your sister spend one more moment with the Kronock than is absolutely necessary."

"Really? You'd come with me to find Sasha?"

"You don't even need to ask. Of course, I'm coming. But first, I need to have a plan. *You* need to have a plan. And that means we have to find out where they're keeping Sasha."

Ariana exhaled loudly. "How do we do that?"

Without thinking, I walked into the room. "I can help."

Both Fiona and Ariana looked up from where they were sitting on the foot of the bed, startled that I'd materialized.

Only a beat behind me, Morgan strode in. "I can help, too." She cut her gaze to me and nodded. "We're Assassins. We know how to find information. If there's any way of tracking your sister, we can do it."

Ariana's eyes swam with tears as she smiled at us. "Thanks."

Fiona hooked an arm around her shoulders. "See? Leave it to the Assassins. We'll find your sister."

Ariana twisted her head to give Fiona a serious look. "I promise I won't fly off looking for Sasha on my own, but as soon as we have a good idea of where she might be, or can narrow it down to a few sites, I'm going. Got it?"

"Totally fair." Fiona gave her shoulders a squeeze. "But not without me, remember? And I'm guessing your boy toy will want to join the party?"

"Volten?" A laugh burst from Ariana. "I'm sure he'll insist on coming, but you have to promise me that you won't refer to him as my boy toy."

"I can only promise that I won't call him that to his face. When it's just you and me, all bets are off."

Ariana groaned but she was smiling while she did it. "I can't wait until you pounce on one of these Drexians, and I get to make up a pet name for him."

Fiona made a face. "You and me both." She turned her attention to us. "What about you two? Any gorgeous cadets catch your eye?"

Morgan and I both shook our heads quickly, our hasty denials becoming a jumble of nos.

Fiona's eyebrow lifted, but she didn't comment on the fact that we both protested a bit too much. "Good to know. That means none of us will be distracted by boys. We have all the time in the world to hunt for Ariana's sister." Then she added with a stern expression. "After classes, of course."

Classes and my forced tutoring sessions, I thought. At least I had plenty to distract me from the battle of the schools, which I was already dreading.

CHAPTER
EIGHT

Torq

Volten thumped a hand on Kann's back. "I appreciate you volunteering so quickly, but there cannot be a rescue mission to get Ariana's sister."

"Why not?" Kann shook his head.

To a Blade, a fight was almost always the answer, and Kann was ready to fly into battle. I understood Kann completely. When it came to our enemy, rarely did the solution *not* involve a bloody fight. Even though I'd never thought of myself as a Blade before being chosen, I now saw that it was a better fit than I could have imagined.

"I am with Kann," I said. "Why are we not gathering a strike team?"

Volten cocked his head at me. "You have been a Blade for

less than a day, and you are ready to join a strike team to go into Kronock space?"

Kann grinned at me. "A Blade is a Blade. It doesn't matter how long he has worn the insignia."

I instinctively touched the emblem of double blades that was now pinned to my uniform, pride surging through me. I was a Blade, and proud to be one, no matter what my family might think about it.

Volten crossed his arms, and his gaze shifted between me and Kann. "Before the two of you rush off with blasters blazing, we cannot mount a rescue because we do not know where Ariana's sister is being held. The information Zoran told us was scant. The only things we know for certain—almost certain—are that Sasha did not die when her ship exploded, she was transported out by the Kronock, and they are keeping her alive."

"Transported her out?" Kann's voice dropped. "The Kronock have the technology to do that?"

"You know those scaly bastards," Volten said. "Just when we think they are beaten, they return with new technology that makes them harder to defeat."

Heat buzzed my skin at the talk of the Kronock. I'd never encountered one of the creatures, but I knew Kann probably had when he had flown with Inferno Force. The elite fighters were usually the ones who battled it out with the Kronock, although all of the Drexian military had fought the enemy when it attacked Earth.

Kann stiffened, as if recalling memories of the Kronock. "I had hoped never to see the monsters again, but we cannot allow them to take our females and hold them captive."

Volten grinned for the first time since we'd seen him. "Do not let Ariana hear you refer to her sister as one of our females, and I am pretty sure you do not want her sister hearing you say that either."

"But the human females do fall under our protection," I said. "The entire planet does after we signed the treaty that established the tribute brides. We would keep their planet safe from Kronock invasion, and they would provide us with brides."

Volten nodded slowly. "Things have changed a bit since that treaty. We no longer take brides in secret. Now they volunteer. And the humans fought with us when the Kronock did finally invade."

"That does not change the core part of the agreement." Kann glanced at me. "The cadet is right. Earth is still under our protection, which means all the females from Earth are ours to protect. Abducting Ariana's sister is an act of war by the Kronock." Then he glanced at Volten and winked. "You know how I love a good fight and how much I hate when others touch my females."

Volten dragged a hand across his face and through his hair. "Sasha is going to love you."

Kann ignored the sarcastic tone. "Of course, she will. All females love me."

Volten let out a reluctant laugh. "Promise me when we do find out where Sasha is being held and mount a rescue party that you don't lead with the whole 'no one touches my females' line when we find her."

Kann ignored Volten, instead musing to himself. "I hope this Sasha is as hot as her younger sister."

Volten growled, but Kann just gave him an innocent smile. "You know I would not dream of touching your mate, but I'm not blind."

"Sometimes, I wish you were," Volten said under his breath.

"How do you plan to find her sister?" I asked, talking loudly and hoping that Kann had not heard his friend's comment.

Volten rocked back on his boots. "That is not exactly my area of expertise. I can fly you anywhere, but I need coordinates. Right now, we have no coordinates."

Kann shook his head, his levity gone. "The Kronock have so many outposts and occupied planets, even if they abandoned a lot of them, searching them all would take forever."

"We cannot even be sure she is at a location that is known to us. Since they have been in retreat, they have been better at hiding." Volten frowned. "I honestly do not know how we are going to find Ariana's sister, but I fear telling her that. If she knew how difficult it would be, her heart might break."

"This is not the first human who's been taken by the enemy," I reminded them. "Do you not remember that tribute bride who was snatched off the Boat?"

Both Drexians gave me blank looks.

"You know, the one who was taken to an old Kronock outpost for medical experiments?"

More wide eyes.

"I have not been paying much attention to tribute bride gossip," Volten said. "And I have never been to the Boat or the Island."

"Neither have I." I couldn't believe both Drexians had missed a story so big. "But my family talked about nothing but the rescue that Kax from House Baraat pulled off."

Volten's expression darkened. "Maybe they were interested because he was a High Commander and from one of the elite houses."

Was that it? My father had been friends with Kax's father before he had died, so maybe we had been more aware of the actions of his High Commander son than most Drexians. "That is not the point. The reason I brought it up is because a rescue of a human from the Kronock has been done before. Why don't we talk to the Drexian who pulled it off?"

"I think I remember this." Kann snapped his fingers. "But I think Kax left the High Command after the rescue, and after he took the woman he had rescued as his mate. He went back to intelligence work."

"Which means he will be hard to find," Volten added.

"I can find him," I said, before considering my words. It was not that I could find him as much as I knew Drexians who could find him. My father could find him.

Then it struck me that my father still didn't know that I was a Blade and not a Wing. He still did not know that I had failed to do what I had been raised to do. Once he knew that his last son had not carried on the clan tradition of joining Flight, how would he react? There was a good chance he would not be inclined to help me find a missing human.

Kann blinked at me a few times. "You can connect us with Kax?"

I squared my shoulders, summoned the confidence that had always helped me mask the doubts that swirled beneath the surface. "Absolutely."

CHAPTER
NINE

Jess

I stood in the back of the darkened lecture hall, waiting for a beat at the top of the stairs to let my eyes adjust. "Are we late?"

Morgan was next to me as we peered at the completely circular classroom, with rows of seats ringing a space below that held a single, clear lectern. "Not according to my schedule or all the empty seats."

"Maybe we're in the wrong room?" I'd had my introduction to military strategy in the Assassins building during the last term, but I hadn't spent much time exploring the school. However, I was relatively confident that this was the Oculus Room.

Unless I was wrong, in which case we'd be late for our first official day of classes as Assassins. Not a good look.

"You're in the correct room."

I jumped a bit as Admiral Zoran swept past us and down the stairs toward the center of the room. I only saw him at the weekly academy dinners, but it was impossible to miss the silver in his temples and the general air of authority he wore like a cloak.

He paused when he was halfway down the stairs and glanced back at us. "Will you be joining me?"

Morgan and I both snapped into motion and started to follow him down the stairs, but my mind was racing.

"Is *he* our teacher?" Morgan whispered, as the admiral lengthened the distance between us with his long strides.

I shrugged. "Maybe he taught strategy before he became the Academy Master."

"If not, he's the hottest sub I've ever had."

I shot Morgan a look as we slipped into an empty row of chairs near the front—but not so close that we'd feel like we were on top of the instructor, especially if it was the admiral. More cadets were trickling in behind us, loud chatter dropping to whispers as everyone spotted Zoran standing at the lectern with arms long and his hands grasping both sides.

I pulled my tablet from my bag, and when I looked up, the admiral's assistant was standing off to one side. I nudged Morgan. "When did he get here?"

"Two seconds ago. The guy is stealthy—and hot. I wonder if he was an Assassin, too."

I knew almost nothing about Zoran's ever-present assistant, aside from his name, Tivek, and that he had left the academy before he graduated and been taken underwing by the admiral. But I wasn't about to tell this to Morgan when the guy was within earshot. I also didn't know any more than that, and Morgan would want to know more. The girl was a stickler for details.

I cut my gaze to her and noticed her tracking Tivek. Did she have a thing for the admiral's assistant?

Zoran cleared his throat and the hush of conversation vanished in an instant. "Welcome to your first day as an Assassin. I've used my considerable pull as Academy Master to serve as your guest lecturer today."

I fought the urge to sigh audibly. I was getting used to big, intimidating instructors at the Drexian Academy, but the admiral made me nervous. Maybe it was the fact that he held the power to decide who stayed and left the school that made me so jittery, especially since I refused to fail. Not when I'd come so far.

I shifted in my seat, aware that others around me were breathing easier. Morgan's shoulders sagged as she slid down in her seat, which told me she might think he was hot, but she was also glad he wasn't going to be teaching us every day. At least it wasn't only me.

"If you got in the School of Strategy, I have no doubt you're all clever." Zoran swept his gaze across the class. "You're also probably shrewd and cunning. Maybe you were called sneaky when you were young, or maybe you were smart about hiding the fact that you noticed patterns in everything and could spot everyone's mistakes almost before they could make them."

There was a smattering of laughter.

I hadn't been called sneaky as a kid precisely because I'd figured out early on that being smarter than everyone—and letting them know it—didn't win you friends. It didn't even impress my parents, who thought I was acting too big for my britches. So, I'd hidden my intelligence until I needed it to get the hell out of there.

"Assassins see things others don't, but instead of punishing you for it, we reward you," Zoran continued.

My pulse quickened. I'd found my place. The idea of an

entire school devoted to strategy made my fingers buzz as I held them over the surface of my tablet, eagerly awaiting something to write down.

"You are the ones who will have to out-think our opponents, out-smart the enemy forces. You are the future warriors who will help us defend Earth and defeat the Kronock."

Cheers went up around the room, and Morgan and I joined in. Our first class was turning out to be a bit of a pep rally, and I was there for it.

"I'm not going to start you off with more war techniques or history of famous battles." The admiral released a small groan and the corners of his mouth quirked. "You'll have enough of that to come." He flicked his gaze at Tivek, who stood. "Today, we're going to play a game."

A game? If this was the part of the class where two extremely handsome cadets were going to pick teams, leaving me and any other geeky kids for last, then I was going to have serious flashbacks to elementary school and maybe a panic attack.

Now my heart was hammering in my chest like I was being chased. It wasn't a surprise that Drexians would make everything some kind of competition, but I hoped that it wasn't the kind that involved serious physical skills. I'd hoped that after going through my basic battle class last term—and after-hours coaching for the maze—I could relax into my Strategy classes, which should have been more cerebral.

"Pair up," the admiral announced as Tivek produced a box that had been tucked behind the first row of chairs.

Morgan and I immediately grabbed each other's arms, laughing at how fast and urgently we were grasping. At least I would only be competing against my friend. That couldn't be so bad, unless this was a Drexian version of the three-legged race and Tivek's box was filled with rope to bind our ankles together.

When he handed us a deck of cards, I stared at it for a beat. "A card game?"

"You have played Drexian cards before?" Tivek eyed me, and I could have sworn I noticed a hint of a smile teasing his mouth.

Morgan and I both shook our heads as my friend inspected the cards, which appeared to have the four emblems of the academy schools printed on them instead of suits.

"Do you think this is like poker?" I asked Morgan.

She flipped up the flat writing surface that had been tucked between our seats and fanned the cards out, then flipped them over so they fanned out in the other direction. I had the sinking suspicion this was not her first rodeo when it came to cards.

"I fucking hope so." She winked at me. "Full disclosure, Jess. I did take a trip to Vegas with some college buddies to count cards. Honestly, poker isn't my game. But if this is anything like blackjack, then I'd like to apologize in advance."

I laughed. "You're assuming you'll win?"

She leaned closer to me. "Don't tell me you're an ace at blackjack, too."

"I've actually never been to a casino or bet on a card game in my entire life."

She blew out a breath as she started to shuffle the cards on the mini table between us, removing and slotting small groups of cards into the deck over and over. Then she divided the deck and riffled the two stacks together at the corners and folded them into each other so neatly that I almost gaped. She tapped the shuffled deck and placed it on the table with the bronze Drexian Academy emblem facing up.

Morgan looked so pleased with herself that I felt I had to

tell her. "I've never been to a casino, but I have read a decent number of books on card strategy." When her smile fell, I added. "And I have an eidetic memory."

She cursed under her breath. "Now I wish I'd known you when we went to Vegas."

CHAPTER
TEN

Torq

I swiped the back of my hand across my forehead, the slickness coating my skin. If I'd thought the introduction to battle class during the first term had been an intense experience, my first official class as a Blade had taught me otherwise. My side ached from the nonstop sparring against the much more skilled and considerably less forgiving Blade instructors, and it even hurt to suck in a breath.

The steel cage rattled, as a cadet crashed against it, and the floor trembled as another cadet was knocked off his feet. I snatched a sip of steamy air that carried the remnants of sweat and the tang of blood before lifting my arms high in a defensive stance.

The Blade instructor facing me grinned. "You want more, cadet?"

I managed to nod, even though every molecule in my body

screamed for mercy. But I refused to admit how hard it was, I refused to back down. If I was a Blade, I was going to be the best *grekking* Blade the school had ever seen.

I'd spent my entire life being told what I would be and what I deserved. I'd believed that I was destined to be a Wing. I'd believed my clan entitled me to whatever I'd desired. And I'd wanted to be a Wing. At least, I'd thought that's what I wanted. It was what I'd been programmed to want.

Being chosen to be a Blade had shocked me into the reality that I was entitled to nothing at the academy. Being high-born entitled me to nothing that was not earned. Not even survival.

Now I understood that the academy would give me nothing I did not deserve, which oddly made me more determined. I'd been chosen by the Blades because they saw the potential within me to be a great warrior, and I would not fail them. I would not fail as a Blade.

Before my opponent could lunge for me again—and no doubt land another hit—the class leader clapped his hands. "That is all for today. Well done, cadets." He swung open the iron door. "You are all still breathing."

I slowly surveyed my fellow first-year Blades as I lowered my fists. They all looked as exhausted and battered as I felt, their bare chests displaying welts and the precursors to bruises. I put a hand to my own side, flinching at the tender spot that would undoubtably turn blue.

The instructor who'd bestowed the bruise on me threw an arm over my shoulder as if we the best of friends. "Nice work, cadet. You have got good instincts, even if your technique needs work."

I managed to mumble thanks, even though I wanted to punch him in the mouth.

He must have sensed my hostility because he grinned broadly. "It is understandable if you want to kill me. I felt the same way about my sparring instructors." He elbowed me in the side, sending pain shooting through me. "It means you are a Blade."

The final jab should have made me want to flatten him, but it didn't. His words sent pride pulsing through me. I was a Blade. I had found my place, and the instructor saw it as much as I felt it.

I joined the shuffling procession of cadets from the raised sparring ring and down the few steps, grabbing my towel from the floor and wiping off the sweat from my bare skin, moving gingerly as my muscles screeched in protest. I could only imagine how sore I would be in a day's time—and how bruised.

"You heading to the dining hall?"

I twisted to face another first-year, Kort, who had been in my flight class from first term. I'd never paid much attention to him since he hadn't been one of the cadets who'd given me the due I'd demanded. But those cadets had washed out or been killed in the maze, and I didn't care so much about being treated like a high born anymore.

From what I'd seen so far, no one in the School of Battle cared about your clan. They certainly didn't hit me softer because I came from a prominent family. Part of me wondered if they might actually be coming at me harder.

"Is it time to eat already?" I pulled on my sparring Blade shirt—black with the emblem emblazoned across the chest—and waited as Kort did the same. "Time passes quickly when you are fighting for your life."

Kort laughed. "They say it gets easier."

"When?"

He started walking toward the door. "It is nothing some food and drink cannot cure."

My stomach growled at the reminder that I hadn't eaten

since a quick sip of juice and a bite of toasted bread that morning. "I will meet you there." I walked beside him from the sparring chamber and down the corridor toward the entrance to the school and the main hall. "I have something to do first."

"Do not take too long. I cannot promise I will leave much of the good stuff."

I laughed, trying not to flinch from the ache in my side. "I will not."

We separated in the main hall, Kort headed up the stairs two at a time while I strode through the hall toward the School of Strategy. I hadn't forgotten the deal I had made with Jess, and I needed to be sure she had not either. She had promised to tutor me, but I had not seen her since, and it was time to remind her of our deal.

She is the last thing you need.

I ignored the voice in my head, the voice that knew I should focus on my classes and on surviving my Blade training. I knew I did not need her, but I wanted her, and I had not been able to deny myself all my desires in service to my new school. Not yet.

I spotted Jess before I entered the School of Strategy. She was walking under the archway with the Assassins emblem of the blade and mask carved into the black stone, and she was deep in conversation with the blonde from the maze. I searched my mind for the female's name, finally remembering that it was Morgan and that she'd been one of the women to decipher the climbing wall pattern. Now I could see that she had made it into the Assassins along with Jess, which made sense.

Jess's gaze flitted to me and then away just as swiftly. Was she ignoring me? I recognized the sting of rejection and then my automatic reaction to it, my instant need to cover the pain with bravado. I moved to step into Jess's path, but she stopped short, said something to her friend, and then Morgan continued without her.

Jess waited for a beat before walking to me and pulling me into the shadows beneath the stairs. "What do you want?"

Her hostile tone made it impossible for me to curb my own version of hostility. "I wanted to remind you of our deal."

She would not meet my eyes as she slunk further from view as cadets streamed past us. "Is that what we're calling it?"

"You are helping me; I am helping you."

She glanced at me, her eyes flashing. "You mean, you're not ratting out me and my friends."

Jess was much less agreeable than she had been when she had been a little drunk, but I liked this feisty side of her. "I would like to start tonight."

"Tonight?" She nibbled her bottom lip, and then nodded. "Fine. I'll meet you at the Stacks."

The Stacks. Had I ever been inside the academy's collection of books? Did I remember where it was? This was more evidence that I had always been destined to be a Blade.

"After dinner at the Stacks. I will be there." I couldn't stop myself from putting a finger under her chin and lifting her face so that she was forced to meet my gaze. "Make sure you are, too."

CHAPTER

ELEVEN

Jess

B ritta sat down across from me and Morgan in the cadet dining room. "Was that you I saw talking to the hot Drexian in the main hall?"

My heart lurched. I'd been so sure no one had seen me. Fucking Torq and his bullshit deal. Blackmail was what it was, even if he wanted to slap lipstick on that pig and call it helping each other.

"It's Torq, right?" Britta continued before I could deny it. "The guy who was with us in the maze."

I saw my easy out and took it. "Yeah. He wanted to congratulate me for becoming an Assassin."

"Really?" Britta flipped her long, silvery hair off her shoulder. "You guys looked pretty intense and not super friendly."

I attempted to laugh it off, but my laugh sounded strangled. "You know Drexians. They're always intense."

Britta swept her gaze at the Drexian cadets surrounding our table of human women—the loud laughter, the pounding on the tables, the heated discussions that seemed on the verge of exploding into a torrent of flying fists. "You're not wrong about that."

Morgan nudged me. "You sure you and Torq don't have something going on? You did pair off to fix the ships in the maze, and it was you he helped when we were almost gassed."

"Because I was standing beside him." I shook my head. "There's absolutely nothing between us. Besides, cocky guys who know how hot they are aren't my type."

Britta snorted out a laugh. "Then you might be shit out of luck at the Drexian Academy because this place is chock-a-block full of gorgeous, buff Drexians who know it."

"I don't know," Morgan said. "I thought Torq wasn't half bad in the maze. He pulled his weight and didn't call me babe or honey, which is more than I can say for some human cadets."

"Agreed." Britta reached for her goblet. "Before the maze, I thought he was a class A douchebag, but after working together in the maze..."

I'd thought the same thing about Torq before he'd found me outside the initiation celebration banquet. I'd thought he'd changed after going through the maze and proclaiming that he'd go into battle with any of us. I'd thought he'd reformed his arrogant ways. But then he'd pulled his blackmail crap on me, showing me that he was just as big of a dick as he'd always been.

My mouth went dry when I thought about him pinning me in and telling me that he might require more from me than tutoring. Then I thought about him lifting my chin in the main hall, his gaze hot as he'd warned me not to stand him up at the Stacks. I grabbed my goblet and took a drink of the chidi berry tea, wishing it was something much stronger. Why didn't thoughts of Torq enrage me? Why did they make my core heat and my heart trip? Why did I want a guy who would never desire me the same way?

"Enough about the cadets, what do you all think about the Drexian instructors?" Britta asked, as she leaned down and lowered her voice.

"Just as hot, but off-limits," Morgan said.

"Are they?" Britta's gaze locked on a group of Blade instructors who'd just entered the cadet dining hall. "Is there a rule against hooking up with the Drexian teachers?"

"Forget the Drexian teachers." A human cadet with dark skin and hair cropped close to her head joined us, sliding her tray onto the wooden table. "Seriously, you should forget them unless you want to end up on a transport back to Earth."

Britta frowned. "Party pooper."

Zalina gave her a playful shove with her shoulder. "I like a party as much as the next girl. What this academy needs are some gorgeous Drexian women."

I smiled at Zalina. "If you aren't into guys, there's not much love for you here."

Morgan held up a strip of fried padwump. "It's the ultimate sausage fest."

Zalina wrinkled her nose as Morgan took a bite and cracked off half of the strip of meat. "No, thanks."

I was grateful that the women had changed the subject and had forgotten about Torq. I was able to breathe easier as the conversation turned to the few mysterious Drexian females that remained in the society and how Zalina might score one, which was much more entertaining.

It was almost entertaining enough to distract me from the fact that I had to meet Torq at the Stacks later. At least we'd be in a public space, even if we'd have to hide ourselves deep within the towering shelves to avoid notice. Because as furious as I was with the Drexian, I did not trust myself with him. And I definitely did not trust him.

CHAPTER
TWELVE

Torq

T he moment I walked into the dining hall, I sensed her. Even as I fought the urge to look at her, my gaze was drawn to her like a magnet.

"Torq!"

Kort's booming voice snatched my attention and pulled my gaze to where he sat at a table of Blades, their broad shoulders practically touching. There was no doubt that the Blades were the loudest table in the hall, but the volume made me breathe easier. I would not be distracted by Jess's presence if I was surrounded by a bunch of rowdy Blades.

Kort motioned to a plate of food at the empty place next to him, and I crossed the bustling room to join him. "I hope you like *poplack* hoppers."

I glanced at the plate, bracing myself to see the quivering

dish. Thankfully, there was only some thick *gurley* stew and rounds of puffy Drexian bread. "Good one."

Kort laughed as I slid the chair out and sat, grateful that I was facing away from the table of humans, even if I did sneak a brief glance at Jess before turning to my food. She was not looking my way and didn't seem to know I was there, which was annoying. How was it that I could not stop thinking about her and she did not seem to care about me?

I recalled how her eyes had flared when I had tipped her head up to mine. I had thought—no, I had hoped—that it was arousal, but now I was thinking it was only irritation.

Maybe you should not have blackmailed her, idiot.

I growled, hating that even I knew that I had gone too far. But it was too late now, especially since it seemed to be the only way to get her attention. And for some inexplicable reason, I needed the woman's attention.

"Don't you think, Torq?"

I only caught the tail end of what Kort had said to me, but when I looked up the entire table was staring at me. "Yeah, of course."

They all grinned and nodded, and I wondered what the *grek* I'd just endorsed.

"Torq knows a few of them," Kort continued. "They went through the maze together."

We must be talking about the human females. I had not spoken much about my time in the maze. After the revelations about the sabotage and the involvement of the High Command, the trials were something that was muttered about darkly. Aside from the cadets who did not make it through, I knew almost nothing about what had happened to the other cadets in the maze.

"Does that mean you have an in?" Zenen eyed me, as if I might have the keys to the kingdom.

"Not really." This was no lie, although I might have lied even if I did have a tighter connection to the women.

The Blade visibly deflated. "You are telling me you cannot introduce me to the one with the dark hair who looks so serious?"

I stiffened. He meant Jess. She was so studious and unconcerned with how she looked that I was surprised that any other Drexian had noticed her.

"I would like to give her a few reasons to abandon her books," Zenen said, with a nudge to the Blade beside him.

"Or maybe just one big one," his friend added, and they both laughed.

A possessive rage tore through me, and I fisted my hands on the table at the thought of either of the Blades giving Jess anything.

"Torq?"

I managed to look at Kort, whose brow was furrowed as his gaze moved from my face to my tight fists. I quickly uncoiled my fingers. "Memories of the maze."

He nodded, as if thinking of what we had gone through explained my sudden change. "We were lucky to get out alive." Kort pointed to a pair of Blades at the other end of the table. "If it had not been for those two, I would have been eaten alive."

The mood at the table shifted, the conversation going from the pretty humans and what everyone wanted to do to them to tales of surviving the maze. Even though I had not talked about my experience so far, it felt good to hear others share their near-misses with death. As long as I did not let thoughts of the maze turn into thoughts of Jess, which was almost impossible.

I forced myself to focus on the stories and not on memories of holding up Jess when the toxic gas was enveloping us, the warmth of her body pressing against me as she started to go limp. At the moment, I had been so distracted by how right it felt to hold her that I had barely registered the fact that we were about to pass out or die. I had barely cared, as long as I could keep her in my arms.

I gave my head a curt shake, dislodging the memory and bringing myself back to the loud dining hall, the clattering of silverware on dishes reminding me that the maze was in the past. I stabbed a chunk of stew meat and took a bite, as Kort regaled the table with his maze survival story.

Then the group of females walked by our table toward the doors, and my gaze locked onto Jess. Her long hair fell down her back, and her ass swayed as she walked. The chatter slowed to a stop as everyone watched the females, and I knew that mine was not the only gaze on Jess.

You should not care. The human is the last thing you need.

Staying away from Jess was the smart move, but it was the one thing I did not believe myself strong enough to do.

CHAPTER
THIRTEEN

Jess

I paused at the bottom of the stairs, holding my breath and listening. Most of the other cadets were tucked away in their quarters, but some were still leaving the dining hall from dinner. When I was confident the corridor was empty, I hurried along it as light flickered from the sconces on the wall and sent long shadows stretching and writhing across the ceiling.

This was a mistake. I was too smart to be wrapped up in something as ridiculous as this, especially at my age. It was one thing to be sweet-talked into doing the quarterback's homework when you're a geeky freshman in high school, something I might have done, but it was another to still be doing the bidding of the hot guy when you were over twenty and one of a handful of women sent from Earth to the Drexian Academy.

I almost turned on my heel and headed back to the female tower, but then I remembered what Torq knew and what he could reveal. Now that we'd all made it through the trials and into schools, there was no way I could allow that to be put in jeopardy. Not if I could prevent it by doing a few tutoring sessions.

"How hard can it be?" I whispered to myself, as much to hear some sound aside from the soft tapping of my feet on the stone floor as anything. "I help the guy learn Kronock, and he keeps his mouth shut."

When I said it like that, it seemed easy. When Torq said it, when he locked his hot gaze on me, when he touched me and his flesh made mine burn, it did not seem easy.

I rounded the corner, so caught up in thoughts of Torq that I didn't stop to listen, and I walked straight into Reina.

She threw up her hands as we both staggered back. "I didn't see you there, hon."

I managed a smile at the Vexling, who was dressed in one of her usual dresses with so many bright colors that it almost hurt to look at her. "No harm. No foul."

Reina tilted her head. "What a funny expression. Earth language is so colorful. Now, by foul do you mean birds?"

It took me a beat to make sense of her question. "Like chickens? No. It means a foul like in sports."

"You have birds in sports?" Reina's eyes grew even larger than normal. "How bizarre."

I didn't have time to explain sports and fouls to her. Not when I was already running late. "We're a weird planet."

She giggled and her blue, vertical swish of hair quivered. "That you are, hon."

"Well, I'd better go." I backed away with a wave.

Reina swiveled her gaze around the dark and empty corridor, as if noting for the first time that I was the only cadet around. "Shouldn't you be in the female tower? Do you want me to walk back with you, since these corridors are so dark and spooky?"

I shook my head. "Nope. I'm fine. I don't mind the dark corridors." I did, but I couldn't tell her that.

"Are you sure?" She stepped toward me, as if she was going to join me regardless of my protest.

"I'm actually not going to the female tower."

That stopped her. "You aren't?"

I hated lying, especially to the Vexling who'd been nothing but nice to me, so I told her a half-truth. "I'm headed to the Stacks. I need to do some research."

Her confused expression fell away, replaced by merely a curious one. "What are you researching?"

I remembered what I should have been researching. "I'm helping Ariana search for potential sites where the Kronock could be holding her sister. The Stacks have records of all the Kronock outposts and colonies, and which ones have been abandoned. I'm trying to narrow the field of possibilities."

Reina pressed her bony fingers to her chest. "Aren't you the sweetest thing?"

I was reminded that Reina had spent a lot of time with human women as a tribute bride liaison on one of the Drexian space stations, so I wasn't completely caught off-guard by the fact that she sounded like she'd stepped off a wraparound porch in Savannah with a glass of sweet tea.

"I'm happy to help. So is Morgan. She's working with me."

Reina glanced around, as if I'd hidden Morgan somewhere nearby.

"Not tonight. Tonight, she's busy."

Reina nodded, and I knew I needed to stop while I was ahead. If I keep blabbering, I'd talk myself right into a corner.

"Then I hope your research goes well. I'm on my way to the kitchens to get Noora her evening tea."

I wasn't a tea drinker, but I wouldn't have minded a soda. Not that Drexians drank soda, or much of anything with sugar, one of the great failings of their society.

"Thanks. Tell Noora I said hello." I wasn't sure why I said that. I was pretty sure the Academy Master's wife had no clue who I was.

Reina gave me a final wave and hurried off in the opposite direction. I drew in a breath to steady myself and then continued, poking my head around the next corner before slipping around it. I'd almost reached the main hall when I heard heavy footsteps pounding toward me.

I ducked behind a pillar and held my breath in the shadows as the footsteps grew louder. The academy's security chief, who'd been proven not to be involved in the sabotage of the maze, strode by me without looking left or right. His silver hair glinted in the faint light, and his profile was sharp and stern.

Once he'd passed me, and the slapping of his boots had faded, I shuddered and took a breath. The Drexian might not have been guilty of anything, but he still terrified me. I craned my neck to see if there was anyone coming and started to emerge from the shadows, but I was jerked back into the darkness. A hand snaked around my waist and another clamped over my mouth, as I was tugged flush against something warm and hard.

Then breath tickled my neck and sent a shiver sliding down my spine.

CHAPTER
FOURTEEN

Torq

I held my hand flat against her stomach, fighting the urge to move it higher as I lowered my mouth to her ear. For a moment, I considered kissing the soft skin on her neck, but I thought better of it. "Don't make a sound."

My words had the opposite effect on her. Jess started squirming and making sounds against my palm, finally jabbing one elbow hard into my hip. When I loosened my grip and she whirled on me, she reminded me of a spitting *zerren*. "What the hell are you doing grabbing me like that?" Her words even held the same low growl as the striped felines made before attacking.

"I was trying to keep you from making a scene." I rubbed my side, which was unfortunately the same place I'd taken most of my hits in sparring earlier. "So much for that."

She put her hands on her hips and tapped her toe on the

floor in rapid-fire. "You thought groping me would be the best way to keep me from making a scene?"

"I did not grope you." I had wanted to—*grek* had I wanted to—but I hadn't.

"You touched me." Her eyes were narrowed at me, and I was surprised fire wasn't shooting from them.

I remembered the full contact grappling session that had left me bruised and breathless. "This is the Drexian Academy. If you cannot handle being touched, you are in the wrong place."

She huffed out a breath, glancing furtively left and right. "I agreed to tutor you in Kronock in exchange for you keeping quiet about what you know. I did not agree to being manhandled, so if you don't think you can keep your—"

"I promise I will not grab you again." I held up my hands in surrender.

She studied my face, as if searching for signs of deception. "Fine." She jerked her head to one side. "The Stacks are this way."

I shook my head. "We are not going to the Stacks."

She gave me another suspicious look. "Why not? That was the deal."

"The Stacks were never part of the deal. Tutoring was the deal." I cut my gaze from side to side, although the corridor remained empty. "I do not think either of us want to advertise what we're doing, and the Stacks might not be the most popular place in the academy, but they are not private."

"Where do you suggest?"

"We cannot go to the female tower. It is too suspect if I'm seen there."

"And you've been told to keep away," she reminded me.

"But I can get you into the cadet dormitory without being seen."

She choked back a laugh. "You want me to go to your room?" Then she cocked her head. "What about your roommate?"

"He did not make it through the trials."

Her eyes widened. "Oh, shit. I'm sorry."

One of my shoulders jerked of its own accord. "Not everyone makes it through. That is the hard truth of the trials, especially the last ones."

Jess relaxed her stance. Maybe she was remembering how we'd worked together in the maze, or maybe she was feeling some sympathy for me since my roommate had died.

I pounced on her hesitation. "I promise that I do not have anything in mind but tutoring." That was a lie, but the truth was that even if I wanted to act on my desires, I would not. I could not.

She nibbled on her lower lip, drawing my gaze to her mouth, which was not helping. "I'd rather not have to admit that I'm tutoring you or why. It would prompt too many questions. But if you try anything, you should know that I'll scream."

Grek, why did she have to say that? Now I was thinking about how much I wanted to hear her screams of pleasure. Even better? Her screaming my name as I—

"Torq? Did you hear what I said?"

I tore my gaze from her mouth. "Every word. You can trust me."

She made a face that told me she didn't. "You were great in the maze, I'll give you that. But I remember you cornering me at the bottom of the female tower, and I remember you hitting on our flight instructor. Your reputation isn't exactly stellar."

I wished I could tell her that I acted like an overconfident ass because I was the opposite of confident. Deep down, I was sure that without my clan and status, I was nothing. My greatest fear was that everyone would realize what a fraud I was once they peeled away my clan name and false confidence.

I had been able to reveal more of my true self in the maze, mostly because I was convinced we were all going to die, and I hated the idea of dying with people who despised me. But now I was a Blade, and I could not let anyone think I was weak. I could not bear if Jess felt pity for me, even though part of me ached to tell her the truth.

I thumped one hand across my chest. "I give you my word as a Drexian and a Blade, I will not lay a hand on you." Then I dropped my fist and gave her my silkiest smile. "Unless you ask me, and then who am I to deny you your deepest desires?"

She rolled her eyes back in her head. "Trust me, I'm not going to ask, and there's no way you could ever fulfill my deepest desires."

My pulse spiked as she started walking ahead of me toward the cadet dormitories. Why had she said that? Why had she issued a challenge that was going to torment me every moment of every day until I proved her wrong? Why did I now want nothing more than to fulfill her deepest, darkest desires and hear the screams she'd teased me with earlier?

Because you know it can never happen, and you're a glutton for punishment, I told myself as we walked toward my room, and what I could only guess would be the most exquisite torture cleverly disguised as tutoring.

I was a *grekking* fool.

CHAPTER
FIFTEEN

Jess

I hesitated on the threshold of his room, but then hurried in ahead of him in case someone poked their head into the hall. When the door slid closed behind me, I had to fight the urge not to make a run for it.

This is by far the dumbest thing you've ever done, I told myself.

Not that there were a lot of impulsive mistakes and foolish choices to choose from, since I'd been the quintessential good girl for my entire life. Unlike most of the girls in my hometown, I hadn't snuck out to go drinking in high school or fooled around behind the football stadium. I hadn't flunked out of school, or gotten knocked up, or gotten a DUI. I hadn't gotten so much as a parking ticket, and I hadn't been kissed until I was eighteen.

So, why was I in a Drexian cadet's room now? I'd managed

to steer clear of trouble when I'd lived in a place where I couldn't take a step without tripping over it, and I hadn't even made it through my first year at the academy before I was sneaking around and breaking rules.

"You can relax."

I swung my head to Torq, who was sitting on the bed. He might as well have been sitting on the end of a pickup truck and swinging his legs.

Oh, hell, no. I took a step back. "I'm relaxed."

Torq eyed my crossed arms and a laugh burst from him. "Are all human females as tense as you?"

I bristled at this. "I'm only tense because we were supposed to meet at the Stacks, and now we're in your room. I agreed to tutor you. Nothing else."

His smile dimmed, and he stood again. "Right. Tutoring."

As he pulled out the chair to his desk, I swept my gaze around his room. It wasn't much different from mine in the female tower—two beds, two desks and chairs, a pair of tall chests with personal items scattered on top of one. The empty desktop and lack of items on the second dresser reminded me that Torq's roommate hadn't made it through the maze. I didn't know which Drexian he was, as I hadn't gotten to know many of them during the first term, but it still struck me as sad.

My gazed snagged on a shiny emblem propped up next to a digital image of Torq and what must have been his family—a bunch of tall, handsome Drexians who smiled like they owned the universe. The emblem wasn't that of the Drexian Academy or even of the Blades. Those symbols I knew. This one was a sun surrounded by wings.

I touched the shiny embossed sun. "What's this?"

Torq paused in dragging the second chair to his desk. "My

clan crest." He joined me at the dresser. "House Swoll has produced proud Wings for a long time."

I could hear a hint of bitterness in his voice, and I noticed that he didn't touch the clan crest. "If my family had a crest it would be a bottle of Jack Daniels surrounded by Coke cans."

He tilted his head at me as I forced myself to laugh. "Is this Jack Daniels someone famous on Earth?"

My uncomfortable laughter died on my lips. "No, it's a type of liquor." I looked away as my face warmed with embarrassment. Great. I wasn't any less awkward on Drex than I was on Earth. "I was making a joke."

"So, your family crest does not have this Jack liquor on it?"

"We don't have a family crest. Maybe some families on Earth have them, but mine doesn't. We're not exactly what you would call a clan with a proud history."

Torq's gaze was penetrating, and now it wasn't just being alone in a guy's room that was making me feel weird. "You do not come from an elite family, but you were chosen to come to an elite warrior academy?"

"Things are a bit different on Earth." I released a breath as my thoughts reluctantly returned to my past. "If you work hard and are smart enough, you can make it without family connections or money. It isn't as easy, but you can do it."

"And you did that?"

How had this tutoring session become an exposé on my hardscrabble childhood and journey from nothing to the top? "Yep. I came from nothing and busted my ass to get as far away from that as possible, so here I am."

Torq's usual cocky expression had become curious and confused. Had he never met anyone who hadn't come from a fancy family like him? I knew the academy wasn't filled with only elite Drexians, although they did appear to stick together.

"I am not used to spending time with..." he paused, as if searching for the right word.

"Poor kids?" I asked in an attempt to finish it for him.

One side of his mouth quirked up. "I was going to say, females so smart they beat out everyone else."

"Oh." I studied his face to determine if that was what he was actually planning to say, but the Drexian appeared sincere, which was not a look I was used to on Torq. "Well, I'm not used to hanging out with rich kids."

Now his half smile grew into a full one, and the arrogant tilt of his lips returned. "There were no *rich kids* where you lived on Earth?"

"Literally none," I said, memories flooded my mind of the small Midwestern town that had been withering on the vine when I'd lived there and was probably now all but dead.

"I grew up surrounded by Drexians from elite families just like mine." Torq's expression flickered something unreadable for a beat. "You might have been the lucky one."

I snorted out a laugh then put a hand over my mouth. I wasn't trying to impress the guy, but it would be nice if I didn't repel him. "I've never thought of myself as lucky for having to struggle."

"Maybe you should."

I wasn't sure if he was serious or not. From everything I'd seen of Torq so far, his clan—and its status—were important to him. It defined him. He exuded arrogance that was only possible from someone who'd grown up with so much privilege that their innate superiority had never been questioned. The only hint I'd seen that there was something underneath all that entitlement had been in the maze when clan status couldn't fight off a monster or get him across an open pit of burning lava. Then he'd been different. Then he'd been real.

I cleared my throat, aware that we'd strayed far from the reason I was there. "We should probably get to the Kronock."

He blinked at me a few times before it hit him what I meant. "Kronock language tutoring. That's right." He held my gaze for another moment before he turned to the desk and finished dragging the second chair to it. "Let's begin."

For a second, I wondered again if I was really there because he needed help with Kronock. Then I brushed the thought aside. Why else would a gorgeous, elite Drexian need a nerdy girl with a no-account family like me?

CHAPTER
SIXTEEN

Torq

" Tell me again why this is your favorite holo-chamber program?" I dodged a flying ape with slashing talons, as Kann pivoted and stabbed it with his blade.

"Volten loves visting Ancarra." He swiped at his sweaty brow and grinned at his friend. "Is that not right, Volt?"

Volt jumped down from a branch in one of the leafy jungle trees and landed on the dirt with a thud. "What can I say? I love the climate here."

Sweat beaded across my bare chest and along my upper lip, and rivulets of it rolled down my spine and below the waistband of my sparring pants. "You enjoy this heat?"

"More than I enjoy the apes." Volten lunged toward an ape as it sailed through the air overhead, dispatching it quickly with his blade.

I shook my head. I was trying to remain flattered that the two instructors had invited me to join them in their weekly holo-chamber simulation, but I hadn't been aware that their idea of fun was being attacked nonstop in a jungle so hot and humid that I was sure we were being steamed alive. As a Blade, I enjoyed sparring as much as the next Drexian, but I was unaccustomed to doing it with sweat dripping into my eyes.

"This is good practice, Cadet." Kann tossed his blade from one hand to the other. "Not all battles will be on cold worlds like Drex or sterile battleships. Holo simulations like this will make you a better Blade."

"I am grateful that you invited me to join you," I said, which was entirely true.

Volt grinned and wiped his slick blade on his pants. "But you would have preferred the Corvaa Arctic simulation?"

Arctic? That didn't sound much better.

I tried to focus on the fact that the two instructors had included me, which had been a surprise, but I knew it was due to the unusual bond I shared with Volten since surviving the maze together. It had been a strange path to go from antagonists who'd actively disliked each other to reluctant allies in the maze to something akin to friendship after working together to survive the trials and get the rest of our group out alive.

I remembered my early days of the academy when Volten had glared daggers at me whenever I so much as glanced at Lieutenant Bowman. Now that they were openly together, his hostility made sense. But back then, I'd merely seen him as a low-class upstart who was daring to challenge me. Memories of my behavior made my face heat even more than it already was, if that was possible, and I was once again glad that I'd shed that part of myself. Well, most of it.

There was something about Jess that provoked both the

dominant side of me and the vulnerable one. I found myself opening up to her about my family but then demanding that she tutor me in secret and holding a threat over her head.

Because you know you're not worthy of her. You know she would never spend time with you unless you made her.

I growled, despising myself for my insecurity and weakness. A weakness that my family would have reviled and rejected. They would have told me that she was the one who was not worthy, and that any female should be honored to be with a Drexian of my status.

But I knew that was false. Jess didn't care about status. She didn't care about clan. Most nights when she was bent over my desk quizzing me on Kronock verbs, I didn't think she cared much for me.

"Have you made any progress on finding Commander Kax?"

I snapped my head to Volten, as he caught a smaller ape by the neck and tossed it aside. For a moment, I didn't know what he meant. Then I remembered what I had promised. I had assured Volten that I could use my connections to locate the Drexian who'd rescued a human from Kronock territory. The only problem was that it involved my father, and he had not responded to me since I'd left word that I had been inducted into the Blades.

I tried not to let it bother me. I tried to ignore the pain of his silence. I tried to tell myself that I was worth more than my school.

"I have not heard back from my source," I admitted and kicked a curling vine from my leg.

Kann heaved in a breath. "Who is your source?"

I considered lying to them, but that was the action of the old Torq. I wanted to be better, even if it pained me.

"My father is my source. He has known members of Kax's

clan for a long time, and he was close to his father." I drew in a breath of the air that was so warm it burned my nostrils. "He has been slow to respond."

Kann's jaw tightened. "He was not pleased you were inducted as a Blade."

I could feel his outrage for me even through the dense holographic jungle. "Our clan has always produced Wings."

Volten strode to the entrance of the holo-chamber and tapped on the panel until the simulation around us evaporated taking the cloying warmth and loamy scent with it. "I understand a bit about family not being pleased with your decisions."

Kann walked to me and slapped a hand on my back. "I come from a long line of Blades, so I do not know exactly what you're going through, but I can tell you that your school is more than just your classes. The Blades are your new family. We will be with you through it all." Then he grinned, his expression becoming both terrifying and heartening. "No one should cross the Blades. Not even House Swoll."

I'd spent my entire life devoted to my clan, but Kann's words made my chest expand with pride and my throat tighten. I nodded mutely, unable to form words.

Volten turned and gave me his own nod. "You will find that it is your academy family and your school that stand by you through everything." He winked at Kann. "You will even discover that Blades and Wings can be as close as blood brothers."

"Closer," Kann added, his voice hoarse.

I managed to smile at both Drexians as we left the holo-chamber. As much as I appreciated their words, their support made me even more determined to get the information for Volten. I had made a promise, and I intended to keep it, no matter how my father felt about me being a Blade.

At least my family would never know that I desired a female from the human equivalent of a low clan. Then there would be no returning to their good graces if they ever discovered that. I would be cast aside for good.

Which is why you should be glad that there is nothing between you and Jess, I told myself. Nothing to push you further from your clan. Nothing to widen the chasm between you and your family.

Then the wicked voice in the back of my head—the one that had always plunged me into trouble, the one I could never fully suppress—chuckled. *Not yet.*

CHAPTER
SEVENTEEN

Jess

"I might be going blind." Morgan let her head flop between her shoulder blades as she hunched over an oversized book that was bound with what looked like snakeskin. Her blonde hair was pulled high in a messy topknot, which bobbled as she dropped her head.

I stole a glance above us at the hanging wrought iron chandeliers suspended from the vaulted stone ceiling of the Stacks, and then at the flickering lamp on the table between us. We'd been poring over documents for hours, and my eyes were starting to burn. I inhaled the distinct scent of dust and leather, a smell that seemed to permeate libraries no matter what planet they were on. "We should take a break."

Morgan lifted her head and released a mournful sigh. "How can we take a break? We haven't made any progress."

I eyed the stack of books I'd already scoured as well as the tablet that glowed at me from where it sat on the long, dark wood table. "Just because we haven't found clues to where the Kronock might be holding a prisoner doesn't mean we haven't made progress." I held up my tablet. "I've been keeping a list of all the outposts and colonies we've ruled out. That's something."

Morgan straightened and blew a loose strand of hair from her eyes. "I guess you're right. Eliminating options is a form of progress, but are we sure none of these places are possibilities?"

I swiped a finger down the screen. "Every location on this list is one that's been reclaimed by the original inhabitants or is currently being rebuilt by the Drexians, so I'm pretty confident."

Morgan nodded. "You're right. This is progress."

"Which is more than I can say for my Strategy homework." I put down my tablet and arched my back into a stretch.

My friend let loose a string of colorful curses. "Is that due tomorrow?"

"No, but it's due the day after that, and I haven't started it."

More curses from Morgan. "Same, but I'm sure Fiona will give us a pass, right?"

"Why am I giving you a pass?"

We both jerked to attention, almost knocking our chairs over in an attempt to push them back and stand at attention. Before we could injure ourselves, both Fiona and Ariana emerged from behind one of the towering bookshelves.

"At ease, Cadets." Fiona held up her hands. "What have I told you about saluting me and standing at attention?"

"Not to do it." I shared a grateful glance with Morgan, who'd also forgotten the captain's request. Saluting and snapping to attention were second nature after being in the military, and none of the cadets who'd been sent from Earth weren't already officers.

"Since we live in the same tower and on the same floor, we'd spend half our days saluting," Ariana added with a half-smile. She hadn't smiled fully since she'd learned that her sister was being held by the enemy, and the line between her eyes had become a deep groove. But she'd been convinced to wait until there was a target to mount a rescue, and she continued to teach her classes.

Morgan was halfway to standing and sank back into her chair. "I don't think I could handle it if we added nonstop saluting to my plate."

"Does this have something to do with the pass I'm giving you?" Fiona crossed her arms as she swung her gaze from Morgan to me.

"That was partially a joke." Morgan's cheeks mottled pink. "We've been so busy researching potential locations the Kronock could be holding prisoners that we might have forgotten to start our Strategy homework."

Ariana sucked in a breath, as she cut her gaze to the books piled on our table. "This is all research to find my sister?"

"Like Morgan said, we went down a bit of a rabbit hole." I shifted from one foot to the other since I'd remained standing. The thought of turning in an assignment late made my skin prickle with unease. I hadn't gotten where I was by slacking on anything, ever, for any reason. "But that doesn't mean we're not going to complete our work for your class, Captain."

Fiona's stance had relaxed. "If anything deserves a pass, it's this." She touched a hand to Ariana's arm as the woman gaped at our research. "Have you found anything?"

As I said 'yes,' Morgan said, 'not really,' which made the other women eye us with confusion.

I looked at Morgan who mimed locking her lips and

pointed to me. "What we mean is we haven't found any solid leads but we're making a list of places we can eliminate." My own pride at this withered when I saw the hope in Ariana's eyes fade. "But that means we're closer to finding sites that we can consider."

Fiona squeezed Ariana's arm. "She's right. Narrowing the field is crucial when we're talking about the entire galaxy."

Ariana flicked us a weak smile. "I appreciate all your hard work. I really do." She jerked a thumb at Fiona. "But I don't want to be responsible for this hard ass flunking you."

Fiona gasped in mock horror. "Hard ass?" Then she swiveled her head as if staring at her own ass. "I mean, it's firm, I'll give you that."

Ariana rolled her eyes but released a small laugh.

"This research is exactly the kind of work that I'd expect from Assassins, although I can't stop assigning you the same homework as the other cadets simply because you're doing this." Fiona flipped her golden waves off her shoulder. "However, I can offer you extra credit for your extra work, and some extra time for your homework."

As much as I appreciated the captain's offer, I knew that I wouldn't be turning my work in late, even if I had to stay up all night to finish it. I'd been too self-programmed to do all the right things to let something slip, even now.

"Thanks, Captain." Morgan relaxed into her chair and waved a hand at the book in front of her. "What happens when we do find some possible targets? What then?"

"Then I lead a mission to check out every site until we find Sasha." Ariana's expression hardened with determination. "We infiltrate the site, kill as many of the scaly monsters as we can, and we bring my sister home."

That seemed long on emotion and short on tactical details, and the strategist in me twitched.

"Typical pilot," Fiona groused, casting a fond look at her friend. "Flying in guns blazing without thinking of the strategy." She pivoted to face us. "There's more to it than that. We're developing a plan for the incursion based on various scenarios. We won't know which one we'll need until we determine the type of prison or facility we're dealing with, and we won't know that until recon missions scout out the sites."

"But in every plan we kill the Kronock and get my sister," Ariana added.

"Have you considered making this an assignment?" I asked.

Fiona cocked her head at me. "You want an additional assignment? I thought you had too many already."

"Not an additional assignment just for us." I slid my gaze to Morgan. "What about giving the task to the entire School of Strategy?"

Fiona's eyes widened as she rocked back on the heels of her boots. "Now that's a thought."

"Imagine if you had all the Assassins working on the plans." Morgan bobbed her head with enthusiasm and swept a hand wide over the table of books. "Imagine if they were all helping us with this."

"Could you do that?" Ariana asked. "Could you harness the power of the academy to find Sasha?"

"I don't see why not." Fiona was smiling brightly. "The Kronock are the sworn enemy of the Drexians, after all, and Sasha was captured when she was fighting against them. I can't think of a better reason to use the talents and resources of the academy than this."

Ariana threw her arms around her friend. "I could kiss you!"

Fiona laughed as she hugged her friend back. "But what would Volt say?"

"If Drexians are at all like guys on Earth, he'd love it," Morgan said under her breath with a mischievous grin to me.

When Fiona extracted herself from Ariana's hug, she narrowed her eyes at me and Morgan. "Did you just manage to sweet talk your way out of work?"

Morgan shrugged and gave her a look of pure innocence. "What can we say? We are Assassins, after all."

"Well played," Fiona said.

Morgan twisted her neck until it cracked. "Now can we please get out of here so I can get my beauty sleep?"

Before I could tease her about her beauty sleep, I remembered where I was supposed to be and who I was supposed to meet. Panic shot through me as I grabbed my tablet and leather bag. "I forgot something I need to do. I have to go."

I didn't wait to see anyone's reaction or linger for their questions. I only hoped that I dashed from the Stacks fast enough that they couldn't follow me, as I rushed through the darkened halls of the academy to Torq's quarters.

Torq

I SNUCK another impatient glance at the timepiece on my nightstand, the small moons circling the perimeter while the numbers in the center remained motionless. She was late.

She's not coming. She's tired of your deal. She's tired of you.

I brushed aside the traitorous thoughts that lurked in the depths of my mind, the ones that had always told me that I wasn't strong enough, that I wasn't smart enough, that I wasn't fast enough. That I wasn't enough.

I suppressed them the only way I knew how, the only way

TANA STONE

that had always worked. I reminded myself that I was an elite
Drexian from House Swoll. I was born superior and anyone
who didn't recognize that was clearly beneath me.

But that wasn't true either. Jess wasn't beneath me. Even
thinking that made me want to fly to her rescue and defend her
against...myself?

I growled and scraped a hand roughly through my hair.
How had I let this happen? How had I let myself become so
distracted by the prospect of a female—a *human* female—
coming to my room to tutor me that I couldn't think about
anything else, including the weapons homework I should have
been completing?

"Concentrate, Torq." I dragged my chair back to my desk
and bent my head over the tablet that displayed the various
types of weapons I needed to label and explain. I started with
the easiest one—the throwing dagger—and quickly outlined
its optimal uses and the advantages of various grips. Thinking
of how I'd have to demonstrate my skills with the dagger
helped keep my mind on the blade and far from Jess.

The only things preventing me from going mad and
obsessing about the woman I could never have were my battle
classes and my fellow Blades. I'd become fast friends with the
other first-years in the School of Battle, which had lessened the
blow of losing my roommate and losing the chance to see Jess
daily during the intro classes we'd had during the first term. I
hadn't realized how much I'd looked forward to watching the
dark-haired human from the corner of my eye, or how I'd
always taken a seat in the lecture halls so I could see her.

Now she was in the School of Strategy, and I was in the
School of Battle, and the only way I could ensure that our paths
crossed was to insist she tutor me nightly. I didn't need to be
tutored nightly, especially not in Kronock, which would play a
minuscule part in my curriculum. But I didn't mind pretending

to be thick when it came to the language, as long as it meant being in the same room with her.

I needed to breathe in her scent, savor the occasional brush of her finger against mine, and watch her nibble her bottom lip when she was deep in thought. I needed it like I needed blood to flow through my veins, and I did not know why. I could not have explained why this particular female had drawn my attention so completely, but whether it was her unadorned beauty, her intelligence, or the way her eyes flared when they met mine, I was helpless to fight it.

A furtive knock on the door made me spring to my feet, my heart racing as I pressed the panel to open it. I was prepared to reprimand her for being late, but there was no need.

"I'm really sorry." She rushed inside with a glance over her shoulder. "I lost track of time."

That stole the thunder from my indignation, which was fine since seeing her swept away all my irritation within an instant. "You did not have second thoughts about our deal?"

She shook her head. "No. The deal is still on, so don't even dream about spilling my secret."

I had no intention of telling anyone what I had surmised about her and the other humans training for the maze, but I could not tell her. Instead, I gave her my silkiest smile. "You hold up your end, and I pledge to hold up mine."

She turned away, clearly not charmed by my smile, which continued to bother me. Most females, especially Drexians, found me irresistible, but Jess did not. Jess also didn't care about my clan status, which might have had something to do with it. I was starting to realize that I'd relied on my clan name to impress females, and this one was not impressed.

"Let's get started." She retrieved a tablet from her bag and sat down at my desk. "We left off with the various forms of 'kill,' and in Kronock, that's a lot."

I didn't join her at the desk. "No verbs tonight."

She looked at me, her brows pressing together. "Why not? Is this because I was late? I told you—"

"It is not that. I think we need a break from Kronock." I noticed that her eyes were bloodshot. "I think we both need a break from studying."

Jess released a sigh. "Seriously?" When I held out my hand, the relief in her face morphed into panic. "What kind of break?"

I was a bit hurt that she seemed horrified by the thought of doing anything with me but studying, but I laughed it off. "I am not suggesting anything scandalous."

She tilted her head slightly, obviously unconvinced.

The version of myself that still couldn't believe she wouldn't want to be pursued by an elite Drexian like me leaned down so that I could drop my voice to a whisper. "When we end up in my bed, it will be you who has begged me."

She jerked back, as a bark of laughter burst from her lips. "Well, that will never happen."

A primal need to toss her on my bed and tear her clothes from her body stormed through me, but I stifled it, merely emitting a grunt in response. I straightened and extended my hand again. "Then you have nothing to fear."

She stood without taking my hand and dropped her tablet back inside her bag. "What kind of break did you have in mind?"

"You dislike surprises?"

"So far, the surprises at the academy have included being attacked by alien beasts and having to climb across an open lava pit, so it's fair to say I'm not a fan of *Drexian* surprises."

Her hesitation was understandable. "I promise this is not as scary as that."

"Low bar," she muttered as I opened the door to my quarters.

I questioned my own impulsive idea as I peeked into the dim corridor, which was empty and silent. I was taking a risk by leaving my room with her. I was chancing us getting caught. But I needed to convince myself that there was more to our relationship than tutoring and keeping secrets, although this was one more secret we'd both have to keep.

"You have heard of the unofficial graduation requirements, correct?"

Jess narrowed her eyes at me. "I might have heard whispers about them, but I also might have thought the whole thing was a myth."

"No myth." I stepped into the hallway and motioned for her to follow me. "There are four requirements that every cadet must fulfill before they leave the academy."

"Or what?" She asked in a hushed voice as she joined me.

Of course, Jess would challenge the requirements. The woman seemed to question everything I had been taught to accept without question.

I closed my hand around hers and tugged her forward as I started down the corridor. "You would never fail to complete a requirement, would you, Jess?" I shook my head, knowing I'd pegged her correctly from the start. "You have always been a good girl, haven't you?"

Her quick inhalation told me I'd hit the mark. She'd always been a good girl, and I'd always been a bad boy. Which was why I couldn't resist her, and why she was hurrying down the halls of the school after-hours with me.

CHAPTER
EIGHTEEN

Jess

"You could tell me where we're going." I stayed close behind him as we hurried along the dark walls of the academy, the light from the sconces sending undulating shadows dancing across the ceiling.

"If I did that, you might refuse to come."

Well, that wasn't comforting. It was bad enough that I was sneaking into the cadet dormitory tower every night, but now I was running around the slumbering school in the dead of night.

Torq had been right. I had always been the good girl who played by the rules. I'd been the smart girl who busted her ass and always did everything right so no one would remember that I came from nothing. I was not a rule-breaker or a trouble-maker. I'd never been rich enough or spoiled enough to get away with those types of things. There would have been no one to bail me out if I'd gotten in trouble, so I'd never set a toe out of line.

That is, until I'd come to the Drexian Academy. Since I'd been at the alien school, I'd been involved in secret coaching sessions and late-night tutoring sessions in a cadet's room. Now I was skulking around the depths of the building with a Blade I had no business trusting.

So much for being a good girl.

I'd hated that Torq had pegged me as one though. It made me sound so boring and predictable. Not that anyone—least of all me—could have predicted that I'd become entangled with one of the hottest and cockiest Drexian cadets in the academy. I still had a hard time believing that I'd gotten roped into making a deal with him. What was sometimes harder to believe was that he'd stuck to his end of the bargain and hadn't given me a reason to slap him.

"The night is young," I said to myself as we jogged down a twisting flight of stone stairs.

"What?" Torq swiveled his head as we reached the bottom.

I glanced at the narrower corridor, and recognition tickled the back of my brain. "How much farther?"

"Not far." A smiled teased his mouth.

He was enjoying this. Of course, he was. Torq was exactly the kind of entitled rule-breaker who never gave a second thought to doing things that could get them into trouble. A high-born like him had probably never gotten in serious trouble in his life. Which begged the question why I was with him, since I was neither entitled, nor high-born, or likely to emerge unscathed if we got caught.

The floor sloped down, and the air became cooler. A chill passed through me, as I realized where we were going moments before we turned another corner, and I spotted the rusted gate.

I pressed my lips together to keep from revealing that I knew where we were and what requirement Torq had brought me to fulfill.

"The secret passageways underneath the academy." His voice was a hush as we walked closer. "There are a few entrances, but this one is the safest."

I nodded. It was also the one from which we'd emerged after using the passageways to sneak out of the school and see the maze the night before the trials. Even though I'd been there before and already fulfilled this unofficial requirement, I couldn't tell Torq.

He might already know that there had been some type of coaching for the human cadets before the trials, but he didn't know how extensive it had been, or that Kann had taken us through the underground tunnels to see the maze. I didn't know if that would make a difference to the Drexian, but I couldn't take the risk that he'd find that detail too much to keep secret. We hadn't gone into the maze or previewed any of the challenges, but Torq might not care.

He might think that we'd had an unfair advantage. He might think that the new information was reason to break our deal. Or he might think that it meant he was now entitled to more from me to keep him quiet.

I followed behind Torq, dreading what I already knew was coming—a low ceiling dripping with water, darkness so complete I wouldn't be able to see my hand in front of my face, and uneven dirt beneath my feet interspersed with puddles. I breathed in the loamy scent of soil as we entered the passages, not minding the warmth of Torq's hand closing around mine.

"How far do we have to go?" I asked, my voice echoing back to me. I'd already been to the end and back, so technically I'd already checked off this requirement, not that I could admit it.

"Some say all the way until it ends, but I never have. I have heard that it is caved in at places, so who knows if it is even possible to reach the end anymore."

It was possible, but I kept my mouth shut. The sooner this was over, the better.

We shuffled along in total blackness for a few more steps until a laugh bubbled up in my throat. "So this is your idea of a fun break?"

Torq stopped. "You do not think this is better than drilling Kronock vocabulary?"

One of my feet landed in a puddle, splashing cold water on other pant leg. "No, I do not." I mimicked his more formal speech. "It's cold and dark and it smells like something has died down here."

Torq was silent for a beat then he chuckled. "I suppose you are right. It does smell pretty dank."

"Why can't one of the requirements be sneaking into the kitchens and snagging some food from under the cooks' noses? Now that I could get behind."

Torq laughed harder. "Stealing food is not a very Drexian challenge."

"It's a very *me* challenge." My stomach growled at the thought of warm Drexian bread, and it hit me that I'd been so busy in the Stacks that I'd forgotten to eat dinner. "I'm starving."

"Then we can get out of here and go to the kitchens."

I released a breath. "That's the best idea you've had all night."

We pivoted in the other direction and started retracing our steps in the dark. Torq was slightly in front of me, but he'd dropped my hand as we groped our way along the damp walls. The toe of my boot caught on the uneven ground, and I pitched forward with a yelp.

Before I hit the dirt, Torq caught me and pulled me up until we were facing each other. His arms gripped the sides of my arms as we both breathed heavily.

"Thanks." I couldn't see his face, but I could feel how close he was to me.

Torq didn't speak. Instead, he cupped my face in one hand, running his thumb over my lips as if he was trying to see me by touch.

My heart hammered in my chest, and I was sure he could hear it. His body was so close to mine, I was sure he could feel it.

Torq closed the scant distance between us and crushed his mouth to mine with a groan, but I could barely hear his hungry sound over the pounding of my heart. He wrapped one arm around my waist and pressed his palm to the small of my back to hold me to him as he deepened the kiss. When he backed me against the damp wall, I remembered where we were and who he was and why we couldn't happen.

It had been a hot minute since I'd been kissed, but this was unlike any human kiss. His lips were soft but even they felt more forceful, stronger, more dominant. And he tasted like everything dark and forbidden that I'd been avoiding my entire life—like velvety smooth whiskey with a fire chaser.

I pushed him away and gasped for breath once he broke the kiss. "I thought you said I was the one who would beg you."

He ran his fingers through my hair as he dragged in uneven breaths. "You will, but that is when we end up in bed together. I never said anything about stealing kisses."

Of course, the Drexian was a cheater. I despised cheaters. But why could I not bring myself to despise him? Why did I only want more of his stolen kisses?

CHAPTER
NINETEEN

Volten

I leaned against the corridor wall as I finished the last warm roll that I'd confiscated from the kitchens. There was nothing like getting Drexian bread straight from the ovens, and even though my stomach was full, I was tempted to go back for another basket.

"Don't push your luck," I told myself as I started back to my quarters, even though there was no rush. Ariana would be spending another late night in the Stacks working with Fiona on a plan to rescue Sasha. I'd gotten used to her crawling into the bed with me so late at night I'd already drifted off or even when first light was starting to creep through the windows, but I would never complain that I missed her sleeping next to me. I knew how important it was for her to find her sister. I only wished I could do more to help.

Aside from being ready to pilot a rescue ship at a moment's

notice, my assistance was limited to emotional support and shared outrage. So far, we had not been able to reach the High Commander who had rescued a human from the grasp of the Kronock, but I had faith in Torq's contacts. He was high born, after all, and they tended to stick together.

As if thinking of the Drexian had summoned him, I spotted Torq slipping from a dark corridor. I caught myself from calling out when I saw that he was holding the hand of a female and leading her behind him.

I instantly recognized the human who had been with us in the maze, the one who had been inducted into the School of Strategy, the one who was assisting Ariana in the hunt for Sasha. "What is Jess doing sneaking around after hours with Torq?"

Aside from Torq pairing up with her in the maze to fix the ships, I had not been aware that they had become friends. I had not seen them together in the academy corridors or eating in the dining hall together. As far as I had noticed, they did not purport to be friends during daylight hours. But from the way he held her hand, I suspected they were more than friends or soon would be.

I wondered if I should say something to Ariana about Torq and Jess. Since Jess was one of the human cadets, Ariana naturally took a special interest in her, and they lived in the same tower. But what if Jess wished to keep her relationship secret for a reason? Ariana and I had kept our feelings just between us, and I had relished the time when we had not been fodder for academy gossip. Then there had been more salacious gossip to eclipse us, so it did not matter. But I understood wanting to keep things private.

"I'll keep your secret," I said aloud, but to no one in particular since the corridor was empty again. "For now."

But I would keep my eye on Torq. He had proven himself to

be brave in the trials, but he had also shown himself to be capable of manipulation. I had forgiven the way he'd gone after Ariana, but I had not forgotten it. High-borns were used to getting what they wanted. They were not accustomed to hearing no. If I discovered that Torq was behaving badly toward Jess, he would have to answer to me.

I nodded to myself, pleased with my decision, and turned to go when a hand closed over my arm.

CHAPTER
TWENTY

Ariana

Volten jumped and spun around, grabbing my hand and twisting it behind my back so quickly I didn't have time to shriek.

"What the hell?"

He was holding me close, but his grip relaxed when he heard my voice. "Ariana? What are you doing here?"

I wriggled from him. "Of course, it's me. I was looking for you, and the kitchens are always a safe bet. Who else would be grabbing you?"

He shrugged. "It is the Drexian Academy. It is not uncommon to be jumped in dark corridors."

I shot him a look. "Maybe when you were a cadet."

He closed the short distance between us and took my hands in his, examining the wrist that he'd clutched. "Old habits die hard. Did I hurt you?"

I shook my head, the heat from his hands already sending

tingles up my arm. "No. You know I'm not a fragile flower."

He pulled me flush to him. "I do know that." He backed me up until my ass hit the stone wall. "And I know that it turns you on to be somewhere that we could be caught."

My heart pounded as he pressed his body to mine. "Are you sure that isn't your turn-on?"

He twitched one shoulder. "Why can't it be both?" He dipped his head and kissed my lips softly then proceeded to kiss his way down my neck.

I glanced up and down the dimly-lit corridor. It was late at night, and there would probably be no one else creeping around the lower levels after hours, but that didn't mean we couldn't be spotted. The thought made my pulse flutter. Damn Volten for being right about me. "Are you serious right now?"

The lieutenant continued kissing his way down my body and finally dropped to his knees. "I am very serious. You need to release some stress, fly girl."

"Oh really, fly boy?" I laughed, the throaty sound reverberating over the stone. He was right. I'd been consumed by stress since learning that my sister Sasha was being held captive by the Kronock, but I also knew that being miserable didn't help find her any faster.

Volten hooked his fingers on the waistband of my pants and panties and yanked them down to my knees.

I gasped. "What are you...?" My protests were silenced when he buried his face between my legs, making it very clear exactly what he was doing. I tipped my head back as he worked his tongue expertly over my clit, surrendering to the sensations as the thrill of being caught pulsed through me.

"Typical pilot," I murmured as I tangled my hands in his hair. "Always chasing danger."

He only hummed and flicked his tongue faster. My heart pounded as I held his head to me. Anyone could round the corner and see us. Anyone could hear my breathy sighs as Volten licked my pussy while I was pressed to the wall, and it made my entire body throb with excitement.

Part of me wanted to get caught. Part of me relished the thought of someone else watching my Drexian boyfriend please me. The adrenaline junkie part of me that made me a great pilot also gave me a bit of an exhibitionist kink.

The more I thought about being caught, the more my body trembled with pleasure until I was shaking and spasming, my moans echoing around us as I came. "That was—"

Volten didn't let me finish as he stood up and flipped me around so I was facing the wall. He tipped me forward and grasped my hips in his hands, tilting my ass up so he could drive into me from behind.

I sucked in a breath from the sudden intrusion, but I was so aroused that I instinctively rocked into him. "Anyone could see you fucking me, fly boy."

"Good," he husked in my ear as he bent over me. "Let them watch me take what's mine."

I rolled my head back as he continued to thrust his cock hard into me, the frenzy of his movements matching my own hunger. I needed him hard and fast. I needed to burn off the energy that had been roiling through me.

I flattened my palms to the cool stone and bent over more so he could get an even deeper angle. "You are a bad influence on me, Lieutenant."

"And you love being a bad girl, don't you?"

I twisted my head to meet his hot gaze. "Not as much as you love fucking a bad girl."

A growl slipped from his lips as he thrust deep into me, and my body clamped around his cock as another release barreled through me. I threw back my head as he pistoned hard once more and then held himself deep as he exploded inside me.

The corridor was filled with the sounds of our panting as Volten slumped over me, curling one arm around my waist and kissing my throat as I leaned my head back onto his shoulder. "Do you have to go back to the Stacks?"

"No. Why?"

"Because we need to finish this in my quarters."

"Finish?" The Drexian was still inside me and still hard, but I knew that didn't mean anything since Drexians didn't get soft immediately the way humans did. "We're not—?"

He laughed low. "Not even close, fly girl."

CHAPTER
TWENTY-ONE

Torq

I slapped my hands together and a cloud of chalk puffed from them, provoking a hard cough as I inhaled the particles swirling around me. It was not only my chalk dust that filled the air. All the first-year Blades were preparing to practice grappling on the climbing wall with daggers, which meant the air was hazy and the mood edgy.

I strapped a sparring dagger to my thigh, the blade duller than ones I'd take into a real battle but sharp enough to sting on contact. Snug athletic pants were all I wore. They were all any of us wore, and the mats were crowded with sweaty, bare chests, many of them covered in dark tattoos. The Drexian Academy emblem etched on my shoulder was small in comparison to some of the markings that stretched down arms and across backs.

My nerves jangled at the prospect of scaling the vertical

wall that rose high above me, its geometrically domed ceiling glinting hard and black. It wasn't that I felt unprepared for the challenge. I didn't doubt my climbing skills or my ability to wield a dagger. I questioned my ability to focus on anything but memories of kissing Jess the night before.

I hopped from leg to leg, trying to get my blood flowing and my brain working but as many times as I told myself that I needed to get my mind in the game, all I could think about was the softness of her lips, the way she'd yielded to my touch, the almost imperceptible sound she'd made when I'd torn my mouth from hers.

Grek. I stopped bouncing from side to side as my cock strained my pants, and I bent over at the waist to hide my arousal. If I didn't stop remembering touching Jess, every Blade was going to think I had a thing for them or for climbing walls.

It wasn't like I could explain to my fellow cadets that I'd been remembering the sweet taste of a human cadet, the very same cadet I'd blackmailed into tutoring me because I knew a secret I'd promised not to reveal. That was *not* something I could reveal. Not to my fellow Blades. Not to anyone.

"You will ascend the walls one at a time," Kann announced, as he strode toward the wall and thumped one of the holds. "Speed is your friend—if you can make it up the wall before the next cadets catch you, then you won't have to engage in a dagger fight—but speed can also be your down-fall—literally. You have no ropes to keep you on the wall, so one misstep means you could be down on the mats with us again."

I gulped as I tipped my head to mentally measure the height of the wall. Too high for an enjoyable fall, even if there were mats at the bottom to cushion the landing.

Fear had doused my arousal, so I straightened and started to study the holds and map out a possible route. I wouldn't know how good each hold was until my hands were on it, but I could attempt to form a plan. Jess would have a plan.

I made a low sound in the back of my throat, disgusted with myself that I'd lasted all of two seconds before thinking of the human again. Would I last as long on the climbing wall? Would my distraction make me the first cadet to fall from the wall and plummet through the air?

"At least the holds do not move," I said to myself.

Kort snorted out a laugh as he strode up to me. "Do not remind me about that wall in the maze."

I swung my head to him. "You had to go over the lava?"

Kort shuddered and rubbed his chalky palms together. "When I got there, bits of alien monster were still being devoured by it." He inclined his head to the towering wall dotted with holds. "This is a dream in comparison."

He had a point. This challenge would not be easy, but we were Blades. It should not kill us. Unlike the trials, which had been intended to end us all. "It feels good to have the trials behind us."

"But the battle of the schools is still ahead of us." Zenen had joined us, but he looked almost excited when he gazed at the wall.

I'd almost forgotten that the end of our second term—and the first full term as Blades—would be marked by a competition that pitted the schools against each other. My gut clenched with the reminder that I would not be able to go through with the same group of cadets who'd been in the maze with me. Those cadets would be my opponents because each of them was in a different school. Jess would be my opponent.

Thoughts of battling against Jess brought memories of being in the secret tunnels slamming into me. How was I supposed to work to defeat her when the only thing I wanted was to hold her, protect her, make her mine? The better question was how was I supposed to go back to being tutored by her in my room without wanting to touch her and kiss her and feel her body pressed against mine again?

A bellowed name brought me back to the climbing wall, as Zenen grinned, ran to the wall, and started moving up hand over hand. Then Kort's name was called, and he grinned at me.

"See you at the top."

I shook out my arms as more names were called and more Blades started their ascent. By now, the cadets who'd been first up the wall were engaging in one-armed dagger fights, and those of us left on the mat had to leap aside as the first cadet up the wall came crashing down. He roared and slapped his hand on the mat after he landed in a crouch then he raced back to the wall.

My tentative route was all but forgotten when my name was called. The wall was swarming with cadets, and more were dropping from above, making even getting to the wall to start a bit of an obstacle course. I eyed the cadets clinging to holds and decided to take a different approach. Instead of leaping for a hold, I leapt for a cadet.

He yelled in protest as I stepped on his shoulder, but I was already jumping onto a second cadet's back. Body parts were easier to grasp than wall holds, so I was able to catapult myself from cadet to cadet until I was almost halfway up the wall where there were fewer climbers.

I paused for a breath, glancing below to assess any threats. Apparently, the cadets I'd used as human holds hadn't been happy about it, and they were all coming straight for me. One held a sparring dagger between his teeth so he could move quickly and be ready to slash when he reached me.

Using my feet to push myself higher, I climbed to one side around a pair of grappling Blades until I reached Kort, who'd just forced a cadet off the wall. For a moment, I wondered if he'd try to dispatch me as well, but he tucked his dagger into the sheath on his leg and nodded to the ceiling. "Together?"

I grinned at my friend and reached for an overhead hold. That was when I felt a searing pain across the back of my calf, and my leg slipped from its hold. Kort turned at my scream, reaching out a hand with wide eyes as I fell from the wall. The air rushed around me as I pinwheeled my arms and tried to right myself, but the pain from my leg overtook me. Until the pain from hitting the mat consumed that.

CHAPTER
TWENTY-TWO

Jess

The hot water beat on my shoulders as I stood under the shower with my head bowed and let the pressure melt away all the tension of the past few days. Tension that wouldn't have been there if I could stop obsessing about Torq and what had happened in the hidden passageways.

I swept my hands across my face and down my hair as I pivoted, breathing in the steamy air and the scent of lavender soap, one of my few girly indulgences. Why was I making this such a big deal? So what if he kissed me? So what if my knees became jelly and my brain short-circuited the moment his lips touched mine? So what if I actually moaned out loud?

I squeezed my eyelids together as I remembered my throaty sound echoing back to me in the stone tunnel. So much for playing it cool. Not that I'd ever been great at being any kind of cool.

I'd always been the nerdy girl who studied all the time and never got noticed. I'd been the one who didn't go to dances or get asked to prom. So why was a hot, hunky Drexian kissing me?

It couldn't be because of the tutoring. He'd already conned me into that. It wasn't like he had a secret that I was keeping for him either.

I shook my head. Did he actually like me? Was it possible that the gorgeous alien was into me?

Flipping off the water, I stood dripping in the shower before daring to step outside and into the cool air. I swiped at my eyes before opening them. I wasn't going to find any answers by staying in there, and I wasn't going to get them by hiding out in my quarters, which was what I'd been doing since the night in the tunnels.

"I'm not hiding," I said, challenging my own assessment of the past two days, as I stepped an inch from the stone shower enclosure and snatched a towel off the hook. "I'm regrouping and reevaluating."

Yeah, right. Regrouping, reevaluating, and running was more accurate.

Then again, as my mother would have said, running was what I did best. I'd run as far away from my going-nowhere-fast small town as I could as soon as I could. Then I'd left Earth and taken a place at the Drexian Academy that was literally across the galaxy.

"If you're going to do something, do it right." I muttered, as I dried myself off and wrapped the towel around my chest, tucking it in under my armpit.

But just because I'd skipped tutoring Torq since he took me to the tunnels didn't mean I was running. It did mean that I needed time to think and figure him out. And figure out what kind of game he was playing.

The Drexian cadet was one contradiction after another. At first, I'd been convinced he was a spoiled rich boy who didn't deserve his place at the academy. Then he'd fought off deadly creatures in the maze, and I'd had to rethink my assessment. I'd been sure that he would reveal what he knew about the secret coaching sessions before the trials, but he hadn't. I'd been certain that he was only using me for my brains so he could get ahead in class, but then he'd kissed me.

I could not unravel the mystery of Torq or his intentions, and as an Assassin, that drove me nuts.

One more surprise—I'd been positive that he would have hunted me down before now. I'd skipped two tutoring sessions, but instead of sending me a message or coming to my room, I hadn't heard a peep. It helped that I'd done my best to avoid him, skipping meals, darting from the female tower to the School of Strategy and hiding in groups of tall Drexians so I wouldn't be seen. Okay, when I said it like that, it sounded like I was hiding.

I slipped into soft, black pants that were not part of my academy uniform and a matching tee that had the Assassins emblem emblazoned on the front. Wrapping the towel around my wet hair, I coiled it into a turban on top of my head and prepared to finish my latest Strategy homework.

A hard knock on my door stopped me from pulling out my desk chair. So much for Torq not tracking me down. I expected as much, and had thought he'd show up sooner, but that didn't mean my heart wasn't beating wildly as I pressed my hand to the side panel to open the door.

As I braced myself to explain why I'd been so busy and no, I hadn't been avoiding him, thank you very much, Britta strode into my room. My mouth had been open to launch into an explanation, but I clamped it shut as she held out a bundle wrapped in cloth.

"You missed dinner again, so I brought you some food." The woman's long, silvery hair was in a high ponytail, which made her dark eyes and olive skin look even more striking. "None of the stew, obviously, but the bread is the best part, anyway."

My stomach rumbled, apparently my automatic reaction to any mention of food. "Thanks, that was sweet of you." I took the bundle and unwrapped it to reveal several rolls and golden pastry twisted around strips of padwump. I didn't hesitate to bite into one of the twists and was rewarded with a burst of savory flavor and flaky pastry that crumbled in my mouth. The Drexian Academy might be tough when it came to curriculum, but their food was better than any military mess hall I'd ever visited.

I waved a hand at the chair as I chewed, and Britta sat down.

"You've been MIA for a couple of days." She eyed me, as if expecting me to look sick or incapacitated. "Morgan said you're fine, just busy."

Guilt stabbed at me for abandoning my friends. I was being ridiculous, and Britta showing up at my door with emergency rations proved it. "Sorry. I've been catching up on work, but I'll be joining you all again for breakfast."

Britta smiled as she watched me gobble up the bread. "If you miss too many meals, you miss out on all the gossip."

My pulse quickened. There wasn't gossip about me and Torq, was there? He wouldn't have told anyone what happened between us, would he? "Oh, yeah? What's been going on? Anything juicy?"

Britta tipped her head back and forth. "I wouldn't say juicy, but there has been drama. I mean, it's the Drexian Academy. When is this place not full of drama?"

I forced myself to laugh as I sank onto the foot of the bed, but it came out a strangled squeak. "Any drama with the Irons?"

My friend joined me in laughing. "The School of Engineering? You know I love being an Iron, but we aren't exactly known for being dramatic. That's Blade or Wing territory. I would say Assassin, too, but you all are too stealthy to let anyone know the drama."

"So, things are going well for you in Irons?" Britta wasn't the only human who'd gotten into the School of Engineering, but she was the only female.

Her smile brightened. "I love it. We work on the coolest tech and talk about cutting-edge designs that Earth isn't even close to developing."

Britta's excitement was infectious, and my anxiety at being part of the school gossip had faded. She would have mentioned it if I was the subject of the academy scuttlebutt. "That sounds amazing."

"Hopefully, some of the new tech can help to track down Ariana's sister."

That caught me off guard. "You're working on finding her sister?"

"I offered to help. Ariana said that you and Morgan are already doing a deep dive into possible targets for the rescue mission. What we're developing would make it possible to scan for human life forms from much farther away than we normally can detect them."

I thought about how much of a game-changer this could be for our search. "Do you think you can do it?"

Her eyes sparkled. "We're close."

"You're right." I glanced at the empty cloth. "I have missed all the good stuff by skipping meals."

"That's not all you've missed." Britta crossed her legs. "Did you hear what happened in Battle?"

"Battle?" I repeated, even though I'd heard her perfectly. My spine already tingled with dread as Britta nodded.

"They were doing these crazy grappling bouts on the climbing wall and one of the cadets took a bad fall."

"Did he die?" My voice cracked as my body went cold.

"No, but he's out for a while. Bad luck for a Blade, right?"

"Who was it?" A part of me knew before she uttered his name, a part of me could feel it in my gut.

"Torq, that Drexian who went through the maze with us. You remember him, don't you?"

CHAPTER
TWENTY-THREE

Torq

I shifted my weight on the bed and flinched from the sharp pain in my leg. Grek, the gash in my calf still hurt, even though the academy surgeon assured me that it was healing quickly. I cursed again as I thought of him telling me that I needed rest to fully recuperate and ordering me to avoid strenuous activity. That meant he was ordering me to miss every Blade class until I recovered, which meant I had been stuck in my quarters since being stabbed and falling.

I could not blame the surgeon. I could not even blame the cadet who had slashed at my ankle. He had been trying to beat me, which was the point of the exercise, and he had used the sparring dagger that we'd been given. He had managed to jab it hard enough to break flesh, lodge in my leg, and bring me off the wall.

I had not been the only one to fall, but I had been the only one not to get back up. The shame of my failure washed over me like scalding liquid, and I rammed my head back onto the pillow. First I'd failed to make it into Wings, and now I was failing as a Blade. The possibility of washing out of the academy entirely made me want to scream.

It was bad enough that I'd been injured, but what added to my frustration was the fact that I had not seen Jess since kissing her in the tunnels. After we'd parted that night, I had been sure that she felt the connection as much as I had, I had been sure the kiss had meant something to her.

But she had not shown up for our regular tutoring session the next night. She had not even come to see me after I'd been hurt. Then she hadn't appeared again tonight, when I had been sure she would. I told myself that she would care that I had been injured. I had assured myself that she cared about me.

"*Grekking* fool," I said angrily to myself as I lay in my room alone.

I'd been an idiot to think that Jess was spending time with me for any reason other than blackmail. She didn't want to hang out with me. She didn't like me. She was only protecting her friends and keeping me quiet, and I'd been fooling myself if I'd ever thought it meant more.

The kiss had been a mistake. I saw that now, even if I'd been too caught up in the moment to realize it when we were in the tunnels. I'd been too overwhelmed by the closeness of her, the scent of her, the heat of her body next to mine. I'd been tricked by her breathy moan into thinking that she wanted me as much as I wanted her, but I'd obviously been mistaken.

If she wanted me, she would have returned. If she desired me, she would have come back. If she cared, she wouldn't have left me to suffer alone.

"You have no one to blame but yourself," I muttered darkly, as I stared at the door that had only opened for the surgeon,

Kort, and Kann since I'd fallen. "You ruined everything, as usual."

Why couldn't I stop myself from pushing things? Why couldn't I leave well enough alone? Why couldn't I stop sabotaging myself?

Jess had been the best part of my days, and she'd become the best part of the academy for me. And I'd scared her off. Like usual.

My leg throbbed as I readjusted it and sat up fully in bed. If I stayed here wallowing in self-pity for much longer, I'd go mad. I grabbed the tablet on my nightstand and swiped a finger across the screen to open it.

The School of Battle was heavy in experiential learning—it was a school of fighting, after all—but there was some written work I could do while I waited to return to full strength. I scanned the document on various attacks with swords, even though Drexians rarely battled with long blades anymore. Still, it was something we'd have to demonstrate, and I didn't plan to fail an assessment again—ever.

My one comfort was that my family did not know about my fall. I had managed to convince the surgeon not to report my injury to my parents, and since it was not life-threatening, he had agreed. My family had never been big on sympathy, so I would have gotten nothing from them but scorn. Since I was already shedding the last pile of derision they'd heaped on me, I was glad I had been spared more.

When my brain started to tire of sword attack techniques, I instinctively switched my screen to the last Kronock lesson I'd been on with Jess. I might despise the look and sound of the language of our enemy, but I had grown strangely fond of it because it was the reason I got to see Jess. Even reviewing the verbs for "kill" sent a hum of pleasure through me.

I shook my head at my twisted reaction. "I have got to get out of here."

Glancing back at the screen, I focused on the alien verbs until a knock on the door made me look up. Kort usually checked on me after dinner. Last night he'd brought me some contraband Noovian whiskey, which we had drunk together until I couldn't feel the pain in my leg. I hoped he would have more tonight. I would welcome anything that dulled the ache in my leg and my heart.

"Come," I bellowed. "It is open."

When the door slid back, it was not Kort or Kann. It was Jess.

My heart hammered in my chest at the sight of her, but I could not staunch the hurt from bubbling up along with the relief and happiness. I steeled my expression and crossed my arms. "You are late."

CHAPTER
TWENTY-FOUR

Jess

My hair dripped down my back as I ran along the corridors, the boots I'd hastily shoved onto my feet slapping the stone floor. There were a few cadets still drifting from the dining hall and a few more headed for the Stacks, but I didn't pay them much attention. They glanced at me, eyebrows peaking as I ran, but I didn't care. At least my hair wasn't still wrapped in a towel. That would have drawn stares.

I'd have to apologize to Britta later for rushing her from my room and feigning sudden exhaustion. I was pretty sure she hadn't bought my lame act, and I wouldn't be shocked if she'd heard me dash from my room only minutes after she'd left.

That was nothing compared to the apology I owed Torq. How long ago did he fall from the wall? Britta's voice had become an incomprehensible buzz as I'd realized the reason

Torq hadn't come looking for me, the reason I hadn't bumped into him around the academy. It hadn't been because I'd been slinking around like a coward and avoiding him. It was because he was injured.

He might have been killed, and I wouldn't have known. The thought made my stomach churn, but I didn't slow my pace as I reached the cadet dormitory tower and took the stairs two at a time. I almost fell on my face, barely catching myself at the last moment, but I didn't stop.

Only when I was standing outside Torq's door did I pause to draw in a breath and ask myself why I was in such a panic. From what Britta had said—although she only had sparse details—he hadn't been seriously injured. He was healthy enough to recover in his quarters instead of the surgery, which was a good sign. Of course, it had taken a trip to the surgery—after I'd located it in the cavernous academy—for me to discover that he'd been discharged to his room.

It wasn't so much Torq's condition that had me so flustered, it was the thought that I hadn't known. I hadn't known, which meant he hadn't heard a word from me since he'd kissed me. He must think I'd heard about his fall but didn't care, and that made my stomach do an uncomfortable flip. I might be a nerd, a geek, a brainiac, but I'd never been a mean girl.

I rapped my knuckles on the door and slowed my breath while I waited for it to open. Then I heard a muffled voice. "Come. It's open."

I pressed my hand to the side panel, and the door glided open.

Torq was sitting up on one of the beds with a stack of pillows behind him. When he saw me, he didn't smile or even give me his trademark cocky grin. He crossed his arms over his chest. "You are late."

All of my guilt and regret evaporated like a puff of smoke. I stepped inside and returned his frown with one of my own. "I went to the surgeon first."

He relaxed his shoulders and expression. "You thought I was at the surgery?"

"I was told you fell. How did I know you were fine?"

He mumbled something about not being completely fine. It was then that I noticed that the lower part of his leg was wrapped in bandages and some of the sympathy I'd felt when I'd seen him laid up in bed returned. "Are you going to tell me what happened, or should I leave?"

Torq released a breath. "We were practicing grappling with daggers on the climbing wall."

I shook my head at the absurdity of that statement. "Fucking Blades."

He angled his head to one side, as if waiting for me before continuing his retelling.

I waved a hand at him as I pulled out his desk chair and sat. "Go on."

"Like I was saying, we were on the climbing wall, and I'd used a few other cadets to leverage myself halfway up the wall when—"

I held up one palm. "I'm sorry. You did what?"

"I climbed the cadets instead of using the climbing holds. There were too many of them ahead of me and it was a faster way to get up the wall."

I couldn't stop the laugh that spilled from my lips. "That was actually a pretty clever strategy. Too bad you're so buff and aggressive, or you could have made a half-decent Assassin."

He grinned at me, the cockiness instantly reappearing. "You think I'm buff?"

"And aggressive. Don't forget that part. And I only said half-decent, so don't get a big head about it."

Torq touched a hand to his face. "Why would my head expand?"

"Big head means you think you're God's gift to the universe."

His brow furrowed. "Which god?"

I groaned. "Never mind. Just don't get all cocky about it. All Drexians are buff."

"And humans have very strange expressions." He grinned without any trace of arrogance. "But I am pleased you liked my strategy."

I fought the urge to roll my eyes, although there was something sweet in how happy he was with my approval. "I take it not everyone liked it as much as I did?"

He cut a look to his wounded leg. "They did not. One of the cadets I used as a stepping stone decided to slash at me with his sparring dagger. They are not as sharp as fighting daggers, but he put a lot of force in his attack. It sliced my calf and made me lose my balance and drop from the wall."

I cringed at this, imagining plummeting off a climbing wall. "At least it didn't kill you. I feel like death is an actual possibility for some of your training."

He shrugged. "Usually only during the trials. Occasionally during the battle of the schools. Rarely during routine training."

Rarely was not never. "How long will it take to heal?"

"Drexians are fast healers, but I cannot return to regular Blade training for a few more days."

"Then you have plenty of time to study Kronock."

His eyes widened. "I thought you..."

I knew exactly what he'd thought. He'd believed the reason I'd stayed away was because of the kiss. "Got scared off by a little kiss?"

He studied me, his eyes narrowing. "I would not call it a little kiss."

"It was dark, we were close together, it happened. No big deal." I didn't tell him that it had been a big deal. I didn't tell him that I hadn't been able to think about anything else since. I didn't dare tell him that it had been the best kiss of my life, not that there was a ton of competition in that regard. If I told him any of that, his big head wouldn't fit through the door.

"It was no big deal?" His tone told me he didn't believe me.

My pulse fluttered as I remembered my wobbly legs and ragged breath and racing heart. I managed to let out a light laugh that didn't shake. "It was one kiss. I think we can move on from one kiss."

"Move on?"

Okay, now I wondered if the fall had effected his brain and was making him repeat everything I said. Either that, or he was having a hard time believing me. "Well, you still have a lot of Kronock to learn."

Part of me wanted to ask if he was willing to release me from our deal, but a tiny part of me wanted a reason to continue seeing him. Coming to his room at night, even though it was skirting the rules and was not at all in character for me, had become part of my routine. I looked forward to sitting next to him and hearing him recite alien words in his deep voice. I even thrilled when he would sometimes drape his arm across the back of my chair when he leaned closer to read something. And that kiss...

He loosed a long-suffering sigh that didn't sound so tortured. "I guess I have nowhere to go."

I stifled a grin, stood, walked to his nightstand, and picked up the tablet. "Where were we? The verb kill, right?"

Torq rattled off a series of Kronock words that were exactly right. When I gaped at him, he only smiled. "Like I said, I have had nowhere to go, and I was not sure if you were coming back."

I glanced at his desk and his injured leg stretched long in front of him. With his leg bandaged, he wasn't much of a threat, not that I'd ever felt he was. At this point, I suspected I could take him. I glanced at his broad shoulders. Maybe not.

I nudged him as I sat next to him on the bed, and he scooted over without protest so we could sit side by side. "Just for the record, this is not you getting me into bed."

He laughed and the sound rumbled into me. "Is it not?"

TWENTY-FIVE

Torq

Kann leaned against the wall of my room with his arms folded as he watched the surgeon assess my leg.

"I told you I am fine." I stood on my injured leg, putting all my weight on it as the Drexian academy's medical officer inspected the gash that had healed into a faint scar.

The surgeon grunted and sat back on his heels. "He is right. His cut has healed, and he has regained full motion in his ankle. I do not see any lasting damage or any reason he cannot return to training."

Kann gave us both a curt nod. "If you are sure."

The surgeon stood. "I am sure. You could try sending me fewer cadets to mend, though."

Kann's serious expression morphed into a crooked grin. "We are Blades."

The surgeon shook his head, knowing that was explanation enough. The School of Battle wouldn't be easing its training regimen. It couldn't, not when the Blades were the warriors who rushed headfirst into every battle. The first line of Drexian defense had to be the toughest one.

After the surgeon had given his last few warnings to me—unhelpful ones like recommending I avoid falling from climbing walls and I learn to dodge daggers better—he left, but Kann stayed.

"I have bad news for you."

I rolled down my pantleg and sat on the end of my bed. What now?

"We have moved on from grappling on the climbing wall." Kann's lips twitched as he tried not to laugh. "You won't have the chance to climb over your fellow cadets again."

"I stand by that strategy." It had worked beautifully, until I'd been knocked off.

"Of course, you do." Kann did laugh now. "You're a Blade. We're stubborn and thick-headed."

I'd been called stubborn many times by my father, but I'd always thought that was just because he hated when anyone defied him.

"If we're not working on the wall, what are we doing?"

"Holo-chamber simulations to prepare you for the battle of the schools."

The reminder of the upcoming contest that would pit Blades against Assassins and me against Jess made me frown. "What kind of simulations?"

"Since the battle takes place outside the academy and ranges from the Restless Sea to the Gilded Peaks, we must ensure you are exposed to all the various environments you might experience."

I hadn't heard as many tales about the battle of the schools as I had the maze trials, primarily because when my father had been a cadet, the Wings had never won one of the end-of-year competitions. He'd always grumbled about it and shared scant details about the event, although I did know it was different every year and it always took place beyond the walls of the academy.

"Will we have to figure out challenges like we did in the maze?" If there were going to be technical tasks then I feared the Blades might not stand a chance. On the other hand, if we needed to fight off more vicious beasts, we would certainly be victorious.

"No challenges." Kann picked up my tablet from my desk, wrinkling his nose when the latest Kronock lesson flashed onto the screen. "You definitely will not have to translate Kronock, but I'm impressed you want to continue to hone skills outside of Battle."

I didn't comment. What could I say? I could not tell Kann that I was only studying the alien language as an excuse to see another cadet who was much better at it. I could not tell him that because then I would have to explain why Jess felt compelled to tutor me, and I doubted that would make me look great. It might even get me booted from Blades.

"If there are no challenges, then what—"

Kann held up his hands. "I cannot reveal anything else. Partially because it would not be fair for me to tell any cadets what they need to face, but mostly because I do not know."

I huffed out a frustrated breath.

The Blade instructor placed my tablet back on my desk. "You should not worry. The battle is set up so that every school has an equal chance of winning. There should be no elements that give one group an advantage over the others. It is a test of general warrior abilities, which every cadet should possess, and it is a test of adaptability, another vital skill for a warrior."

That was both comforting and aggravating. "Then I look forward to the simulations."

"They will be less dangerous, if nothing else. Your goal with them will be to get through the environments as a team." He turned to my door, pressing his palm to open it. "You might want to put in some extra time on the climbing wall just to make sure you are comfortable doing vertical assents. During the battle of the schools my first year, we had to scale the highest point of the Gilded Peaks." He shivered at the memory. "I am not saying you will have to do that, but you should be prepared."

"Thanks," I said as he stepped into the corridor. "And thank you for checking on me."

Kann inclined his head at me. "You are one of my Blade brothers now. Besides, Volten holds you in high regard, and he is slow to warm to others, so that tells me a lot about you."

Then he was gone, and the door glided shut behind him. I stood motionless for a few moments, basking in the pleasure of his words. Volten held me in high regard. I was Kann's Blade brother. Both of those made my chest swell with pride, but not the usual pride that was puffed up to mask my fears and insecurities. This was genuine pride. Pride at who I was and who I was becoming. And those were things that had nothing to do with my clan, a fact that made me happier than I could have imagined.

A knock on the door snatched my attention, and my gaze darted to the tablet on my desk. Jess.

My pulse spiked at the thought of sitting with her on the bed while she drilled me in Kronock verb tenses and unusual nouns, then I remembered that I was healed. I didn't need to remain in bed. We could return to sitting at my desk in chairs side by side.

My excitement faded. That wasn't the same as feeling her

body press against mine and breathing in the scent of her hair. It wasn't the same as her body heat pulsing into me and her hip flush with mine as we sat close on the narrow bed.

But she didn't know I was fully healed or that I didn't need to sit with my leg outstretched any more. She thought I was still wounded.

I jumped on the bed and slid up so that I was sitting propped against the headboard. What would it hurt to enjoy one more tutoring session next to her? What was the harm in savoring her touch and closeness one last time?

I wouldn't have to lie. I wouldn't have to say anything. She would see me on the bed as usual and assume that I was recuperating. And if she asked? Then I would tell her the truth. Of course, I would. At least I liked to think I would. I liked to believe that my Drexian honor would override my desire for her, but even thinking of her climbing on the bed with me had my heart racing.

I cleared my throat. "Come."

CHAPTER
TWENTY-SIX

Jess

I wiggled higher on the bed as Torq held the tablet between us and conjugated the Kronock verb for disembowel, which was shockingly not the only word in the language that meant to rip out someone's internal organs.

Once he finished, he dropped the device on his lap. "I think I might have had my fill of Kronock verbs."

"They have a lot of dark ones." I hadn't been tutoring him for as long as our usual sessions, but he seemed more restless than usual. Being cooped up and unable to attend classes must have started to get to him. "We can stop here if you want."

He put the tablet on his nightstand and twisted to face me, which meant he was practically looming over me. "I have a confession."

This was interesting. Torq had always struck me as the kind of Drexian who pushed the envelope and got in trouble often, which meant he was the exact opposite of me. It made sense. He was a Blade, which meant he struck first and asked questions later, if at all. I was an Assassin who made strategic plans for everything I did.

"Does this have to do with what happened in the tunnels?"

He cocked his head a touch. "Why would I have a confession about kissing you?"

I bobbed one shoulder. "I don't know. Maybe you kissed me on a dare." I'd said it as a joke, but as soon as the words left my mouth I wondered if they were right. "Wait, is this whole thing a dare? Did you bet some of your Blade buddies that you could trick me into coming to your room, and then sweet-talk me into the tunnels, and then—"

He clamped a hand over my mouth before I could continue rambling. "No. There is no dare. None of my Blade brothers know about you or about this."

I allowed myself to breathe again, but his hand was still over my mouth, so I tugged it away. Despite his assertion, I wasn't sure if I trusted him. He was blackmailing me to be there, after all. "Then what's your confession?"

He hesitated. "I don't regret kissing you, even if you regret letting me."

"I never said I regretted it." Had I regretted it? Maybe a part of me had at some point, but it was more that I'd regretted what the kiss might mean or how it might change things between us. Despite how our meetings had started, I'd come to enjoy spending time with Torq, especially since he'd been injured. "Is that your confession, that you didn't hate kissing me?"

His lips quirked into a grin. "No, but I would never put it that way. Far from not hating kissing you, it was one of the most enjoyable things I have done in a long time."

My cheeks flushed with heat. "Oh, well, thanks." Were we

seriously discussing our kiss? "I still don't know what you're confessing to me."

His eyes had darkened as he held my gaze. Then he flipped himself over with his hands on both sides of my hips, pinning me in.

"What the hell?" How had he moved so fast with a bum leg? He hadn't flinched or favored his injured side. Was he on some powerful Drexian pain-killers I didn't know about?

His gaze was molten. "My confession is that I've been cleared to go back to classes and training. I'm healed."

My jaw dropped. "What? Since when?"

"Just before you came. I was going to tell you but..."

"But what?" I couldn't believe he'd let me think he was still bedridden. I couldn't believe he'd tricked me.

He leaned down so that our lips were close. "You did say you didn't regret me kissing you."

"I'm rethinking that." It was hard to think clearly with him on top of me and his very kissable mouth so close to mine.

"Aren't you curious how good we could be together? Don't you want to know what would happen if I kissed you again?"

My heart hammered in my chest as if trying to escape. "I know exactly what would happen, and I know it can't happen."

"Why not?" His voice was a low hum that slid over my skin like silk. "Tell me why, Jess."

Reasons. I could give him logical reasons. "For one, we're cadets. We're not supposed to be hooking up. I know I was told that there could be no fraternizing with Drexian cadets."

"That's not an academy rule."

Of course it wasn't. The Drexian Academy didn't have rules to account for female cadets since they'd never had them before, although I had serious doubts the Drexian academy hadn't had hookups that were kept quiet. "For another, it's too distracting for both of us. We just got inducted into our schools. We need to focus on our work."

"We cannot work all the time. It is not healthy. We need breaks, and I cannot think of a better break."

I narrowed my eyes at him. "You're a Blade, and I'm an Assassin. We're preparing for the battle of the schools. Aren't you worried that being emotionally attached to an opponent might be a weakness?"

"I can separate my life as a Blade and my personal life. I do not intend to go easier on your school just because you're in it. Would you go easier on me?"

"Never," I said quickly.

"Then we're agreed." He lowered his lips to my neck, but I pushed him away.

"We're not agreed. I can't do this."

His eyes narrowed, heat flaring within them. "You don't want me to kiss every bit of your body and make you screa—"

"I've never done this before," I blurted out before I could think better of it. "I've never been with anyone."

Torq stiffened, a deep wrinkle forming between his eyes. "How is that possible?"

My cheeks flamed with embarrassment. This was not something I'd wanted to admit to him. This wasn't something I admitted to anyone.

"I was determined not to end up pregnant when I was a teenager, and the only way to be sure that didn't happen was to stay far from all the horny boys in my hometown who were good at charming girls out of their panties but bad with condoms. Then I joined the Navy and steered clear of hooking up with other sailors, and here I am." I exhaled after saying so much without taking a breath. "Now you know why this is a horrible idea."

"Why would it be a horrible idea?"

"Because I'm a virgin. I have no idea what I'm doing. I'll probably be awful."

Torq smiled at me. "I doubt that very much." He brushed a hair from my face. "Do you wish to remain a virgin?"

That made me think. "No. Not really, but the longer I go, the weirder it gets."

"Then maybe our roles could switch."

I blinked at him. "What do you mean?"

"You have been tutoring me. Now I could tutor you."

I almost burst out laughing before I realized he was serious. "You want to tutor me in sex?"

"I can honestly say I would like nothing more."

A thousand voices were screaming in my head that this was a terrible idea, but I ignored them. I couldn't stay a virgin forever, and here was a gorgeous Drexian offering to be my personal sex tutor. It was almost too good to be true, even if it probably was a terrible idea.

"This stays between us," I said firmly. "And we keep this professional, just like the tutoring. We aren't dating and we definitely aren't a couple."

His eyes flickered with challenge, but he nodded. "If that is what you want."

As hot as Torq was, my gut told me he wasn't boyfriend material, and he wasn't the relationship type. But he was the sex tutor type. I had a feeling he'd be great at that. "I guess we have ourselves another deal."

CHAPTER
TWENTY-SEVEN

Torq

I was not sure if I was more shocked that Jess had not kneed me in the crotch yet, or that she had agreed to another deal, or that the deal she agreed to was that I would tutor her in sex. Most males would sacrifice a limb to have a desirable female ask them for sex but insist that there could be nothing more—no attachment, no commitment, no labels.

Then why had it bothered me when she'd insisted that we be nothing more? Why had it stung when she's been so insistent that we would not be a couple? Why did I care?

I shook off my hesitation. This would be perfect. I didn't want her expecting that there could be anything more between us. I could never be with her, even though she occupied my mind like no one else ever had. She might be brilliant and beautiful but that meant nothing to my family, and I had already disappointed them by failing to become a Wing. I could not claim a mate with no clan who was not even a tribute bride.

Drexians were warriors, we didn't marry warriors.

"You are sure?" I asked, a pang of guilt stabbing me.

Her eyes were wide but they held a determined glint. "I'm sure." She put a hand to the side of my face. "Please, Torq. I want this."

I brushed aside any lingering doubt and embraced my self-assuredness as well as the strange sense of pride that she was trusting me. "Then I am honored to be your first, but I must say that I told you."

Her cheeks flushed and her eyelashes fluttered. "Told me what?"

"That you would beg me to fuck you."

Jess rolled her eyes and tried to push me off her playfully. "I didn't beg."

I scooped an arm under her waist and scooted her to the middle of my bed. "But you want to beg."

She laughed as she shook her head. "I do not."

I sat back and grabbed both of her arms, then I pinned them over her head, holding them in place with one hand. "I think you do."

She struggled against my grip. "I could scream."

I leaned down and sucked her earlobe. "Good. I want to hear you scream." She drew in a quick breath, and I trailed the tip of my tongue down the side of her neck. "I want to hear you scream when I tease you with my tongue."

"I want you to scream when I spread your legs wide and bury my cock deep inside you." I kissed my way back up her throat and nipped at the soft flesh. Her breathing quickened and the vein behind her ear throbbed. "I want you to scream when I fill you and stretch you and fuck you so hard you can't walk."

"Torq." The way she said my name—desperately, hungrily —made my cock thicken.

I moved my mouth to hers, capturing her lips in a hard, claiming kiss. Just as she had in the tunnels, Jess surrendered her mouth to mine, parting her lips and sighing as my tongue stroked hers. She tasted as sweet as I remembered, but I wanted more. I wanted to taste more.

When I broke our kiss, her eyes were half-lidded with desire and her chest heaved.

"Torq," she said again, just as urgently. "What if I can't?"

I blinked down at her for a beat. "What if you can't what?"

Her cheeks were pink as her gaze dropped. "What if I can't take all of you? What if I can't do those things you want?"

I fought the urge to smile. Instead, I kissed her gently, charmed by her innocence and aroused by her desire to please me. "You do not think you'll be able to take my cock?"

"I've heard that Drexians are bigger than humans—a lot bigger." Her voice trembled slightly. "And I've never..."

"Do you *want* to take all of me?" I locked eyes with her. "Do you want to spread your legs for me like a good girl?"

Even though her pupils flared, she moved her head up and down.

"Then don't worry, *cinarra*. I'll make sure you're ready for me, and I'll teach you just what to do."

"*Cinarra?*"

I hadn't meant to let the Drexian term of endearment slip out. I'd never used it with a female before. It had always felt too intimate, but with Jess it felt perfect. "A Drexian word that doesn't have an exact translation in your language."

"Is it a nice word?"

My heart squeezed, and doubt niggled at the back of my

brain that I would be able to keep from becoming more attached to her. "It is, but that is the only nice word you are going to hear from me. The rest of them will be as bad as all the things I am going to do to you."

Her mouth opened in surprise, but her eyes blazed as I released her wrists and moved down her body. I tugged her shirt from the waistband of her pants, pulling it up until I revealed her bra and the nipples straining against the sheer fabric.

With a moan, I set my mouth on one tight peak, sucking it through the transparent fabric before moving to the other. Jess arched her back and tangled her fingers in my hair as she emitted breathy sounds. I switched to the other hard nipple, giving it a small nip before lifting my head and stealing a glance at her half-lidded eyes.

"That's right, I want you to let go for me, Jess. I want to hear every moan."

I slid farther down her body, unfastening her pants and dragging them over her hips, then I sat back and pulled her pants all the way off and tossed them to the floor. When I saw the triangle of sheer fabric between her legs and the string sides begging to be ripped in two, my heart pounded, and my cock ached.

I wanted to tear them from her body and thrust inside her, but I would not do that. I would not make her first time so rough, even if her lush body did make me feel feral. I wanted this to be good for her. I wanted to be good for her.

It may not be something I could wear as a badge of honor like my clan or my school, but it was something that I would know. I would know that I had bedded her well and taught her well, even if I would not be the mate enjoying her.

I brushed this thought aside and met her gaze as she lay on my bed. "Did you wear these for me?"

"No." She shook her head, but her words were unconvincing.

"If you are lying, I might have to spank you."

She bit her bottom lip, as her chest heaved. So that did not scare her.

"Did you ever imagine me taking them off you?" I asked, pinning her with my gaze. "And do not lie to me again, Jess."

She nodded without speaking.

I bent down, grabbed the thin straps on both sides, and slid them down the length of her long legs. Then I sat back. "Open for me, *cinarra*."

She hesitated, her breath hitching. I dropped between her legs, kissing my way up her thighs and gently parting them as I went. If she was shy, I would tease her open like a flower, softly, tenderly, patiently.

When I reached her sex, I pressed a long kiss to the thin strip of neatly cropped hair. "Has anyone tasted you before?"

She drew in a quick breath. "No."

Their loss, I thought as I inhaled the sweet scent of her and battled against more primal urges to take her in a single, hard thrust. But when I ran my tongue through her and tasted her honeyed juices, I forgot all about rushing to fuck her. And when she scraped her fingers through my hair and hooked her legs over my shoulders, I remembered what I'd heard about human females.

I remembered the talk of their arousal button, the bundle of nerves between their legs that could produce the most exquisite pleasure and the most enticing sounds. More than wanting to be buried inside her, I wanted to hear her sounds and feel her tremors.

I explored with my tongue until I found a swollen nub of flesh. Jess's sharp inhalation of breath and her nails digging into my scalp told me I'd found the magic spot. I took my time swirling and flicking until her hips twitched restlessly and her breathing was thready.

I raised my head. "I'm going to prepare your perfect little cunt for me now." I slid one finger inside her, my own eyes rolling back in my head at the tight, wet heat. "Relax for me, Jess."

She whimpered as I slid my finger out and in slowly, curling it slightly to stroke her. "Torq, I..."

I loved hearing my name on her lips almost as much as I loved hearing her gasp and feeling her writhe beneath me. For a female who'd never done any of this before, she didn't seem to have any problem surrendering to the pleasure. "That's my good girl. You're doing so well. Now I want to feel you come. Can you do that for me?"

She nodded before arching her back. She was close, which made my cock stiffen and my heart race.

I returned my mouth to her, continuing to move my finger in and out as her moans intensified. I didn't slow my pace as her body jerked and spasmed, her legs tightening around my head until the sound of her crying my name was muffled. Only when her thighs released their grip on my head and her entire body went slack was I sure she'd climaxed.

Sitting back, I took in the sight of her with her dark hair fanned around her head and her cheeks flushed. Her legs were still open, and her chest rose and fell as she tried to catch her breath. I'd never wanted someone more in my life, and I had to remind myself that I needed to go slow. I did not want to scare her off.

I moved up her body on all fours, lowering myself to whisper in her ear. "Now you're ready to take my cock like a good girl, aren't you?"

CHAPTER
TWENTY-EIGHT

Jess

His words should have sent up alarms. They should have made me second guess such an impulsive decision. They should have reminded me that Torq was a bad boy at heart. But my heart was pounding too hard, and my body was buzzing with desire. I didn't care what others thought about him or even what I'd thought. I'd seen a different side of him. Even if he was bad, he was my bad boy.

Besides, I'd let fear keep me from experiencing love—or even just a good lay—for too long. Avoiding guys had served me well in getting me away from my dead-end town, but now I'd gotten out. Way out. It was time to have some fun.

"I'm ready," I whispered, my voice breathy as I recovered from my entire body imploding. I reached down and tugged his pants down so that his cock sprang up, hard and hot. I fisted it, even though my fingers couldn't reach all the way around the thick base. "I want to take you like a good girl."

As if he'd been released from invisible restraints, Torq crushed his mouth to mine. I tried to breathe as his mouth plundered mine and his tongue parted my lips, but he rendered me breathless.

He lowered his body between my legs, and I had to let go of his cock, but within a moment it was between my legs. I instinctively rocked my hips into him, an ache of need building between my legs. Hunger surged hot as the hard bar of his cock dragged across my clit and sent fresh tremors through me.

One of his hands slid up to tangle in my hair as he moved his hips to slide his cock through my slickness, and he pulled me deeper into the kiss. I gripped his shoulders, my finger slipping over his academy insignia tattoo and then sliding down his back and reaching around to feel his nodes. I'd seen the hard bumps that ran along his spine when he'd taken off his shirt in the maze, but I'd never felt them before.

Torq let out a desperate growl, as I stroked my fingers over the firm bumps. He broke our kiss, panting. "You are going to drive me mad before I can fuck you."

My pulse skittered wildly, power surging through me as I worked his nodes harder and savored the instant response. His body jerked and his breathing hitched.

Torq pulled back, and his molten eyes locked with mine. "You are making it impossible for me to go slow."

"Who said I want it slow?"

Torq squeezed his eyes closed and gave a small shake of his head. "I did. Now are you going to obey me and be a good girl?"

I might have been a rule-follower most of my life, but I'd never been big on obeying. But I didn't mind obeying him. Not when he made it feel so good. "Are you going to fuck me, or do I need to find another Drexian to do the job?"

He growled and swallowed my words with a deep kiss, his tongue stroking mine as he centered the thick crown of his cock at my entrance. I sucked in a breath, startled by its size and by how desperately I wanted it inside me. My heart was racing so fast, I was afraid I might explode if he didn't fuck me.

My hands roamed his back, tugging up his shirt so I could feel the flesh of his nodes and the fiery heat as his arousal grew. I loved the dark rumble in his throat that grew louder the faster I stroked.

"Jess," he rasped after tearing his lips from mine, his body trembling as his cock teased my entrance. "I do not want to hurt you."

"You won't." I was so hungry to have him inside me, I didn't care how much it hurt.

His jaw was tight as he shook his head, but I hiked my legs up and circled them around his hips. "Better?"

Torq growled and crushed his mouth to mine again as he pressed his cock into me without breaking our kiss, his tongue caressing mine. I could feel myself stretching as he pushed his rigid length slowly inside, the burning sensation making my breath catch.

He paused and pulled away, panting. "You are so tight, Jess." The torment was clear on his face as he held himself inside me without going deeper. "You make me feel wild. It is all I can do not to fuck you like a beast."

Part of me loved the fact that I was pushing him to the brink, but another part of me wasn't sure if losing my virginity to a huge Drexian was a bad plan.

Too late now, Jess. He's inside you. You went big. There is no going home.

"Do it fast," I whispered, hoping this would be like ripping off a Band-Aid.

He gritted his teeth and closed his eyes for a beat. "Do not tell me that."

I ran my hands across his nodes. "I want you to, Torq."

He captured my lips again as he thrust the rest of the way in. A sharp pain arrowed through me, but he swallowed my scream, as he held himself deep. I twitched my hips, as if I could escape the massive intrusion, but he had me pinned down with his cock. After a few seconds, the pain subsided, and a warm sensation of pleasure washed over me.

"Are you okay?" he asked, his voice tight when he tore his mouth from mine. It was taking an effort for him not to move inside me.

"Mmhmm." I hummed my answer as I relaxed my grip on his back. "You?"

He rasped out a laugh. "I have never felt better in my entire life." He touched his forehead to mine. "I did not hurt you too much?"

I lifted my legs higher around his hips, pulling him deeper as he emitted a strangled sound. "You can hurt me like this any time."

"Do not say something you don't mean." His warm breath feathered over my cheeks. "I might want to fuck you all the time."

I relished the feeling of being filled by him so completely. I loved having his big cock inside me and our bodies locked together. Even though he was the one on top of me, I felt a rush of power from being able to take him. "If you're going to teach me everything, you might need to."

With a growl, Torq started moving inside me. "You feel like you were made for my cock. That is something that cannot be taught."

"Maybe I was." I moved my hands from his back to his hair,

scraping them through it and then holding onto his neck. "Maybe I was always meant for a Drexian."

"For me," he said quickly. "You are mine...for now."

I thrilled at hearing him call me his, even though I knew he was only going to be my teacher. "For now."

He moved one hand to my hips and guided me to rock my hips to match his thrusts. "That's it. *Grek*, you're taking me so well."

How had I gone from barely able to stretch around his cock to eagerly meeting his strokes? Pleasure made me lightheaded as his pace quickened and beads of sweat appeared on his brow. I moaned as tremors started to ripple through me again, my second release just as powerful as the first.

Digging my fingernails into his back, I clenched my legs around him as my body shattered and my pussy pulsed around his cock. I'd barely stopped gasping when I pulled his head down so I could bite his earlobe and whisper in his ear. "Now it's your turn. Fuck me like you know you want to, Torq. Fuck me like I'm a bad girl."

With a roar, his self-control snapped. He reared back and drove into me a few more times until he finally thrust hard and pulsed into me. He propped himself on his elbows as his head fell forward, and he sucked in breaths. "I think you might have a real future as a bad girl."

CHAPTER
TWENTY-NINE

Torq

A splash of salty spray drenched my face as a wave crashed over the bow of the small boat. I swiped the back of my hand across my mouth to rid myself of the briny taste, but my hand was also wet. Readjusting my grip on the wooden oar, I heaved the paddle through the turbulent water in time with my fellow cadets. This was not what I'd imagined when Kann had mentioned that we'd be using the holo-chambers to prepare for the battle of schools.

"The Restless Sea is even more unpleasant than it looks," Kort yelled over the howling wind, as he craned his neck to look at me over his shoulder. Before I could answer, he turned back around and resumed rowing.

I would have reminded him that this wasn't actually the Restless Sea, but he knew as well as I did that we were inside the holo-chamber. I still wasn't sure why this was part of our training, but it made me anxious about the upcoming face-off between the schools. They wouldn't send us out in some kind of regatta in the actual Restless Sea, would they?

I was glad I could swim, but I was sure there were Blades who couldn't, and those cadets were glancing furtively at the white-capped waves and churning water. Of course, they wouldn't drown. Not in the simulation. The water might feel like water, and the boat might feel like a real boat, but they were still energy made solid and could be disabled at any moment. But you could drown if there was a challenge that took place in the real sea that bordered the academy. I liked to think that after what had happened in the trials, that more lives wouldn't be risked in the next cadet challenge. But this was the Drexian Academy, after all.

"Faster!" The cadet at the front of our ship pointed at a massive wave bearing down on us. "We have to crest the wave before it breaks."

My heart was beating double time as I rowed faster, my gaze riveted to the impending wall of water barreling toward us. We weren't going to make it. My arms burned as I pulled as hard as I could, and my back ached from throwing myself back to get more leverage. I hadn't thought that I'd be treated softly on my first day back to Blades training, but I hadn't expected this.

The tip of our boat lifted as we rowed up the swell of water that was starting to resemble a wall as it grew larger, but I could sense that we were not going fast enough. If we didn't get the nose of our boat over the crest of the wave, we'd flip backward and get crushed by the water. Considering the amount of water already on my face, I braced myself to be rolled by a massive wave.

"Almost there!" The cadet leading the charge could barely be heard over the crashing waves and the grunting of the cadets that filled the two sides of the long boat. His voice was snatched away and tossed into the whipping wind.

I pushed my feet into the floor of the boat to get more traction as I rowed and, my leg wailed in pain. I ignored it and kept my gaze on the wave. The wave we were not going to go over in time.

Gritting my teeth, I pushed myself to move my arms faster, even as the boat started to tip back and the white froth topping the wave began to crash over us. Kort stopped rowing in front of me and appeared ready to leap over the side.

"End program."

The stormy sea vanished, the boat vanished, the oar I was holding vanished, and we were all unceremoniously pluncked down onto the hard floor of the holo-chamber. Even though droplets of water were still splattered across of our faces, the holo-chamber was dry. It was a good thing I was a Blade and not an Iron because I would never understand holo-technology and the ability to transform energy into matter and back again so seamlessly.

There was some grumbling as we all readjusted to being back on dry land. I stood and rubbed the small of my back that ached from hunching forward and yanking back over and over while Kort shook out his arms.

"I think I have a splinter," he said, as I offered him a hand to pull him up.

"I have questions," I said in reply, but not loud enough for the Blade instructors to overhear.

I didn't have to wait long for another cadet to ask what the point was in the exercise.

An older Blade instructor with scruffy cheeks and long, dark hair pulled into a topknot eyed us with little sympathy. "Not all battles take place in space or on open fields or even on sheer rock walls. There have been occasions for Drexians to take to the seas in battle. Although it isn't common, you should know what it is like."

"But that wasn't a battle," a cadet pointed out.

The instructor grinned, his teeth flashing white. "It would have been if you'd made it over the wave."

I exchanged a look with Kort. Was missing a battle on the other side of a huge wave supposed to be a bad thing? Blades were supposed to love a good fight, but I doubted any of us would have loved that.

"The battle of the schools won't involve the Restless Sea, will it?" Kort asked when he'd stopped inspecting his hands for splinters.

The instructor just grinned at him. "I have no idea, but I make no promises. Past battles have used the sea and the mountains."

I walked with Kort as the class dispersed through the open holo-chamber doors, aware that most of our boots were making squelching sounds as we walked. So much for the Blades sneaking up on anyone today.

"Torq."

I turned at the gravelly voice that hadn't come from the instructor. It took me a beat to recognize the Drexian cadet who'd stabbed me on the climbing wall and knocked me off. I'd only gotten a flash of his face as he'd lunged for me, but I recognized the malicious glint in his eyes.

Kort stopped with me, tensing as he must have also recognized the cadet. "What do you want, Dom?"

I was surprised that my friend was so hostile to our Blade brother. Sure, the Drexian hadn't checked on me when I was out, but I hadn't taken that personally. We didn't know each other, and apologies were awkward.

"I wanted to talk to Torq."

Kort crossed his arms. "Well, you got both of us, so talk."

"About that day on the wall," he started.

"Don't worry about it," I told him before he could finish. "I'm over it."

The Drexian's gray eyes narrowed. "You're over it? Who says I'm over it?"

I didn't know what this cadet was going on about, but he was obviously mad. Had he gotten in trouble for what he'd done? Did he blame me for his punishment?

He leaned closer and pointed a finger at my chest. "You thought you could climb over me like I was nothing. Well, you got what you deserved."

"You didn't like that I got ahead of you?"

"You cheated." He spat out the words, flicking his gaze between me and Kort. "If I were you, I'd watch my back."

He pushed past us and stomped through the doorway, leaving me in openmouthed shock. "He drove a dagger into my leg, and he's mad at me?"

"Ignore him." Kort shook his head as we walked from the holo-chamber. "He's *grekked* off because you proved you were smarter than him by using other cadets as climbing holds. Everyone else thought your move was pure Blade. Maybe with a touch of Assassin, but mostly badass Blade."

I thought of Jess hearing my tactic on the wall and telling me I would have made a decent Assassin. Being tossed around in a violent sea had distracted me enough that I hadn't thought about Jess for the entire class, but now memories of her naked and beneath me flooded my brain.

"You ready for some makeup work?" Kort elbowed me. "I bet we'll be the only ones on the climbing wall if we go while everyone else is eating."

"Great plan," I deadpanned. "And when do we eat?"

"Don't pretend that you don't sneak down to the kitchens for extra food."

I hesitated. I could not tell him that I had taken Jess there.

Kort barked out a laugh. "I forgot you were a high-born. Have you ever been inside a kitchen?" Before I could tell him that I had—although only a few times in my own house, which was something I wasn't planning to mention—he gave me a friendly punch in the arm. "Don't worry. That's why you need a friend like me."

CHAPTER
THIRTY

Jess

T he lights came up in the classroom, and I blinked a few times as my eyes readjusted from the darkness. The holographic image of the land war diagram faded in the brightness as Fiona sat on the edge of a wooden desk. "The next test will include all the battle strategies from Earth medieval era and Drex Dark Times."

Morgan swiped her tablet closed and tipped her head closer to mine as we sat side by side in the front row. "The Dark Times on Drex seem a lot scarier than the Dark Ages in Earth history."

"That's because we didn't have dragons or griffins on Earth." I waved a hand at the hint of the hologram hovering in the air, the outlines of eagle-headed lions in the depictions of the Drex battle.

Morgan tightened her blonde ponytail. "You don't think

that's real, do you? I mean, those are mythological creatures, right?"

I shrugged. "After the creatures we encountered in the trials, I honestly would believe anything here."

"But they aren't on the planet now." It was a statement, but I sensed it was also a question.

"I think someone would have mentioned if dragons roamed Drex."

Morgan snorted out a laugh. "Are you kidding? How many things have the Drexians failed to mention already?"

She made a good point. The Drexian Academy wasn't known for being forthcoming about its traditions or long-held secrets, which made me wonder if they were hiding things about the planet, as well. Still, I'd seen no evidence of dragons or griffins, and those seemed like large things to conceal.

While we were debating the existence of mythological creatures, the rest of the class filed out and left the half-moon shaped classroom virtually empty. Only Fiona sat behind her desk flipping through a stack of yellowed parchment that hadn't been there during the lecture.

I walked to her, unable to keep my curiosity at bay. "More research into the Kronock?"

She tipped her head up, grinning when she saw it was us. "Don't tell anyone, but I snuck these documents from the Stacks so I could review them between classes."

Morgan joined me at the desk. "Why didn't we think of borrowing things from the Stacks? Not that I don't love reading by the dim lighting in there."

"Maybe because we aren't instructors?"

She bobbled her head at my point. "Right."

Fiona smiled. "I'm pretty sure I'm not supposed to take papers from the Stacks either, but I trust you two not to rat me out."

"Who hasn't broken a rule or two?" Morgan slid her gaze to me. "We already broke about a thousand last term with our after-hours coaching."

And I was breaking more rules by sneaking into Torq's room, I thought, as my heart pattered. I hoped my cheeks weren't flushing and betraying me as I shifted from one foot to the other, but I couldn't staunch the flow of memories from the night before—of Torq's head between my legs, of him inside me, of him coming inside me, which would have freaked me out if I didn't have a birth control implant and know that he had one, too.

Morgan elbowed me. "Jess freaks out even talking about breaking the rules."

"I do not," I protested, even as my cheeks warmed.

Fiona eyed me but only smiled wider. "Rule-breaking doesn't always come easy to Assassins at first. We're used to playing games by the rules and winning on skill alone."

"I don't mind a little bending of the rules." I glanced at the papers on her desk and tried to change the subject. "Have you made any progress?"

Fiona sighed. "If by progress you mean adding even more possible sites to our list, then yes."

"That's the opposite of our lack of progress," Morgan said. "We came up with a long list of places that wouldn't work. At least you've found some targets."

Fiona didn't seem comforted. "Too many targets mean it will take forever to narrow it down, but I can't ignore all the locations within Kronock space."

I didn't know a great deal about the enemy's domain. It wasn't a part of space humans—or even many Drexians—had explored. And since the Kronock had been pushed back and weakened, I'd hoped that the space they controlled had shrunk, but that might have been wishful thinking on my part.

"Is there anyone at the academy who has experience with Kronock space? Maybe the Academy Master can help narrow the field."

Fiona frowned. "There's one Drexian here who has been to Kronock space, but he's not exactly the type to help out a bunch of humans."

"Vyk?" Morgan asked with a quick glance over her shoulder, as if the silver-haired Drexian might materialize in the classroom at the mention of his name.

Fiona grunted her version of yes. "I hope he was vindicated in the trial scandal, but I can't forget the things he said about humans, or the fact that he went along with the plan to wash out the Earth cadets for so long. He might have gotten cold feet at the end, but that doesn't mean he's changed his mind about us being here."

"What did he say about humans?" I asked. The severe Drexian had always given me the chills, but I don't know if I'd ever heard him speak. My encounters with him had been limited to me scurrying out of the way as he stalked through the halls, and I was fine keeping it that way.

Fiona's frown deepened to a scowl. "It doesn't matter. Just trust me that he isn't a fan of us being here, and he's definitely not a fan of me."

"What did you do to piss him off?" Morgan asked in a furtive whisper.

Fiona squared her shoulders. "I might have told him what I thought about his part in the trials. I might have gotten in his face, and I might have threatened to cut off his balls and use them as castanets."

A laugh erupted from me, and I slapped a hand over my mouth.

"You did what?" Morgan's eyes danced with amusement and disbelief.

"It was at the initiation banquet. I knew he'd been found locked in the dungeons so he couldn't reveal the sabotage, but I also knew that he'd been the reason there were four monsters in the maze. I was still livid that Ariana had risked her life to save the cadets and could have died, and I'd had enough of Drexian superiority bullshit. I walked up to him and let him know exactly what I thought of him."

Fiona didn't look ashamed. She seemed proud, and I didn't blame her. I wished I had the courage to tell others exactly what I thought of them. I wished I didn't feel like I had to run when things got tough. I wished I was the kind of woman that no one would dare mess with.

"What did he do?" Morgan gave her a quick once-over. "You're still standing and you're still here, so that's a good sign."

"He didn't say much." Fiona gave us a wicked grin. "He did seem surprised when I threatened to cut off his balls, and he asked me to define castanets."

"He must not have believed his universal translator implant." Morgan giggled. "I wish I'd seen the Drexian's face. If you ask me, he deserved it."

"That's what I thought." Fiona's grin faded. "But it does mean that I can't exactly ask him for help with this project. I don't think I'm his favorite human."

Morgan and I exchanged wary glances. Neither of us wanted to approach the gruff Drexian who despised humans, either.

"There must be another way to get the information," I said. "He can't be the only Drexian to have entered Kronock space."

Morgan sighed. "But he might be the only one at the academy."

"*Grek* that."

We all turned toward the voice, as Ariana hurried into the

classroom as if she'd run the entire way. Behind her was Reina, wringing her hands and jogging in high-heeled boots that made her blue hair almost brush the ceiling.

"There's more than one Drexian who knows about Kronock space." Ariana stopped when she reached us and put a hand to her side. Then she spun on one foot and waved for us to follow her as Reina sucked in a breath and fluttered a hand at her throat. "Are you coming or what?"

THIRTY-ONE

Torq

"How often do you sneak down there?" I bit into a slightly burned strip of fried padwump as we walked up the staircase from the lower level that held the kitchens.

Kort mumbled something unintelligible as he chewed on a piece of bread, but I took it to mean that his visits were not infrequent. Kort seemed to be liked among the kitchen crew that was mostly comprised of non-Drexians.

He had a way of charming others that I envied. I'd always gotten what I'd wanted through intimidation or flashing my status, but Kort didn't do that. I was starting to see that there were better ways to go about life than the way I'd been taught.

I'd seen firsthand from Jess that status had no part in intelligence or even achievement, especially with humans. As far as I was aware, none of the cadets who'd been sent to the academy from Earth had any sort of name or clout. At first, I'd been offended that I was surrounded by cadets from low clans. Then I'd enjoyed being one of the few elite Drexians in my class. Until I'd discovered why there weren't many high-born Drexians.

No one in our cadet class was supposed to have survived the trials. Including me. Including a cadet from House Swoll. So much for my superior clan protecting me. If it hadn't been for the human cadets, I would have died. That fact haunted me daily.

Kort swallowed his mouthful as we reached the top of the stairs. "I'm surprised your older brother didn't let you in on the secret of the kitchens. Wasn't he here before you?"

Kort said this without a trace of aggression or spite. Either he didn't know my brother had washed out, or he didn't care. Even though I did know about the kitchens, my brother had not told me. He would not have. We did not have that kind of relationship. Actually, we had little relationship. He had no use for a younger brother, and I avoided him and his easily provoked fists.

I eyed Kort, surprised he did not comment more on my brother. If I'd been in possession of the same information, I would have used it as a taunt or worse, to manipulate an advantage. The shame of this realization washed over me and prickled the back of my neck.

That had been the old me, I reminded myself. I wasn't the same Drexian I'd been.

But you did blackmail Jess.

I huffed angrily at this, hating that I'd slipped into my old ways as soon as I'd desired something. As soon as I'd desired her.

"No need to get angry about it," Kort said, studying my reaction.

"I am not angry," I said quickly. "I was thinking of something else."

Kort brows shot up. "Something more interesting than food? What is her name?"

I jerked at his question. "That isn't it. There is no 'her.'"

Kort's face fell. "Too bad. I thought you might have an in with the human females, since you went through the maze with them."

"I do not," I lied.

We started across the open area of the main hall, voices echoing from the dining hall above and bouncing down the sweeping staircase. An inclinator zipped down from overhead, swirling around the inside of the staircase, and stopping at the bottom to let out a compartment filled with cadets. Irons, I noted, as the intense Drexians proceeded off the inclinator and toward the Stacks without glancing at us.

We passed the arched entrance to the School of Strategy as another group rushed out and almost walked into us.

"Sorry," Ariana said, glancing at me and giving me a relieved look. "Oh, it's you, Torq."

Kort didn't hide his surprise as he swung his gaze from me to the flight instructor and back.

"Lieutenant." I gave her a salute by thumping my fist across my chest, even though she wasn't Drexian, and then spotted the human female who taught the Assassins and gave her a matching salute. "Captain." I didn't salute the Vexling in the bright-yellow pants suit, but she gave me a finger wave that seemed unusually friendly.

Ariana glanced at the contraband roll in my hand and then at Kort who held several rolls in his hands. "I don't need to ask where you've been."

I couldn't answer, even though her statement didn't require one. I'd spotted Jess and her friend Morgan behind the two instructors, and my brain had short-circuited. I couldn't think of a sensible word to utter, and I couldn't manage to wrest my gaze from Jess. I could only gape at her as I thought about how she'd looked lying beneath me, her cheeks flushed, her eyes fluttering as she'd moaned with pleasure, her chest heaving.

"Just returning from the dining hall," Kort said after an uncomfortable pause.

Ariana nodded, but I sensed she knew that was a lie. Was I the only one in the school who hadn't been sneaking to the kitchens?

"Don't worry," Reina said in a stage whisper. "We won't tell."

Jess was making a point to avoid my gaze, but it was only when Kort grabbed my arm and tugged me away that I stopped staring at her.

"Have a good night," my friend said, as we allowed the women to pass.

"You too," Ariana called back, as she resumed her fast pace and the rest of the women followed.

Morgan tilted her head at me, flicking a glance at her friend as the group walked by me and continued through the main hall. When they'd gone, I released a breath a bit too noticeably.

"What was that?"

I snapped my head to Kort, preparing to weave an explanation for my off behavior. "You mean the Vexling in yellow? She's the Academy Master's wife's—"

He cut off my convoluted explanation. "Did you see the way the one with gold hair looked at you?"

I blinked at him. "What? The captain?"

Kort shook his head and gave me a look like I was simple

minded. "No, the other one. Wasn't she one of the women who went through the maze with you?"

"Morgan?" I almost laughed in relief. He hadn't noticed my inability to look away from Jess? "I did not notice."

"Too bad. She noticed you." Kort took a bite from one of his rolls. "Too bad the other one didn't look at either of us. She's the one I'd want to try."

I bristled. "Jess? You would want to try her?"

Kort slapped a hand on my shoulder. "Do not look offended. Not all Drexians believe they are so superior they can't enjoy a human female."

"I don't think—"

"We all know what you think of humans," Kort cut me off. "You made it pretty clear last term. Unless that changed?"

Did I tell him that my opinion had completely changed? Did I tell him I now believed the opposite? Did I tell him that I thought human females were fascinating, one especially?

Not unless I wanted my friend to be suspicious. Not unless I was prepared for him to discover the truth. I might not be ashamed of Jess, but I'd promised her that no one would know. Promises had not been something I'd valued before, but I was determined to keep my promise to her.

What I didn't want to admit to myself—what I couldn't admit—was that I had to keep the promise for myself, as well. Jess was a secret that my family could never discover. Not unless I was ready to lose everything.

"I do not despise the humans," I told Kort, "but I will leave enjoying them to you, brother."

Kort grinned at me with his cheeks bulging with bread, and I tried not to think about what might happen if I had to see Jess in public with someone who paid better attention than my Battle brother.

CHAPTER
THIRTY-TWO

Jess

Morgan and I jogged to catch up to Ariana and Fiona, who'd practically sprinted across the main hall and disappeared under the arched entrance to the School of Battle. Reina brought up the rear with her boots clip-clopping on the stone floors. I was so sidetracked by where we were going and why that I barely heard Morgan as she whispered to me.

"Am I the only one who thought that was weird?"

The lights inside the Blades' domain were low since classes were finished for the day, and the corridor that connected the school to the main hallway was empty and echoed our footsteps back to us.

I glanced at her as we caught up to the two instructors. "What was weird?"

Morgan's eyes became narrow. "You really didn't see it?"

I knew exactly what she meant, but the only thing I could think to do was to play dumb and hope she believed me. Considering we were both Assassins, I put the odds very low. "The two Blades? Of course, I saw them. I also saw that they were pilfering food from the kitchens. Is that what you mean?"

She rolled her eyes as we reached the end of the connecting corridor and entered the main building that housed the Blades classrooms, the holo-chambers, the climbing wall, and multiple sparring gyms. Unlike the School of Strategy, which was mostly classrooms and archives, the School of Battle consisted of mostly gyms and training facilities. I suspected that the couple of lecture halls in the school got little use.

"I mean, Torq staring at you." Her voice was low but sharp. "You really didn't notice?"

There were a few ways I could play this. One was to admit everything. Not my first option because then I'd have to explain the whole sordid story. A second option was to deny everything and hope she bought it. But a third option was to admit part of the truth in hopes that it might throw her off the scent.

"Okay." I stopped and pivoted to face her. "I noticed, but I tried to ignore him because he's been weird around me since the trials."

Morgan face pinched. "Weird how? Do I need to kick his ass?"

I put a hand on her arm. "Thanks, but no. I think he might have a crush on me, but I'm managing to ignore him."

"You're telling me that the cockiest cadet in our class is letting you ignore him?"

I forced myself to stay calm and not launch into how much Torq had changed. "I don't think he's so cocky anymore. He did almost die in the maze with us."

"True." Morgan nodded. "He wasn't bad in the maze. I guess I shouldn't judge him by what a colossal ass he was all term before that."

I laughed at her honesty and because it was true. Torq had been a jerk and a bully before he'd had to work with us in the trials and before he'd learned that he had been sacrificed right along with us by the Drexians on the High Command. A part of me wondered how much he'd really changed, and how much I was hoping he'd changed. He was sweet to me now, but was that because I was giving him what he wanted? Would he be so nice if I'd refused to tutor him? Would I be determined to see the best in him if I hadn't decided to lose my virginity to him?

"Are we talking about the handsome Drexian cadets?" Reina asked as she reached us panting.

"I think one of them has a thing for Jess."

I didn't have a chance to protest before Reina was bobbing her head vigorously. "He does, but then, who wouldn't?"

I smiled at the Vexling, who was beaming at me with genuine affection. "Thanks, but he's a Drexian cadet. He probably has a thing for all the women here."

Reina twisted her lips to one side. "I don't think that's true. He's never looked at me like I was a poplov berry dipped in chocolate."

Reina might appear to be perpetually cheerful and bubbly, but I'd noticed that she was also both perceptive and intuitive. She seemed to see a lot that went on in the academy.

"Well, if he tries anything on you, just let me know." Morgan cracked her knuckles. "I have a couple of older brothers. I don't mind a good scrap."

I wasn't sure if picking a fight with a Drexian so much bigger than you would be what most people considered a good scrap, but I appreciated the sentiment. Before I could thank her, Morgan grabbed my arm and Reina's and pulled us forward to close the distance between us and the instructors.

"Where are we going?" I asked, as much to myself as anyone. "And who in Battle knows about Kronock space?"

I realized that I didn't know many Drexian Blades at all, except for Torq and the instructor who'd helped train us for the maze.

"Kann," Ariana greeted the Drexian as he stepped from a doorway in nothing but snug, black sparring pants. "I hoped to find you here."

The Drexian looked startled to see her and even more startled that we were with the lieutenant. "Ariana? Did something happen to Volt?"

She smiled at him. "No, but he told me I might find you here."

I could see from the instructor's expression that Volten might pay for revealing that information, especially since Kann now stood shirtless in front of four human females and one very giggly Vexling. "You found me. How can I help?"

Despite the fact that I'd been up close and personal with a ripped Drexian the night before, I would have been blind not to notice the Drexian's muscular chest and corded stomach. There didn't look to be an ounce of fat on the guy. If there was a single Drexian at the academy who approached dad bod territory, I hadn't seen him.

"I heard that one of your Inferno Force crew mates was taken captive by the Kronock."

Kann wrinkled his brow. "Really? Who's been talking to you about Inferno Force?"

Ariana shifted from foot to foot. "I don't want to reveal my confidential source, but I was told about an Inferno Force crew mate of yours that was held in enemy space. Someone named Jax?"

Reina tentatively raised her hand. "I might have mentioned it to her. I knew Jax at my last space station. I was there when he vanished into Kronock territory."

THIRTY-THREE

Jess

K ann led us into a dark room and then swept his hand over a panel in the wall, and we were instantly engulfed by light.

"Whoa," Morgan said under her breath as she stopped short, and I almost walked into her. "What is this place?"

"This is the circuit." Kann glanced at the massive series of platforms, dangling ropes, incline walls, and parallel bars. Then he smiled at us. "Want to give it a try?"

I suppressed the urge to double over with laughter. I might have made it through basic training, the battle class from last term, and the after-hours, maze coaching sessions, but that didn't mean I considered myself up for a physical gauntlet that looked like it spit out Drexians for fun. The series of challenges looked like something from a cheesy Earth reality show without the bright colors or extra padding.

"Why are we here?" Ariana was practically vibrating with nervous energy as her gaze swept the high-ceilinged space.

The Blade instructor waved to a small area with curved benches for observers. "Battle doesn't have much in the way of seating, and this is the closest place with any place to sit." He walked toward the black benches. "Unless you would rather talk while scaling a rock wall in the climbing gym?"

"Nope." Ariana followed him, running one hand through her hair. "This works. Now what can you tell me about Jax?"

Kann sat on one bench and then turned so he could face the other one. He leaned forward to put his elbows on his knees. "I'd forgotten about his experience with the Kronock. We only shared a ship for one mission before I left Inferno Force to take my post here. I don't even know if he's still in Inferno Force since he took a mate."

Ariana took the spot across from him but the rest of us remained standing since it seemed like almost a private conversation between the two. That is, until Reina plopped down next to Ariana.

"That's a good point," Reina tapped one long finger on her chin. "I don't think he'd want to leave his bride for long. They're quite devoted to each other."

"So, you don't know anything about his time being held by the Kronock?" Ariana sounded deflated, and her shoulders slumped.

"I am sorry to say that I don't." Kann reached a hand and touched it to Ariana's knee. "But he isn't the only one to be held captive by the enemy—or to be rescued from a Kronock prison. A former High Commander rescued a tribute bride from Kronock space. We're trying to contact him so he can share how he did it."

Ariana straightened. "We? Who's we, and how did I not know about this?"

Kann muttered a litany of Drexian curses as he cast his gaze to the floor. "Volt did not tell you?"

Ariana's eyes flashed as she rapidly tapped one toe. "He did not."

"I'm sure there's a good reason, hon." Reina patted Ariana's arm and shot a pleading look at Kann.

"He must not have wanted to tell you until we were sure we could find him. Kax has been on a series of missions that have kept him out of contact for long periods of time. There is no guarantee that we will be able to track him down, but Torq is working on it."

"Torq?" I asked, before I could stop myself. "He's working with you on this?"

Kann looked at me, along with everyone else. "He is. His clan status gives him access to a fellow high born like Kax, so he offered to use his connections."

How elite was Torq's clan? From what I knew of Kann, he didn't come from a low class like Volten, although he didn't flash his clan around like Torq had done when I'd first met him. I was starting to get the idea that Torq's house was more powerful and influential than I'd thought, which was such a strange concept. I'd come from a town where no one had any real status, and I'd never even had a friend who was wealthy. Now I was dating a guy from one of the most important clans on the planet?

Not dating, I reminded myself. That had been my rule as much as his. We were friends with benefits. But were we friends? I'd never have said we were when he'd blackmailed me into tutoring him, but after spending so much time with the Drexian, he felt like a friend. But, again, he'd blackmailed me, which wasn't friend behavior.

Were we frenemies? Was frenemies with benefits a thing? Could sex lessons be considered benefits? They definitely were a benefit for me, and I wasn't being arrogant to say I thought they were for him too.

"So, we wait until Torq's connections come through?" Ariana stood and stamped one foot. "How can I keep waiting when I know that Sasha is being held in an enemy prison?"

"It won't help Sasha if you fly off without a plan or a solid target," Fiona reminded her. "We're all working hard on it. The Drexians are working on finding her, Earth Planetary Defense is working on it. Everyone wants her home."

"Not as much as I do," Ariana whispered.

The pain in her voice was so raw, my stomach twisted in response. Why hadn't Torq mentioned his part in the search for Ariana's sister? But had I told him that I was helping? I guessed we didn't share everything, although now that I knew what he'd promised, I had to talk to him. I had to make sure he was doing everything he could to find this Kax guy.

Now how was I going to shake this group and get to his room without raising suspicion?

CHAPTER
THIRTY-FOUR

Torq

Droplets of water clung to my skin as I stepped from the bathroom with a towel slung low around my hips. The hot shower had done nothing to calm my nerves after seeing Jess in the corridors, but at least I wasn't covered in sweat from my catch-up training with Kort on the climbing wall.

My new friend hadn't made it easy on me, but at least he hadn't stabbed me with a dagger or pushed me off the wall. It had felt good to return to climbing, and my limbs were loose and warm, even though I was sure they'd be sore the next day. The next day in the School of Battle could mean a lecture on sparring technique, but it was more likely to be hands-on training for the upcoming battle of the schools, which meant my muscles would get no rest.

"That's what being a Blade is all about," I said to my empty room, flicking a glance at my clan crest and then forcing myself to look away. The wings on the crest were a rebuke, a reminder that I hadn't lived up to my family's expectations.

Then I remembered what Kann had said. Blades was my new family. My Blade brothers were the ones I had to rely on now. Well, most of them. I scowled at the memory of Dom. That Drexian had it in for me, but I didn't know why. It was possible I'd offended him last term, especially since he wasn't from an elite clan, and that had been important to me when I'd arrived at the academy.

That version of myself seemed foreign to me now. I'd been so sure of my own superiority just because of my family name, which I now recognized as foolish and wrong. I hadn't been superior in the trials. If I hadn't been with the human cadets, I never would have made it out alive. Not that I could explain any of my realization and change of heart to the Drexian who despised me. Mostly because he didn't seem interested in talking.

He was a Blade, after all, and Blades were about action. Unfortunately for me, that action included trying to kill me. I'd just have to watch my back, like my new adversary had advised.

I pulled off my towel and briskly rubbed it over my body before tossing it on the foot of my bed and pulling on a pair of snug, black, boxer briefs that reached mid-thigh. I preferred to sleep in nothing at all, but it wasn't unheard of for instructors to have surprise dorm inspections, and I'd rather not have to stand at attention with my cock hanging out.

A pounding on the door made me wonder if I wasn't about to enjoy one of those surprise inspections now, but I pressed my hand to the side of the door to open it before it was opened for me. I backed up as Jess stormed inside then closed the door behind her, startled to see her.

"I did not expect you to—"

She interrupted before I could ask her if I'd forgotten that we'd arranged to meet. "Why didn't you tell me that you were helping with the search for Ariana's sister?"

I was taken aback for the second time in as many seconds. "What?"

She spun to face me, her gaze locked onto mine. "You offered to use your clan connections to track down some High Commander named Kax who is apparently hard to find?"

"Former High Commander," I said, although I didn't know why I cared about that or why she would either. I cringed at how pompous my words sounded, and then hurried to say something that was less obnoxious. "But, yes, I did offer to help. Volt and Kann were talking about how they wished they could find someone who had pulled off an escape mission into Kronock territory. They mentioned Kax, and I remembered that my father had connections with Kax's clan."

She nodded along with everything I said, but I got the sense that she wasn't focusing on my words. That, or she knew this already. The real question was why this information would bother her so much. "Why does this upset you, Jess?"

She blew out a breath. "I thought it might be something you'd mention to me."

"I didn't think to mention it. We have been very focused on tutoring."

She drew in a quick breath. "If we're going to do this," she waved a hand between us, "then I think we should know more about each other."

"What do you want to know about me?"

She frowned. "I don't know, but I'd like to know important things like you helping Ariana. Have you had any success?"

Shame tickled the back of my neck at the reminder that I had not even asked my father, mostly because he had not responded to my attempts to talk to him. I had little doubt that he was still angry that I was a Blade. "Not yet."

She narrowed her eyes at me. "If you promised to help Ariana, you have to do it."

As much as I hated being reprimanded by a fellow cadet, and as much as my former self would have snapped back with a cutting, superior remark, Jess was right. I had to try harder. "I promise I will succeed."

She grinned at this. "In case you're curious, I'm also helping her. Morgan and I are researching possible places her sister might be held by the Kronock."

Now I understood a bit of her irritation. Why had I not know that she was doing this? "Is this why you're always at the Stacks?"

"Sometimes I'm studying for my classes, but a lot of the time it's for that. There are a lot of potential places." Her gaze finally drifted lower, and she seemed to realize that I was barely dressed. Her lashes fluttered as her gaze lingered on my thickening cock. "And then I'm with you almost every night."

I stepped closer to her. "I didn't think tonight would be one of them."

"I guess I needed to see you," she said as she nibbled her lower lip.

"Because you thought I was keeping things from you?" Now that I'd gotten over the surprise at her arrival and questioning, I loved the fact that she'd stormed into my room demanding answers. It meant that I was more to her than someone she was forced to tutor or someone she was sleeping with for the sport of it.

"I was surprised that you kept secrets." She put one hand to my chest. "I didn't know a Blade had it in him to be sly."

I laughed at this. "We're not just big and dumb."

"I know that." She sounded almost offended, but she grinned at me as she trailed her fingertips down my taut stomach. "Just big."

"So, you didn't come to tutor me?" My voice was hoarse as she brushed her fingers over my swollen cock through the fabric of my underwear.

"I think you might be as proficient as a Blade needs to be in Kronock. From what I've seen of other Blades, they aren't worried about mastering the language."

My cock ached for release so urgently that I didn't even care she'd discovered that my reason for being tutored was an exaggeration at best and a fabrication at worst. I stifled a husky sound in my throat as her fingers stroked me through the fabric. "Then we might have a problem."

"What problem?"

"If I don't need Kronock lessons then I don't know what reason you'd have to be here." I closed my hand over her nimble fingers, pressing her palm fully to my cock. "You don't seem to need any lessons from me on how to arouse a Drexian."

She squeezed her hand around my cock. "I might know how to arouse you, but I think that's the easy part."

She might have a point. I'd started to get aroused by her mere presence in my room.

"I don't know how to do everything you like, but I want to learn. I want you to teach me to be perfect in bed."

I wanted to tell her that she was already perfect. I wanted to make her promise to be perfect for no one but me. I wanted to tell myself that this perfect female would never belong to anyone else but me, but the deepest, darkest part of myself knew that wasn't possible. I knew my clan would never allow it.

But for now, Jess was mine, and I would savor every moment of making her mine. I cupped her face in one hand and dragged my thumb across her curvy, soft lips. "Then let's start with your perfect, little mouth. I have just the place you can put those pretty lips."

CHAPTER
THIRTY-FIVE

Jess

I knelt between Torq's legs as he sat on the bed with his arms braced long behind him. My finger curled around the base of his cock as I eyed it with some amount of trepidation. It was one thing to hear people talk about blow jobs, it was another to give your first one to a massive Drexian. "Tell me how you like it."

He released a tortured sound. "I promise you I will like anything you do."

I frowned at this. Unacceptable. I hadn't gotten as far as I had by winging it. I was a girl who did my homework, did extra homework, and always studied for the tests. "I want you to tell me." I tightened my grip on his shaft. "You're supposed to be teaching me, aren't you?"

He managed to nod as he gritted out words. "Lick it."

Vague, but I could work with it. I dragged my tongue up

the veined length of his cock—and it was a considerable length —before swirling the tip around his broad crown, which was already slick. For something so hard, the skin was velvety soft, especially the head, and I loved the sensation of my tongue going around it.

"*Grek* me." Torq fisted his hands in the blanket covering his bed.

I peered up at him with my mouth still on his cock. "You like that?"

He groaned, the sound somewhere between pleasure and pain. "I think you have lied to me. You have done this before."

I shook my head, reveling in the power I had over the huge, brawny guy. He might be a badass, but I was the one who had him completely in my thrall. "Never, but I think I'm going to want to do it lots more."

Another guttural sound told me that he didn't object to this. "Take it in your mouth, Jess. Just don't use your teeth."

I usually didn't like being told what to do, but I didn't mind him giving me orders. Not when he was teaching me. Not when obeying him made both pleasure and power pulse through me. I used my fist around the base to bring his cock to my lips, and I took the thick crown into my mouth. Of course, I wouldn't use teeth. I knew enough to know *that.*

I slid my lips up and down over the top and then I swirled my tongue around the entire head again, loving his sharp inhale as I sucked it into my mouth once more. Now I understood why some women liked to do this. There was a tremendous sense of power and satisfaction in making Torq this aroused.

His hands moved to the back of my head, and he tangled his fingers in my hair. "Can you take more of me?"

I slid him from my mouth and gave him a confident grin. "I can take all you can give me."

His eyes went molten as I returned my mouth to his cock, sliding it past my lips, taking the crown, and then letting my lips stretch further as he pressed my head gently down. "Your mouth is so perfect and tight."

My face warmed at this, and my pussy clenched. I felt the same flush of accomplishment as I took his cock deeper down my throat than I had when I'd taken all of his cock. Now memories of his cock splitting me made me open my throat and take him even deeper.

Torq hissed out a desperate sound that morphed into a garbled version of my name. "Jess, I can't believe how much of me you're swallowing."

I squeezed the back of my throat, which made Torq loose another hungry moan. Then I moved my lips back up until I could suck on his crown and slide my mouth down his length again. His hands were guiding my mouth without slamming my head down, and they moved faster as his hips started to twitch.

He'd stopped giving me direction, but I didn't need it anymore. I was letting his sounds and movements guide me as much as anything, moving faster and sucking harder as his cock got even harder in my mouth. I squeezed the hand clutching the base of his cock, which was the only part of it I hadn't sucked down, but as I started to pump my hand up and down in tandem with my mouth, Torq released a string of Drexian curses and clenched his hands in my hair.

I didn't falter as he thrust his hips up, holding the base as it jerked and spurted hot down my throat. I'd heard about this part, but I was so caught up in how completely Torq was coming apart in my mouth that I even savored swallowing every drop of his release.

His hands relaxed in my hair, and he bent forward as he hitched in uneven breaths. "Your mouth is *grekking* magic."

I pulled back and guided his still firm cock from my lips, dabbing at the corners of my mouth and feeling proud of myself. "Considering what you did to me with your mouth, I was only returning the favor."

Torq reached down and pulled me up by the elbows. "That reminds me. It's my turn to play."

My body tingled with anticipation. "You can play with me all you want."

He flipped me onto my back on the bed and rolled on top of me. "You're my beautiful little sex toy, aren't you, Jess?"

I shouldn't have liked the sound of that, but I did. I shouldn't have wanted to be anyone's sex toy, but I loved the idea of being Torq's. I loved the idea of him using me for his pleasure and telling me exactly how to fuck him. I shouldn't have desired any guy to boss me around, but I loved Torq telling me what to do to him.

I bobbed my head up and down as he moved slowly down my body, and I closed my eyes as he tugged at my pants. Then there was a thudding on the door, and we both jerked up. Torq leapt to his feet as he tugged up his underwear, panic clear on his face.

We were so *grekked*.

CHAPTER
THIRTY-SIX

Torq

All the euphoria I'd felt evaporated at the sound of pounding on my door. Had someone heard us? Well, had someone heard me? I'd tried not to be loud, and it had taken all my self-control not to roar when I'd come inside Jess's mouth, but that didn't mean my moans hadn't carried outside the walls of my room.

Jess lay on my bed wearing a look of shock. All the sweet satisfaction and sultry smiles were gone, and now panic flitted across her pretty face. I grabbed her by the hand and pulled her to standing, putting a finger to my lips as I swung my head around. My bare bones quarters did not provide much of a place to hide. I snuck a look at the narrow window, but she vehemently shook her head.

No fucking way, she mouthed.

I didn't blame her for that. My heart pounded as I tugged

her toward the bathroom. The floor of the shower was still wet but there was no other choice.

"It might just be my friend coming to tell me something," I whispered, my voice still husky. I didn't think there was any reason for Kort to be popping by, but I didn't want to scare Jess.

She nodded mutely as she squatted below the stone dividing wall that provided some hiding place even if it did only reach my waist. The pounding hadn't stopped, so I strode quickly to the door, afraid that it was a surprise inspection that I would most surely fail, if I didn't end up being sent home. But if it was an inspection, why hadn't they just proceeded to come in? Rarely would a snap inspection show such patience.

I paused, looking down at the damp front of my underwear. There had been no time to do anything but yank up my boxer briefs when my cock was still soaked from Jess's mouth. Even thinking about it made my cock twitch, but I forced myself to push those thoughts aside, as I snatched a pair of soft black pants from my dresser and yanked them on.

Once I was at least somewhat presentable, I pressed my palm to the side of the door and took a steadying breath. The door swished open, but it wasn't an instructor ready to inspect my quarters. It was Kort and a handful of other Blades all fully dressed and in their boots.

"What the—?" I made a concerted effort not to glance back at Jess's hiding spot as the Blades swarmed into my room.

"You're going to have to wear more than that, brother." Kort opened my dresser and tossed a black shirt at me.

"Why?" I asked, as another Blade thrust my boots at me.

"Tonight is the night," Zenen said as if it should have been obvious. "We're knocking out one of the requirements."

This felt like the cruelest turnabout possible. "One of the graduation requirements? You know those aren't official, right?"

Kort shook his head at me, as if that was hardly the point. "Why would that matter? Blades have always completed the requirements. Now are you coming with us?"

I pulled the shirt over my head, as my mind raced with ways I could get out of it, but in none of them did I come out looking like anything but a coward. "Which requirement?"

One of the Blades I didn't know very well gave me a lopsided grin. "We're scaling the forbidden tower."

My heart plummeted to my stomach as thoughts of falling from the climbing wall rushed at me. "What about the dungeons? We haven't done that yet, and I hear the stones are scratched from the beasts that were held there for the maze."

Zenen gave me his usual, lopsided grin. "That's for another night."

I noticed for the first time that two of the Blades had rope coiled around their shoulders. There would be no escaping this. I would not get to lay Jess beneath me on the bed, spread her legs, and lick her sweet juices. I would not get to hear her breathy sighs as her body detonated, and I would not get to fill her and feel her body stretch to take me like she was made for my cock. Instead, I would be climbing up the side of a cold, slick tower and trying not to die.

Grek grek grek.

"Unless you have something better to do." Kort swung his head around my spartan room, his gaze landing on the tablet. "Unless you'd rather study than be with your Blade brothers."

"I would not rather be studying." That was not a lie. I slipped my feet into my boots and leaned over to lace them up, twisting my head just enough to catch a glimpse of the bathroom. No sight of Jess, which meant she heard what was happening and was hiding. "I guess we'll be out pretty late."

Kort cocked his head at me. "You are worried about being out after hours?"

"No. If you don't mind the risk, neither do I."

Kort pounded his hand on my back. "I knew you wouldn't want to miss this."

I made myself smile at him, remembering that my friend had no idea what I was doing. "You know me well, brother."

I put my hand to the panel to open the door, swiping the switch at the bottom to keep it unlocked so Jess could get out. The other Blades poked their heads into the corridor to make sure it was empty before proceeding. I let Kortneys go then I hesitated on the threshold, desperately wanting to say something so that Jess would know I was only leaving under duress and so she wouldn't get caught in my room.

Kort glanced at me over his shoulder, his brow furrowing. "Are you sure you are fine?" He slid his gaze further into my room. "There isn't—?"

I strode forward and threw my arm over his shoulders. "There is nothing I'd rather be doing than scaling the forbidden tower with my fellow Blades."

Now that was a massive lie. I'd rather be doing a thousand different things to Jess instead of sneaking out of the academy and hoisting myself up a rope, so I could scale the side of a treacherously slick and unstable tower. I only hoped Jess would forgive me for leaving her alone in my room. I hoped she would understand.

CHAPTER
THIRTY-SEVEN

Jess

My heart pounded and my knees ached, as I finally stood from where I'd been cowering in Torq's bathroom. They were gone. It wasn't hard to know since the Blades had entered with no lack of noise and chaos, and now the room was enveloped in silence.

"Fucking Blades." I twisted my back to release the tension from crouching on the hard stone and walked into the bedroom, which showed no traces of the loud Drexians who'd stormed in, dressed Torq, and then dragged him out.

I'd heard every word since the bathroom door had been partially open, so I knew exactly why they'd come and where they were taking Torq. I shook my head, partly in disbelief that scaling a tower was one of the unofficial requirements for cadets, and partly because I was relieved he wouldn't feel the need to fulfill that particular requirement with me.

Going into the underground tunnels had been enough for me. I didn't need to visit the dungeons or scale a tower to prove anything, and I was certain they'd let me graduate without those notches in my belt.

"If you don't get kicked out first," I said to myself, remembering that I was currently standing in the quarters of a Drexian cadet, and I was out of my tower after hours. I had no clue how long Torq would be gone, and I had no intention of hanging around to find out.

I was already second guessing why I was in Torq's room, why I was risking my place at the academy, why I was willing to throw away everything I'd worked for just for a few moments of fun.

More than fun, I thought. My pulse tripped as a familiar rush of pleasure and power suffused my body at the memory of taking Torq's cock in my mouth and feeling him lose control. For the first time in my life, I understood why girls ended up doing stupid things for boys, why they lost their ability to think straight, why they fell for bad boys who didn't deserve them.

After everything I'd achieved and after all I'd done, I'd ended up in the same place as the dumb girls in my hometown who fell prey to guys who only wanted one thing. I'd ended up sneaking around just so I could get laid, which made me no better than the giggly girls I'd scoffed at back then.

I tried to tell myself that Torq was different. He wasn't a bad boy. Not anymore. But was that wishful thinking? Had I convinced myself that the Drexian had changed because I needed that to be true? Was I fooling myself because otherwise I'd have to admit that I'd fallen for a fellow cadet who was nothing like me and nothing like anyone I should like?

"Stop overthinking it, Jess. Sex is sex. You had to do it someday." I crossed to the door and hesitantly put my hand to the side panel, holding my breath in hopes that it would open. If not, I was trapped inside with nothing but my dark and swirling doubts. "This was never supposed to be something real or something permanent. This was always a fling, and there's no one better for a meaningless fling than someone you should never be with."

I'd almost convinced myself that I was in control of the whole situation and that I was being rational and reasonable, when the door slid open to reveal the dimly lit, ominously quiet corridor. I peeked my head from the room, swiveling it back and forth to make sure no one would see me emerge from Torq's room.

"Yep, these are definitely the actions of a woman in control." I stepped into the hallway and scurried toward the staircase as quickly as I could. The wall sconces sent shadows writhing across the ceiling, which did nothing to stave off the fear clawing at my throat. What would I say if I was caught? I was nowhere near the Stacks and not even close to the School of Strategy. I could always feign ignorance and claim that I'd gotten lost.

And look like a total idiot who hadn't learned the layout of the academy after a full term. Even if someone would believe that an Assassin wouldn't have memorized the floorplan of the school, I would rather have them know I was sneaking around to see a guy than believe I had crap memory. Unless it meant being sent away and losing everything I'd worked for. In that case, I'd grit my teeth and play the ditzy female card.

I had to make it down the winding staircase, across the main hall, up another flight of twisting steps, across an open bridge between towers and then into the female tower—all without being seen. What had I been thinking going to the cadet dorms so late? There were no straggling cadets leaving the dining hall or drifting from the Stacks or dragging themselves from the sparring gyms. It was only me and my quick footsteps tapping as I practically ran down the stairs.

I reached the bottom and speed-walked across the main hall, but before I could start up another flight of stairs, a figure appeared from the shadows. My heart lurched as I stifled the urge to scream. What was the security chief doing lurking in the shadows?

"What are you doing out after hours?" Commander Vyk towered over me, looking every bit as menacing as he always did, even though I found him marginally less frightening after learning that he hadn't gone along with the High Command plan to eliminate all the cadets during the trials. But it wasn't enough to return my heartbeat to anything close to a normal rhythm.

I ran through all the possible excuses in my head, trying to determine which I should use on the tough, grizzled Drexian. Should I lie and hope he'd believe I wasn't too sharp, or should I tell the truth and hope he'd cut me a break. But telling the truth would be throwing Torq under the bus as well, and that seemed unfair since he wasn't here to speak for himself.

"She's with me."

I hadn't even decided my strategy when a striking, dark-haired woman in a flowing blue dress appeared to float toward me. Her dark eyes locked on mine, silently telling me to go along with whatever she said. I recognized her as Noora, the Academy Master's wife, probably the only woman in the place who got a free pass for almost anything.

Vyk swung his gaze to her, his stiff stance remaining rigid. "This cadet is with you?"

"She's part of the team working on the rescue plan into Kronock territory, which means she puts in late nights in the Stacks."

"She wasn't coming from the Stacks," Vyk growled.

If Noora was intimidated by his gravelly voice, she didn't let it show. "She probably took a break to stretch her legs. Researching possible Kronock prison sites is tedious work." She gave the Drexian a sweet smile. "I'm sure you can understand."

"I didn't know that there was a rescue plan being put together." He stroked one hand down his short beard that was shot through with gray. "Has the admiral authorized the use of force to retrieve the prisoner?"

"I believe stealth is the objective."

Vyk grunted, as if he did not prefer that method. "If the enemy has human prisoners, they will not make them easy to rescue."

"There is always room on our team for an Inferno Force Commander who has experience battling the Kronock and infiltrating their space." Noora's voice was like silk, and I was reminded of a spider silently and expertly weaving a web.

Vyk rocked back on his heels as he considered her words. "You have no one else working on the plan who has been inside Kronock territory?"

"Not yet." Noora smiled at him.

Vyk gave her a curt nod. "I will speak to your...I will speak to the admiral about lending my knowledge to the mission." He cut his gaze to me. "I trust you will return to your tower?"

I bobbed my head without speaking, almost afraid to break the spell that Noora had cast over him. He gave us both a sharp, small bow and strode away from us and up the wide staircase that led to the Academy Master's office.

When his footsteps had faded, I allowed myself a regular breath. "Thanks for saving my ass."

Noora grinned at me, a wide smile that looked nothing like the ones she'd used to lure Vyk into her cleverly laid trap. "You're welcome. I won't ask what you're really doing out here, but I'd be careful about repeating it. Our security chief has a habit of roaming the corridors at night. Zoran says it's because he's tormented by his guilt at being even a small part of the maze sabotage, but I think he likes to catch cadets breaking rules."

"Were you serious about him helping with the rescue?" I hadn't known she knew of it, much less that she could recruit additional participants.

"I might not be the Drexian's biggest fan, but even I can't deny that he has a great deal of experience with the enemy. His experience would be an asset. It would also ensure that he was working with us and not against us."

"Keep your friends close and your enemies closer?"

"Something like that, although I hope he is no longer an enemy of the academy. We have enough challenges from without to worry about those from within."

Before I could ask her to elaborate, she spun on one heel and started to walk away with the hem of her dress fluttering behind her. "Have a good night, Jess."

I had no choice but to resume my swift journey back to my tower, but my mind raced with questions about threats to the academy and how much I trusted Vyk. I didn't think about Torq again until I was slipping under my sheets. Then I remembered that he was scaling the side of a tower with a bunch of Blades, and fresh worry kept sleep at bay until I was certain he was back in his own bed. I refused to think of the alternative.

CHAPTER

THIRTY-EIGHT

Torq

I peered at the looming tower that appeared even more treacherous and unstable in the veiled moonlight. The forbidden tower had been sealed shut so long ago I knew of no one who'd actually seen it when it wasn't unstable and foreboding. I would have dismissed the rumors that it was cursed as foolish, but I could not explain why it had been abandoned yet not destroyed or repaired. The parts of the academy that had been damaged in the Kronock attack had been restored, but the forbidden tower remained untouched and unwelcoming.

"Up to the top window and back down?"

Kort pulled his gaze from the black stone and the crumbling window ledge at the top. "Unless you wish to go inside and be stuck there."

I grunted my thoughts about that idea, as one of our Blade

brothers tied a grappling hook to the end of a length of rope. We all backed up, our feet wobbling on the rocky ground surrounding the tower. Even less pleasant than being trapped in a cursed tower? Falling to the rocks below.

Do not fall, I told myself.

The prospect of falling to certain death made it difficult to think about anything else and impossible to dwell on leaving Jess in my room. I couldn't worry too much about being interrupted just as I'd been about to pull down her pants with the prospect of another, more deadly, fall occupying my mind.

You are a Blade. Blades are brave and strong and rush in where others would not dare.

That didn't mean I wanted to die, especially when I wasn't in battle. Perishing while completing a secret cadet rite of passage was not how I intended to go out. Not that I thought much about death.

The Blade who'd attached the hook heaved it up and into the window, latching it onto the sill on his first attempt. Only when he tugged and some loose stone fell did it occur to me that the window might not hold us.

This wasn't the first time I'd had second thoughts about being a Blade, but I did wonder if the Wings bothered to do this. I'd always been told that it was a point of cadet honor to complete all four challenges, but the tower had not been as decrepit when my own father or brother had attended the academy. Since my brother hadn't finished the academy, had he even attempted one of the four?

"You weren't going to start without me, were you?"

I didn't have to turn to see that it was Dom who'd joined us. I shot a glance at Kort, who avoided my eyes. What was the Drexian who'd already pushed me off a wall once doing here? Hadn't he shown that he couldn't be trusted? Hadn't he proven to be dangerous to fellow Blades?

I considered walking away, refusing to climb, protesting Dom's involvement. But that wasn't what a Blade would do, even if it was what I wanted to do. A Blade would power through any situation and override any fear. A Blade would never run from a fight, even if the fight was in their own house. As I stood in front of the tower, my pulse spiking and my throat tight, I'd never felt less like a Drexian worthy of being a Blade.

"You'll need one of these." Dom slapped a cold steel carabiner in my hand as he wound his way through the group. He didn't glare at me or growl, and I wondered if I'd been imagining the animosity from him. Then I remembered his threat. I hadn't imagined that.

Zenen shuffled toward me so that Dom could get by, knocking into my hand and sending my carabiner to the ground. He handed me his as he bent and scooped up mine. "Sorry, brother."

"No worries," I told him, catching sight of the Blade pendant lying on top of his black shirt and glinting in the faint light. "Do you want to go ahead of me?"

He shrugged one shoulder. "Might as well. My cousin told me that doing this was worse than his trials."

Not comforting. "I do not know any Drexian who has done it. If they have, they have not told me about it."

"Maybe it's time to reassess these requirements, especially with the humans in our schools."

Thinking of Jess going up the side of the tower sent a chill down my spine. Taking her to the underground tunnels so we could be alone in the dark was one thing, this was something very different.

"Ready, Blades?" Kort asked, swiveling to face our group. He'd become our de facto leader, which suited me fine. He turned back around, coiled a smaller length of rope around his waist, hooked it into the rope on the wall, and started climbing.

I accepted the length of rope for my waist and tied it around me, as I watched Blade after Blade plant their feet on the wall and start to scale the stone. Their progress wasn't fast, but each one steadily moved up the wall. When Kort reached the top he hooked a second rope to the wall and rappelled down, passing the climbers still working their way up.

When his boots hit the ground, he glanced at me. "What are you still doing here?"

I'd been so consumed with watching the other Blades go up the wall, I'd forgotten that I was last.

"Unless your injury—"

"I am fine," I cut him off before he could offer me an escape I could not take. Not if I wished any of my Blade brothers to respect me.

I gritted my teeth and strode forward, clipping myself to the rope and twisting the tail over my hand so I could pull it through as I moved up. When there was enough resistance, I put my feet on the wall and began my climb.

One foot in front of the other, I said to myself as I scaled the slick stone. One Blade passed me as they rappelled down and then another. I tipped my head back to see that there was only Dom, who'd almost reached the top, and Zenen remaining.

My leg muscles twitched from the tension, but there was no pain, and as I climbed higher, I breathed in the cool night air and found my rhythm. Slide up the carabiner, pull the rope tight, move my feet. Slide, pull, move. Slide, pull, move.

I paused and stole another glance overhead. Dom had started his descent, which meant there were only two Blades left climbing. Only two to reach the top.

As I slid my carabiner up, the rope jerked. I grabbed it with both hands, tipping my head back to see Zenen pinwheel his arms in the air in an attempt to reach the rope as he fell backward. He didn't scream as his feet left the tower, but gasps from below broke the quiet.

I released one hand from the rope and lunged for him as he plummeted past me, but he was going too fast and was too heavy. My hand tore part of his shirt from his body as he hurtled to the ground, and I squeezed my eyes shut so I wouldn't see him hit.

When I opened my eyes again, I could see nothing, but my Blade brothers huddled around his body at the base of the tower. Even from my height, I could see that his shirt was ripped. I looked at my fist, opening it to see that I had a swath of black fabric and a silver chain with the Blade pendant shining up at me.

My head swam, and I fought the urge to double over. I needed to get off the tower before I became another of its victims. I looked down again, but this time it was Dom who drew my attention. He hung not far from the ground and glared at me with fury—and shock.

CHAPTER
THIRTY-NINE

Jess

I leaned my head in one hand and tried not to slump forward into my breakfast. By the time I'd been able to rid my brain of both worry for Torq and thoughts of Vyk working to find Sasha, it had been late, and I was paying for my scant hours of sleep now. The deep Drexian voices reverberating through the cadet dining hall made my temples throb and the clattering and clanging of flatware didn't help either.

"You look like death." Even though Morgan's pronouncement was grim, her tone was perky.

I squinted to look at her. "Thanks. I feel like it too."

"Are you sick?"

I gave a single shake of my head so I wouldn't make the ache worse. "I couldn't get to sleep last night."

She gave me a knowing look. "Is it the battle of the schools that's making you nervous? You know, it's not supposed to be as deadly as the trials."

"I'd hope not, since we were all supposed to die in those."

"Good point." She snagged a strip of fried padwump from my plate. "So, is that it?"

I removed my cheek from my palm. I wished I could tell my closest friend at the academy why I was so sleepy, but telling her one part of the story would unravel so many secrets that I feared my entire life would collapse. If I told her that I was sleeping with Torq, she'd want to know how that happened, which would mean telling her about the tutoring, which would result in having to reveal that he'd blackmailed me. No decent friend would give that two thumbs up.

"I think it's all of it," I said. "The battle, the classes in Strategy, the research to find Sasha. All of it's important, and I don't think I'm doing a great job of balancing things."

"The elusive work-life balance." Morgan said the words slowly, as if she were a sage sitting on a mountaintop. "Does anyone have that?"

"Does anyone have what?" Britta asked as she sat down next to Morgan, her silvery-blonde hair hanging in a long braid down her back.

"Work-life balance," Morgan said after she swallowed. "Jess is a bit overwhelmed by everything we're juggling."

"I get that." Britta grabbed the end of her braid and brushed her fingers over the tip absently as she talked. "Classes in Engineering have been intense, but I'm not also trying to search the entire galaxy for a missing pilot. How's that going?"

"Impossible," I muttered while Morgan said, "Great!"

Britta looked between us and quirked one brow. "I know you don't need an engineer for this, but I'm happy to help out, if I can."

I ran a hand through my hair as I sat back. "I don't know if tracking Kann down to the giant circuit in Battle requires an Assassin, so don't sell yourself short."

"Giant circuit?"

"It's wild." Morgan put a hand on Britta's arm. "Kind of like one of those ninja-warrior obstacle courses but less cheery."

Britt's eyes were wide. "I had no idea. It seems like Battle has all the cool play areas."

"If you call that playing." The circuit had looked impossible to me, but maybe Britta was more of a thrill-seeker than I knew.

"I don't mind a physical challenge or two. I used to date a rock climber, so our dates were usually at a climbing gym."

"Then you should check out the Blades' climbing wall." I grinned at her. "Maybe you should have been a Blade."

"I like gadgets too much, but I wouldn't mind spending some time in Battle. The Drexians over there are pretty hot."

Morgan made a noise in the back of her throat that told us she agreed. "Don't you have to be hot to join a school devoted to kicking ass?"

Britta laughed. "Didn't the cadet who went through the maze with us end up in Blades? I'm not going to lie and say I didn't notice how ripped he was when he took off his shirt. Not to mention that academy tattoo on his shoulder."

I joined my friends in agreeing that Torq was hot, but an uncomfortable twinge of jealousy made me wish that my friends hadn't seen him shirtless.

Which is ridiculous, since you aren't even his girlfriend, I told myself. We weren't dating, we weren't a couple, we weren't anything to each other. Except he was something to me, which I knew was going to be a big fucking problem.

"He's not the only Blade worth ogling." Britta leaned

forward and lowered her voice. "I wouldn't mind take a big bite out of—"

"More padwump?" Zalina walked up with a plate filled with the crispy strips. "I snagged some before the cadets from Battle arrived."

As soon as she mentioned it, I realized that she was right. There were no Blades in the cadet dining hall, and they were usually taking up at least one long table and making lots of noise. My pulse fluttered with unease.

Britta took a strip then swung her head to take in the entire long hall. "Where are they?"

"You didn't hear?" Zalina's expression turned somber. " One of the cadets from the School of Battle died last night."

Morgan and Britta gaped at her, while cold chills washed over my entire body and sent a shudder through me.

"They were scaling some tower that's supposed to be cursed, and one of them fell."

It couldn't have been Torq. He couldn't have fallen again.

"Was it Torq?" I rasped, my voice cracking.

"Torq?" Zalina crinkled her nose. "The cocky first-year who gave Lieutenant Bowman such a hard time? No, it wasn't him."

I hitched in an uneven breath, and then caught Morgan staring at me as if she'd just fit the last piece into a puzzle.

She knew.

CHAPTER
FORTY

Torq

I squared my shoulders as I stood at attention in front of the wide, black desk and waited for Admiral Zoran to arrive. My eyes burned from lack of sleep, but I wasn't tired. I was too filled with shame and rage to worry about sleep overtaking me.

How had Zenen fallen? One moment he'd been moving easily up the rope, and the next, he'd been falling backward. I closed my eyes as I replayed the moment in my mind, much as I'd been doing since I'd lowered myself to the ground at the base of the tower and learned that the cadet hadn't survived the fall.

Others had whispered darkly that it had been the tower's curse, but I did not believe that. I did not believe in curses, even if I couldn't explain the Blade's fall. Our Drexian ancestors might have held fast to curses and the supernatural, but they'd

197

also lived in the ancient times, when creatures roamed the planet that had died out long ago. Creatures who breathed fire and unfurled broad wings, creatures who ruled the skies and stalked the mountains, creatures who had become the stuff of legend.

Now it was the modern era, and the Drexians were the most technologically advanced species in the galaxy. We had developed jump technology to travel across vast distances in the single beat of a heart, we'd created holograms that were as real as matter, and we had successfully defended Earth and other planets from violent invaders with our superior weapons. Spells and curses and myths had no place in our rational world. Not anymore.

"But neither do coincidences," I said under my breath, as I stood alone in the Academy Master's long office and peered out the tall window to the Restless Sea.

I couldn't help feeling that it wasn't chance that had sent two Blades careening off walls. I knew why I'd fallen, and I was confident that Dom had played a part in the second fall, as well. His expression as he'd looked at Zenen crumpled on the ground and then at me had told me everything I needed to know.

He'd been shocked, but not because of the fall. He'd been shocked that it hadn't been me to fall again. But why did he want me dead so badly? Was it really all over me leaping past him one time on the climbing wall? Was he willing to kill because he'd been bested once?

The thought that it was supposed to be me in a heap at the bottom of the tower made bile tease the back of my throat. I pressed my lips together tightly and took a deep breath. A fellow Blade had died in place of me. Even if I had nothing to do with the fall, I couldn't fight the guilt that clawed at me, the guilt that told me it should have been me, the guilt that repeated the taunts that I hadn't been strong enough, skilled enough, fast enough to save him.

I shifted my weight from one foot to another and clenched my hands behind my back. It didn't surprise me that the admiral wished to speak to me, but it did surprise me that he was making me wait. Every other Blade had already been debriefed. The academy knew what had happened and why we'd been on the tower. My Blade brothers had already been given punishments by the security chief, punishment that I was glad to accept for my part in the death.

But I alone had been sent to the admiral's office to watch the morning break over the turbulent surface of the sea. Only I would be interviewed alone.

A sound from behind made me stiffen and turn my head slightly. It wasn't the door at the other end of the room opening. It was a hidden door in one of the side walls that had slid open and allowed two Drexians to emerge from within. One was Admiral Zoran, and one was my father.

My chest constricted and my jaw dropped. My father had been summoned? As far as I knew, none of the other Blade fathers had been notified. The academy rarely involved Drexian parents in the inner workings of the school, even when danger was involved, even when there was death. Danger was part of joining the academy. It was part of what made it so rigorous.

So why was my father walking toward me with a scowl on his face?

"At ease, Cadet." The admiral strode to his place behind his desk, but he didn't sit.

I unclasped my hands, but I remained ramrod straight as I focused my attention on him and not my father who stood at the end of the admiral's desk facing me instead of by my side. This told me where his loyalties lay, although I should not have been surprised. My father held the academy in higher regard than anything, even his sons.

"There is no debate about what happened last night." Zoran leaned his hands on the desk but didn't break eye contact with me. "A group of Blade cadets—all first-years and including you—went to the forbidden tower to scale the side and complete one of the unspoken requirements."

I didn't make a sound because there was no question, and no facts I would dispute.

"Only three cadets remained on the wall when one of you fell to his death."

I flinched at this cold assessment, recalling the look of terror on my fellow Blade's face as I tried in vain to catch him. I doubted I would ever forget the horror in his eyes when the fabric of his shirt ripped in my fist, and he realized that I had failed.

"The other cadets have told me that no one was near the Blade when he lost his grip on the rope, but that you were the closest. Is this true?"

"It is."

Zoran held my gaze. "They also reported that you attempted to catch him. Is that accurate?"

"It is." I swallowed hard. "But I failed."

The admiral moved his head down so subtly it might have been a twitch. "Did you see why the cadet fell? Did he slip? Did he lose his grip?"

I pushed aside the image of his arms flailing, desperate to find purchase. "I did not see the moment he lost contact with the wall, but if you are asking if he was too weak to hold the rope or if he did not have the skills to climb the wall, then no. He did not slip. He did not lose his grip."

"How can you know that?" My father jumped in before

Zoran could reply, his face twisted in a sneer. "You said you did not see him fall."

I wanted to ask him why he was there, why he'd come all that way just to torment me, but I didn't. "He was not weak. He was not unskilled. He was a Blade who had successfully scaled the climbing wall, won sparring matches, and completed the circuit without falling."

My father's top lip curled. He despised my defense of the Blade because he hated that I was one. That was as clear to me as if he'd painted it on the wall.

Zoran cleared his throat, drawing my attention back to him. "That matches with all the reports about the victim, which makes it odd that he would fall." He folded his arms over his chest. "It is no secret that cadets scale the tower every term, but it has been a long time since there has been a death because of it. And the forbidden tower has never before claimed a Blade."

"Or a Wing," my father added. I sensed he was enjoying the disgrace of my school.

My face flamed at the rebuke, but I ignored it and asked what I had to know. "Was our equipment checked after the fall?"

Zoran's eyes narrowed. "You suspect his equipment malfunctioned?"

Or was sabotaged, I thought but didn't say. I had no way to prove that the carabiner I'd dropped and then he'd picked up had been the reason he'd fallen, but my gut told me that Dom had handed me faulty equipment in hopes that I would fall—again. But a gut feeling was not enough to accuse a fellow cadet.

"All the rope and carabiners were collected by Commander Vyk. If there is anything to learn from them, he will find it." Zoran released a pained breath. "You will join the rest of your

Blade brothers in repairing the damage done to the dungeons last term, and your entire school will be penalized with a delayed start in the battle of the schools."

I thought about arguing that the entire School of Battle shouldn't be punished for the actions of a few first-years, but I realized that the punishment was intended to draw the ire of every other Blade. Part of our penance was to be despised by the rest of the school.

Then I remembered the broken body of my fellow cadet lying on the ground. The punishment was not enough. Not for the one responsible.

CHAPTER
FORTY-ONE

Jess

I was going to kill him. This was the second time Torq had sent me into a panic thinking he was seriously hurt or dead, and now my reaction to him possibly being the Blade who'd died had outed me to Morgan. Not that she'd said anything. Not yet. But I'd seen the way she'd looked at me when I'd thought for a moment Torq had been killed. She knew.

It was my own damn fault, of course. I knew better than to get involved with a Drexian. I had more sense than to hook up with a fellow cadet. I should have known that hiding whatever I was doing with Torq would not be sustainable.

You're no better than those dumb girls you used to make fun of back home, I told myself as I hurried down the wide staircase to the main hall. You fell for a bad boy just like they did. It just took you longer.

I hated that my own judgmental inner voice was turning on me, but what did I expect? I'd spent my life feeling superior to girls who foolishly fell for the wrong guys or tanked their futures for some dick, but here I was obsessing over a hot guy with a huge dick. I fucking hated comeuppance now that it was being served to me on a heaping platter.

I'd managed to weave my way through the crush of cadets heading to class, hoping I could put enough distance between me and Morgan that she wouldn't be able to catch up and question me. I knew she wanted to know what was going on, but I wasn't ready to confess all. Not without telling Torq first.

I reached the bottom step and dodged a cluster of Irons who'd paused to debate some new program, making a beeline for the stone arch leading to the School of Strategy. I hadn't made it across the hall when I caught sight of Torq by the wall and by himself.

Without thinking, I rushed over to him. "You scared the shit out of me." He looked dazed and exhausted but all the irritation at him leaving me alone in his room and the fear when I'd heard that a Blade had died, spilled from me in a torrent. "I thought you were the one who'd died, and I might never see you again and..."

A Blade slowed as he walked past us, and I stopped talking, realizing just how much I was giving away in a very public place. Torq's expression darkened as his gaze tracked the Blade until the Drexian had crossed the hall and disappeared into the corridor leading to Battle. I would have asked him what that was about, but I'd already heard that the entire school was being punished for the misdeeds of the group of first-years. I doubted that would be the last Blade furious at Torq.

I dropped my voice. "I'm glad you didn't die." I lifted my hand to touch his arm but hesitated. "I was worried."

As if he'd just realized where he was and who was standing

in front of him, he lowered his gaze to me. But his eyes held none of the warmth I'd grown accustomed to. Instead, his gaze was cool and haughty, just like it had been when I'd first met him. "Why would you worry about me?"

I opened my mouth and closed it again. Was he serious? I knew that he was probably upset that one of his fellow Battle cadets had died but why was he acting like he didn't know me? Then I remembered that he wasn't supposed to know me. We were in different schools, and no one knew that we had any connection outside of the fact that we'd gone through the maze together. Even that wouldn't have been reason enough to make us close enough that I would worry about him.

I shook off my confusion. "Right. I wouldn't. I meant that I was sorry to hear about your fellow Blade."

Pain twisted his handsome face for a beat then his bored expression returned, flickering only when an older Drexian approached. He wore a uniform, but it wasn't one from the academy.

"You must be one of the new human cadets." He sized me up without hesitation, his gaze going up and down my body. "You are the best your planet had to send?"

It would have been impossible to miss the insult in his question, but I had grown used to Drexians underestimating humans. "One of them."

He arched a dark eyebrow. "Are you a Blade like my son?"

A jolt went through me. I was looking at an older version of Torq's features, arrogant sneer and all.

"There are no female Blades," Torq answered before I could.

"I'm an Assassin."

Torq's father stared at me, as if decided whether that was good enough. "But you know Torq?" He pivoted to his son before I could open my mouth. "You did not tell me you had human friends."

"I do not." Torq's voice was sharp, and he didn't meet my gaze.

I understood why he'd said it, but the rejection still stung. "He's right. We aren't friends. We did go through the maze together but that was more of an accident than anything."

"Yes, the trials." The older Drexian nodded slowly, his gaze locked onto Torq. "Where you proved yourself to be a capable Blade."

Bitterness dripped from his words like acid, and I could almost see Torq flinch, but he didn't respond or look at me. Suddenly, my no-good family didn't seem so bad. At least they hadn't objected to the path I'd taken. They hadn't done much to help, but they hadn't hurt me. Not like Torq's father seemed to take pleasure in doing.

For the first time, I got a glimpse of why Torq could be such an arrogant ass. Every bully has a bully, and his was his father.

"I'd better get to class." I took a step back, making a point not to look at Torq again. I pinned my gaze firmly on his father, challenging him to say something else that would make me want to plot his untimely death.

The Drexian turned his attention from his rigid son, watching me with curiosity that bordered on the disturbing as I backed away. Something told me that he wasn't the type of guy you turned your back on or took your eyes off.

When I finally spun around, I was almost to the archway leading into Strategy, and I almost bumped into Morgan. My already racing heart lurched.

"Who was that?" Morgan was looking over my shoulder to Torq and his father. "Someone related to Cocky Blade?"

"Cocky Blade?" I refused to look back as I led us under the

arch with the mask and dagger carved in stone and down the corridor to the Assassin classrooms.

"A nickname I'm workshopping. So, is it?"

"That was his dad." Now that I was well away from the Drexian I was beginning to thaw out from his glacial stare. "And now I know why Torq can be such a—"

"Cocky Blade?"

I rolled my eyes at Morgan eagerly finishing my sentence. "Exactly."

My friend looped her arm through mine. "If he's such a cocky a-hole, why are you so into him?"

I opened my mouth to protest, glancing around to make sure no one had heard her, but she held up a hand.

"I saw you lose a few shades when you thought he was the one who'd died, and don't tell me it's because we went through the maze together because I also went through the maze with the guy, and I don't look at him like you look at him."

I sighed. There was no point in lying anymore. She knew. I waited until a pair of Drexian cadets passed us and I dropped my voice to a conspiratorial hush. "Promise me that this stays between us?"

Morgan made a criss-cross motion over her chest with one finger. "Cross my heart and hope to be sent to Irons."

I laughed at that. The girl really did not like anything technical. "Okay, but you also have to promise not to hate him."

She scrunched her lips to one side as we paused outside the doors to our class. "I make no promises on that. Not until I hear the whole story. Now spill it, Jess."

CHAPTER
FORTY-TWO

Torq

B lood pounded in my ears as I stormed toward the circuit. I didn't know who I wanted to hit more: Dom, my father, or myself. So much vitriol flowed through my veins that it was like poison burning me from the inside out, and the only way to purge it from myself was to burn off the energy.

The corridor leading to the School of Battle was bathed in shadows with few other Blades walking with me. They were already in class, which was where I should have been. But being around others would not be good for me or them. Not when I was consumed with rage that was begging for release.

I passed the door to the climbing wall and then the ones leading to sparring rings. I breathed a tight sigh of relief when I opened the door to the circuit and found it empty. Stepping inside triggered the lights, which immediately illuminated the elaborate obstacle course that reached high into the air. Our first-year class had practiced on it a few times, but I had far from mastered the route.

I shook out my hands to release some of the adrenaline pumping through me as I strode toward the start of the course and quickly climbed the ladder to the platform. I should have known better than to do anything that required focus and strategic thinking when I was so angry, but I didn't care.

I didn't care if I fell. I welcomed the failure and the pain. Anything to take away the sucking guilt and agonizing remorse. Maybe physical pain would take away the pain that twisted my gut every time I thought of my Blade brother plunging to his death. Now I could add the shame of pretending that Jess was nothing to me. I closed my eyes for a beat but all that flashed in front of my eyelids was her pained expression as she'd realized that I would not acknowledge her in front of my father. I would not let him think she meant anything to me.

"Coward," I growled to myself, as I stood on the platform and eyed the circuit. "You are a *grekking* coward."

My heart raced as I leapt for the first large ring and swung high, letting go at the top and grasping the edge of a hollow cone that rotated. My feet flew through the air behind me, and I savored the rush of air and weightless sensation. I released my grip and landed in a crouch on a suspended disc as it swayed beneath my weight.

I had known that the Drexian Academy would be hard. I'd expected that. I hadn't expected it to almost kill me. I hadn't expected to lose fellow cadets pointlessly. I hadn't expected the human cadets to upend my world.

That's what Jess had done. She'd upset my total confidence in Drexian superiority and human inferiority. I had grown up knowing that Drexians were the strongest and bravest, and that humans—especially the females—were in need of our protection. They were useful as mates but only because we needed them to continue our species. They were not our equals, and they would never be able to outsmart or outperform me.

But Jess and the other humans had destroyed that truth for me. I'd seen firsthand how smart and brave she was, and that she was worthier than my father would ever be able to admit.

My father. I cringed when I thought of how dismissively he'd talked about me becoming a Blade, how he'd practically sneered at Jess, how he'd asked me if I'd fucked her after she'd walked away.

I'd denied it, but he'd only arched an eyebrow and told me that there was no harm in enjoying the weaker species, as long as I remembered my duty to my clan.

Duty. I almost choked on the word as I jumped to the next wobbly disc that was suspended from two chains. My entire life I'd been told the importance of duty and clan, but neither of those had saved me in the maze. My high-born status had done nothing when I'd fought off deadly beasts sent by our own High Commanders to kill us.

My clan hadn't gotten me across the pit of lava or flown me from the maze. If it hadn't been for the humans, I would not be here. And if it wasn't for Jess, I would not have learned that I cared for more than Drexian status.

These were things my father would never understand. Just like he would never understand that I was proud to be a Blade and did not care that I came from a clan of Wings. I was not the same cadet that had walked through the door of the academy, and I did not regret one bit of it.

I lunged for the next disc, crouching as I regained my balance. Before I could leap for the final disc, there was a thud behind me as another pair of boots landed. I twisted my head to see Dom grinning at me maliciously.

"You have been difficult to track down."

My pulse spiked as fresh waves of anger slammed into me. "You. It's your fault he's dead."

Dom's cruel smile faltered. "It was supposed to be you."

I stood, keeping my knees bent as the disc wobbled. "You would kill over something that happened on the climbing wall?"

He gave a mirthless laugh. "You think I care about your stunt on the wall? You think that's what this is about? You are as arrogant and blind as I expected you to be."

What was he talking about? What grudge could he hold against me if it wasn't for the incident on the climbing wall? Before we'd both been inducted into Blades, I'd barely spoken to the Drexian. Was that it? Was he angry that I had ignored him during first term when I only associated with other highborns?

"If I am so blind, tell me. Tell me why you want me dead and why you are willing to kill others to take me down."

He flinched at this. "No one else was ever supposed to die. I am not like your brother."

"My brother?" I blinked at him, unsure if I'd heard him correctly. What did my brother, who hadn't even graduated from the academy, have to do with him?

"Yes, your older brother." Dom's gaze hardened as we both held our arms wide to maintain our balance. "He and my brother were in the same cadet class. But your brother and some of his high-born friends were offended that my brother didn't show enough deference to them, so they ganged up on him after-hours in the sparring ring and killed him."

My blood ran cold. I'd never heard this. I knew my brother had returned home in disgrace after the first term, but I'd always been told it was because he wasn't able to pass engineering. Even though I wanted to deny this story, my gut told me that it was exactly the kind of thing my brother would do. Now that I thought back, he hadn't been the only high-born to be expelled from the academy that year, but it was never talked about, never mentioned.

"You wish to kill me to repay my brother's crime?"

Dom cocked his head to one side. "I did want to kill you. Now I don't. Now, I want you to know what it's like to lose something important, something you value, something that cannot be replaced. Now I want you to suffer while I take away what you love."

Then he lunged for me.

CHAPTER
FORTY-THREE

Jess

M organ dragged me by the sleeve away from the classroom door and toward another door, pushing me into the empty map room as the lights illuminated the space from below. "I'm guessing this isn't something you want to share with the entire military history class."

There were no chairs in the map room, only clear boards lining the circular walls and a large flat disc in the middle with the topography of the Drexian home world and the academy depicted on its surface. The table was a holdover from the days when battles were planned out using the scale model, but there was something solid and comforting about it, even though the Gilded Peaks were sharp, and the Restless Sea looked just as tumultuous forged in metal.

The clear boards around us came to life with the lights, their surfaces illuminated with the most recent star charts and flight plans. I recognized the battle plans from the defense of Earth and several battles against the Kronock that were long past.

"So?" Morgan leaned against the map table and crossed her arms over her chest. "What's the deal with Torq?"

I'd known I couldn't hide my relationship with him forever, but I didn't know what I should tell her. I trusted Morgan with my life and she was my closest friend at the academy, but I didn't know what she'd think if she knew everything. She might not think too highly of me. What kind of badass Assassin lets herself be blackmailed?

"Okay, you're right, there's something going on between us."

Morgan's eyes widened. "I knew it."

"But it's nothing serious. It's more of a proximity thing. We're stuck in this academy together, so one thing led to another."

Morgan studied me for a beat. "An academy fling? I get that." Her lips curled into a grin. "Did the alien bad boy turn out to be good?"

My cheeks burned. Of course, she would want more details. I couldn't exactly tell her that I had no point of comparison. Explaining how and why I'd managed to stay a virgin through high school and my time in the Navy would take too long and create more questions than answers. I managed to return her smile. "What do you think?"

Morgan rocked back and nodded. "The bad ones are always the best. Why is that? Why can't the super-sweet guys blow our minds in bed? Are they too nice? Do we like the challenge of making the bad boys into good ones?"

I shrugged, even though the questions didn't require answers.

"How did this happen?" She asked once she'd stopped

pondering bad boys. "It's not like you're in the same classes anymore. Besides, you've been in the Stacks with me most nights."

"You know how things happen." I hoped my non-answer would suffice. Morgan's brow wrinkled, but I jumped in before she could pepper me with more questions. "What about you? Do any of the cadets do it for you?"

"The cadets?" She shook her head. "Nope. The other humans are a hard no. We have to return to the planet with them and no way do I want to end up with a superior officer I've blown."

"Maybe you'll be the superior officer."

She grinned at this. "You're right. Maybe I will. In which case, I definitely don't want to have to give orders to someone who's seen me naked."

"So, no flings for you while we're here?"

She twisted her lips to one side. "I didn't say that. I just said no cadets."

I forgot all about my strategy to get her mind off my fling. Now I genuinely wanted to know which non-cadets she liked. "The Drexian instructors?"

"I didn't say that." Morgan gave me a coy smile. "Definitely no one in the School of Strategy."

I wracked my brain to think of the other available Drexian instructors. The Academy Master was already taken, the head of security was scary, and the Irons instructors seemed too intense for Morgan. "Lieutenant Volten's friend? The Blade instructor?"

Morgan tipped her head back and forth as if considering this. "Kann? He's pretty hot, but I don't think a Blade is my style. No offense to Torq. I'm sure he's clever enough."

I laughed. "You know the Blades aren't total meatheads, right?"

"I know that." She didn't sound convinced. "And I don't mind a big, buff guy. Maybe one of them would be good for a fling. Does Torq have any friends who are looking for something with no strings attached?"

I thought about my encounter with Torq. He'd made it clear that he didn't want anyone to know about us, and when his father arrived, I understood why. Torq's father clearly didn't have much respect for humans, and I could only imagine how he'd feel to know his son was sleeping with one of them. A part of me had thought that Torq and I had developed something real between us, but that was my wishful thinking. He'd always been clear that our arrangement was just that—a deal, a bargain, an agreement.

It didn't matter that the terms had changed and that he was teaching me. It was still only an exchange. It couldn't be anything more than that. He couldn't let anyone know that he was involved with a human, and I didn't want any of my friends to know that I'd been a twenty-two-year-old virgin who'd known nothing.

Our deal had a shelf life, even if I hated to think about it ending. I would return to Earth to hopefully rise even higher within the ranks of Naval intelligence, and he would go on to be a Drexian warrior. Then I thought about Torq pinning me down to his bed, and my stomach did a somersault.

"You won't tell anyone, will you?"

Morgan looked offended by my question. "And break girl code? Never. Your fling is your business. As long as you banging a Blade won't make it hard when we beat them in the battle of the schools."

I'd been so preoccupied with my dalliance with Torq and trying to help Ariana and keeping up with classes that I'd almost forgotten that the battle was soon. "Never. You know I'm loyal to the Assassins." Panic fluttered in my chest, replacing the fizzy feeling thoughts of Torq had provoked. "The battle is soon, isn't it? Should we be preparing? Have I missed coaching sessions?"

"It's not like the maze. It's not as deadly or as hard." Morgan released a breath. "It's supposed to use skills we all have—or should have—and it's our entire school, so we have the upperclassmen to take the lead. Fiona assured me that it's actually fun."

I doubted that. The Drexian idea of fun was very different from mine.

"Your boy and his Blades don't have much of a chance, especially after what happened last night. Their entire school was penalized with a delayed start in the battle, so it's really just the Irons and Wings we need to worry about beating."

I would have asked how Morgan knew so much more than I did, but the girl was amazing at hearing rumors and scuttlebutt. Another reason why she was a natural Assassin.

"Now, about those friends of Torq's who might be interested in a fling..." Morgan said as she hooked her arm through mine.

I was about to tell her that I didn't know his friends, but we both stiffened when we turned to the door and saw a figure standing silently in the shadow of the corridor, watching us. Dread sent a shiver down my spine. What was the admiral's adjunct doing there, and how much had he heard?

As we hurried past Tivek, I wondered how many academy secrets the enigmatic Drexian knew—and how many of his own he was hiding behind his watchful façade.

CHAPTER
FORTY-FOUR

Ariana

"I don't understand why you think I'll be helpful," Fiona said I practically dragged her along the corridor. "The guy hates me, especially after I threatened to cut off his testicles and use them as castanets."

"I'm sure that's not the worst threat he's ever gotten." The weathered Drexian not only looked like he'd been through a lot, but he'd also served in Inferno Force, which meant he'd been on the front lines against the Kronock.

"It might be the only time a colleague has threatened his nuts, though."

"Vyk is tough." I dismissed her concerns with a wave of my hand. "I doubt your threat even registered in his top ten. Besides, it doesn't matter what you said to him in the past, we need him on our side."

"Do we?"

I stopped when we reached the door to the security chief's

office. "You heard what Noora told us. Vyk is willing to help find Sasha."

Fiona mumbled something about starting to regret sitting with the Academy Master's wife during lunch, but I ignored her.

"Come on, Fi. We need to put our personal feelings aside. Yes, the Drexian has an issue with humans at the academy. Yes, he hasn't been great to either of us in the past. Yes, he's part of the reason I almost died in the trials, but if I can get past it, so can you."

Fiona squared her shoulders and nodded. "You're right. I'm not afraid of this guy, and if he can help find your sister, then let's do this."

I gave her arm a squeeze before I rapped my knuckles sharply on the door. "Thanks. You're the best."

Fiona winked at me. "Yes, I am."

"Come in," Vyk's deep voice boomed from behind the door. I might not have had the altercations with him that Fiona had, but even I shuddered before pressing my hand to the side panel and waiting for the door to slide open.

When we walked inside his office, the commander stood from behind his desk, and his gaze slid from me to Fiona and lingered on her before returning to me. I couldn't keep from glancing at the weapons hanging on the black stone wall we passed on the way to his desk, and I wondered how many of them the warrior had used in battle.

Before he could ask why we'd come, I beat him to the punch. "I heard that you were willing to help find my sister."

He straightened, tipping his head forward only slightly. "I am. No female should be left in the grasp of the Kronock."

I didn't care that his viewpoint sounded a bit sexist, but I could sense Fiona bristling beside me. "What do you know about the human that was taken by them and rescued?"

He waved a hand at the pair of chairs across from his desk and waited for us to sit before lowering himself back into his chair. "I regret that I know little of the location and rescue. I was only involved in getting the human and her Drexian rescuer off the outpost once she was freed."

"Only one Drexian went after her?" I clarified, still amazed that a solo mission had succeeded.

"Only one, but he was well-trained in subterfuge, since he was a—" Vyk stopped himself and cleared his throat, "Drexian warrior."

That hadn't been what he'd meant to say, but I didn't pursue it. "Can you tell me anything more about how it was done?"

The Drexian stroked one hand down both sides of his trim, gray beard as he thought. "I do know that they were certain of the target. That is why the one-Drexian rescue worked."

"See?" Fiona cut her gaze to me. "That's why we're working so hard to find where the Kronock are keeping Sasha."

I didn't respond because a big part of me still wanted to take a ship and start searching. I still had a barely controllable urge to do *something*.

"Your violent friend is right." Vyk didn't crack a grin at this, even though I fought the urge to laugh at Fiona's expression of outrage. "To succeed, the rescue mission must be planned with excruciating detail."

"Thank you." Fiona's words dripped with sarcasm, but Vyk didn't catch that. He merely gave her a curt nod, which provoked a fuming huff from her.

As much fun as it was to watch Vyk and Fiona spar off without actually engaging, I didn't want to waste the security chief's time. "I appreciate your honesty." I stood and Fiona followed suit. "If you can think of anything else that might help us, don't hesitate to let me know."

Vyk also stood. "I do not personally know the Drexian who pulled off the rescue, but his brother is Inferno Force. I could contact him."

"We already have Torq doing that through his father," Fiona said.

Vyk lifted a brow. "Torq has asked his father? I have never known House Swoll to do favors that do not benefit them personally." He squared his shoulders. "It would be no trouble for me to also reach out. In case, House Swoll does not come through."

The way he said it, made me think that Torq would not be successful despite his best efforts.

"I can also make contact with the other members of Inferno Force I know who have entered Kronock territory and escaped."

"Like Kann's friend who was taken prisoner?"

He inclined his head. "Yes, like Jax."

"That would be great. Thank you."

"No thanks are necessary." Vyk gave us a slight bow as we turned and walked from his office.

When we were outside the closed door, I released a long breath. "That wasn't so bad, was it? I'm starting to think he might not be such a bad guy, after all."

Fiona gave what sounded like a harumph as she strode ahead of me. "I still don't trust him."

I followed her, but I already felt better that the gruff commander was on our side, even if it made Fiona crazy.

CHAPTER
FORTY-FIVE

Torq

I winced as I made my way back to the dormitory tower, my leg screaming in pain with every tentative step. At least Dom had left the circuit with as many bruises and as much blood running down his face as I had. At least I'd gotten in as many hits as the deranged Blade.

At this point, I didn't care that I was injured. The fight had purged me of the rage that had consumed me and given me a target for my fury. Battling with Dom across the platforms and obstacles had exorcised the guilt from me, as well. I was not to blame for the death of my Blade brother. It was Dom who carried that. At least, he would, if he wasn't twisted by vengeance.

Part of me wanted to reach out to my older brother on a vid call and ask him what happened. But a bigger part of me knew he was guilty. He'd always despised anyone he deemed beneath him, and since that had often been me when we were growing up, I understood the depth of his wrath. If he'd decided that a Drexian deserved punishment, I had no doubt he'd been brutal.

"And now I get to pay the price." Even mumbling hurt my split lip, and I tasted blood as I swallowed.

As unfair as it was, I understood Dom's anger and his need for justice. My brother and his high-born friends had gotten away with murder simply because of their clans. Drexian honor had been perverted in service to status, which should have been a rebuke to everything our people represented.

But Dom's attempts to punish my brother by killing me was just as much of a perversion of justice. I had nothing to do with my brother's actions, and our innocent Blade brother who'd been killed in my place had been sacrificed for nothing. And now he no longer wanted to kill me. He only wanted to hurt me.

I sucked in a breath of cool breath, flinching from the sharp pain shooting through my ribs, which might have been broken. What did he mean when he said he would take what I loved? I'd loved few things in my life. I'd thought I loved the Wings, but that had been an illusion. I'd only been trained to think I loved the Wings as much as my ancestors had. I now knew that I'd always been destined to be a Blade.

Did Dom plan to go after my family? Doubtful, since he was at the academy with me. That only left my friends, more Blades who were innocent of any crime.

And Jess. The voice in the back of my head was a whisper, as if even it was afraid to admit this out loud. Dom had walked past in the main hall as Jess had rushed up to me. I had not reacted to her, but she had been visibly emotional. Would he think I loved her?

Did I love Jess? I certainly desired her. My desire for her had been an obsession since I'd first seen her. It was an obsession that had driven me to blackmail her and then to pretend to be more injured than I was. It had driven me to accept her deal, even though I'd known that I would never be able to let her go once I'd claimed her.

My mind flashed back to being inside her, and how I'd felt powerful, invincible, whole. My pulse spiked and my heart raced as I remembered her soft moans, her sweet taste, her tight heat that made it almost impossible to retain any shred of control. I couldn't imagine giving her up. I couldn't imagine going without her. I couldn't imagine how I would continue to breathe if anyone hurt her.

I almost stumbled, catching myself with one hand on the stone wall. I did love her. I loved her obsessively, completely, and totally. It didn't matter that she was a human, that she was an Assassin, that she was not even a high-born of her own species. I loved her in spite of all of this. I loved her even though my family would never allow it. I loved her despite the fact that being with her would be impossible.

We were impossible because Dom could never know. He could never find out that Jess was the one thing I could not live without. He could not take her from me. I would kill him first. I would burn down the entire planet if she was harmed because of my clan's dishonor. I would make them all pay.

I staggered to my door and stumbled inside when the door slid open. Before I could collapse onto my bed, Jess leapt up from where she'd been sitting on the foot of it. I stopped and stared at her. "What are you doing here? How did you get in?"

She flapped a hand at the panel on the side. "You disabled the lock last night. It was still disabled when I came to check on you." Her eyes popped wide as she took in my disheveled appearance. "What happened to you? Were you in a fight?"

"I'm fine." My mind raced as I realized that Dom might

have seen her entering my room. Her being around me was no longer a risk to both of us, it was a threat to her life. "You cannot be here."

"Torq." Her voice was soft as she closed the distance between us and raised a hand to my face. "You're bleeding."

I pulled away, fear for her now eclipsing even the strongest desire to feel her touch and hold her in my arms. As much as I wanted to curl into her embrace, I could not put her in any more danger than I already had. My gut churned as I thought what Dom would do if he knew the extent of my love for her. If he knew that hurting her would destroy me, he would not hesitate. "You need to go. Now."

She froze, her face twisting in confusion. "Is this about your father? I know he doesn't approve of humans, but—"

"This is not about him." I made my voice as cold and clipped as I could. She needed to stay away from me. She needed to want to stay far from me. She needed to despise me. "This is about me. I got what I needed from you. You got what you wanted from me. Our deal is done."

"What?" She blinked rapidly, her eyes glistening.

I could not be swayed by tears, even if seeing them made my gut twist in agony. I leaned closer and summoned my cockiest sneer. "You were a decent fuck, especially since I was your first, but we were never anything else but some fun. We both knew that."

"I thought—"

I gave her my most patronizing smile, one I knew would make her want to slap me senseless. "You thought me fucking you meant something? Like I said, you were fun, but I'm done. The end of term is approaching, and I do not want to have any loose ends."

Jess's cheeks mottled pink as she reared back from me as if I'd struck her. "You're done? I'm a loose end—?"

"What? Did you think I would end up with a low-born human? Did you really believe you were good enough for a Drexian?"

She shook her head, as if refusing to believe my words. "I knew you were an asshole. I should have known that you could never change. This was all a game to you, wasn't it? I was a game?"

I forced myself to give her an arrogant grin. "I did enjoy playing with you, but you should know about games more than anyone. Once you win, the game is over."

She pressed her lips together until they turned white as her eyes flashed malice. She pushed past me, pausing at my door. "Thank you for proving my initial instincts right. I guess I now know to trust my gut no matter what some asshole Drexian tells me. Or maybe the lesson here is that all high-born Drexians are liars and cheats." She glanced over her shoulder at me, disdain oozing from her. "Or maybe it's just Drexians from your clan. Or maybe it's just you."

Each of her accusations were like body blows, but I made myself stay silent. I forced myself to watch her stride from my room and bit my lip to keep from calling after her. It was better that she go. It was better that she hate me. At least she would be safe.

When my door glided shut behind her and I was finally alone in my quarters, I shuffled to my bed and sank onto it, letting my head fall into my hands as grief and loss washed over me. I'd just broken the heart of the one person I cared most about in the universe. I'd made sure that she would never believe me, would never trust me, would never love me.

I'd broken my own heart to save her. It was the most honorable thing I'd ever done, and I knew I would regret it, would hate myself for being honorable, and would mourn hurting her for the rest of my days.

CHAPTER
FORTY-SIX

Jess

I refused to let the tears fall as I practically ran down the corridor and down the steps, my boots tapping the stone like rain pattering a window. I wouldn't give Torq the satisfaction of making me cry, even if he couldn't see me. I would know, and I would not let him get the best of me. Would not let him win.

He thought this was all a game, and I was someone who could be toyed with? Well, like he'd said, I could play games with the best of them, and if he wanted to pretend like we were just a bit of fun, then I'd play along. Aside from Morgan, no one had a clue about us, and she wouldn't tell anyone. Especially once I told her that it was over.

Over. I swallowed hard as a lump lodged in my throat. I'd never imagined that I'd be upset that my deal with Torq was done. Since it had started as blackmail that I'd reluctantly agreed to, I hadn't thought that it could have turned into something that I would miss.

I scoffed at this. "Miss that jerk? As if."

I didn't make eye contact with a pair of cadets as I hurried across the open-air bridge toward the female tower, keeping my head down so they wouldn't notice the tears threatening to fall despite my assurances to myself that I didn't care.

This was exactly why I'd never gotten involved with a guy before now. I'd known that it wouldn't be anything but a distraction that ended in heartbreak. That's what it had been for every girl I'd known back home who'd fallen for a bad boy. They'd bought the pretty lies and believed that he wasn't as bad an everyone else claimed, and they all ended up betrayed, broken-hearted, and in most cases, knocked up.

"At least that part won't happen to me."

One of the advantages to Drexian society and advanced tech was the fact that males had birth-control implants. Being pregnant was not part of the plan. Not that hooking up with a total asshat had been, but I needed to count my meager blessings.

I didn't slow when I reached the tower and started climbing the winding stairs, taking them two at a time until I'd reached my floor and was sucking in breath. Now that I'd almost exhausted myself, I'd lost the urge to burst into tears. Now I wasn't hurt. Now I was mad.

Who the hell did he think he was? I'd tutored him in stupid Kronock, even when he didn't need to study the alien language so much. I'd checked on him when he was hurt. I'd worried about him. I'd stood there and taken his father's superior bullshit when I should have told him to go fuck himself.

Now that I wasn't with Torq, I thought of a million brilliant responses and comebacks. Of course. I could barely speak when I was standing in front of him but now that I was halfway across the academy, I was brimming with snappy retorts. I had half a mind to stomp back over and unleash them on him.

I shook my head. "Nope. I'm not going to give him the satisfaction of knowing that I care enough to come up with snarky put-downs."

"That's the spirit."

I jumped when Morgan poked her head from her doorway. "How did you beat me back here? How did you get away from Tivek?"

She inclined her head at me. "You mean after you faked a headache and left me?"

"Sorry." I winced. "I thought you'd be right behind me. Did you get in trouble?"

"For what? Hanging out in the map room? Talking about finding a Drexian for a fling?"

I guess she was right. We weren't breaking any rules aside from being painfully late to class, and the academy didn't babysit cadets. If you missed class, you dealt with the repercussions. "What was he doing in Strategy, anyway?"

"No idea. He didn't say, but I get the feeling he's the eyes and ears of the admiral."

Then I sincerely hoped he didn't hear much of our conversation. The last thing I needed was to be called in to the admiral's office to explain why I was banging a fellow cadet or why I wasn't banging him anymore. That was a topic I'd rather not discuss with anyone.

"So, what were you saying about snarky comments?" Morgan eyed me. "And why do you look like you would love to strangle someone?"

I glanced around the empty floor, noting that all the other doors were closed. "Remember how I told you that I was involved with Torq? Well, I'm not anymore."

Her gaze darkened. "His choice?"

I nodded, my throat suddenly tight and my eyes burning.

She pulled me into a hug that was so fierce I could barely breathe. "I would say that the best revenge is living well, but in this case the best revenge will be beating his ass in the battle of the schools. I know Blades are at a disadvantage with the late start but that doesn't mean it won't be just as sweet when they lose."

I tried to summon some of her righteous satisfaction, but I couldn't suppress the sadness that bubbled up and made it hard to speak. I'd waited so long, and I'd thought that I was being smart about who to trust, but I'd ended up being just another dumb girl who fell for a handsome face and some sweet lies. I'd been so sure I was smarter than that, but I wasn't. My entire sense of self wobbled as I second-guessed my judgment and street smarts, both of which I'd always believed I had in spades. Losing that hurt as much as anything.

I managed to nod as Morgan pulled away, but she gave me a shrewd look. "Don't give the guy a second thought. He's an idiot if he doesn't see how amazing you are, and I'm prone to think he's a bit of an idiot anyway."

I bit back the urge to defend him. Torq wasn't stupid but he also wasn't mine to defend. He never had been. "Thanks, girl."

"It's the truth. You're way too good for him."

"Too good for who?" Britta asked as she emerged from the stairwell. "Are we talking about Drexians we'd like to bang?"

"Drexian fuck, marry, kill," Morgan said, deftly changing the subject away from me. "Who would you pick?"

Britta flipped her hair off her shoulder and tapped a finger on her chin. "Fuck Kann, marry Vorn, kill Vyk."

"Who's Vorn?" Morgan and I asked at the same time.

"Irons instructor. Hot, but not too hot, if you know what I

mean. You can't trust the ones who're too hot. They're only good for one thing."

"Like Kann?" Morgan teased.

Britta lifted her brows. "Exactly. That Drexian has trouble written all over him." She grinned like she would have loved a bit of trouble. "What about you two?"

Morgan jumped in before I was forced to answer. "Fuck Vyk, marry Tivek, and kill Torq."

Britta laughed. "You'd fuck the security chief? He's so scary."

"That's why he'd be so good."

"No way." Fiona walked up from the stairwell with Ariana by her side. "Vyk is all mine."

"She loves silver foxes," Ariana added.

Fiona made a face. "And I'd love to kill that one."

"I'm willing to give him up, but I'd still kill Torq." Morgan slid a quick smile to me.

"Why are we killing cadets?" Fiona asked, as she walked toward her door. "Or should I not ask?"

Britta glanced at us before answering. "Just a quick round of Drexian fuck, marry, kill."

Fiona's eyes sparkled as her door slid open. "That sounds like it would pair perfectly with Noovian whiskey. Anyone up for a glass?"

I normally would have hesitated, especially about drinking with an instructor, but today I didn't care. "Sounds perfect. And for the record, I'd kill Torq, too."

Ariana shook her head. "That Drexian had better watch his back."

My thoughts exactly.

CHAPTER
FORTY-SEVEN

Torq

Tivek's gaze held me as he ushered me into the admiral's office. Even though the Drexian was only the master's adjunct, even though he had no status, even though he did not hold power over me, I withered under the judgment of his gaze.

My clan instinct kicked in. Always fight back instead of showing weakness. Always exert superiority. "Why have I been summoned here again?"

Disdain clung to my voice, but Tivek seemed unaffected by it. "That is for the admiral to convey." His gaze snagged on my split lip. "Do you require the surgeon?"

I shook my head so roughly my ears rang. I'd taken one too many hits to the head to be moving so brusquely. "I am fine. I took a few falls on the circuit."

Tivek cocked an eyebrow, and it was clear he knew I was

lying. Rumor had it he'd been a cadet once, although he hadn't finished, so he was aware that my injuries were not courtesy of the Blade circuit. He walked forward, placing a hand on the stone wall so that part of the wall slid back.

This was where my father and the admiral had emerged from when I'd been waiting to be interviewed. I stiffened at the thought that my father might be inside waiting for me like a Verethian spider waiting to strike at an unsuspecting insect.

"Admiral Zoran would like to speak with you in his private chambers."

I stared at Tivek for a beat then at the opening in the wall and the dimly lit room beyond. I'd heard that the academy had secret rooms, but this was the first proof I'd gotten that the rumors were more than myth. I squared my shoulders, even though the movement made me wince, and walked past him into the admiral's private chambers.

The stone floor gave way to thick carpet, and soon, I was padding toward a crackling fireplace flanked by dark sofas. A wall of books was to my right and to my left was a wall of clear shelves that held a vast collection of bottles, each presumably containing a type of alien booze. A bar fronted the bottles, and the Academy Master stood at it pouring a measure of green liquid into a pair of glasses.

He saw me and stopped pouring. Picking up the glasses, he closed the distance between us, meeting me in front of the sofas and handing me a glass. "It looks like you need this more than I do."

I did not bother lying to the admiral. He would certainly see that my bruises could not come from falls from an apparatus. But if he wondered who had given me such cuts and bruises, he did not ask.

I eyed the green liquid, curious that the head of the academy would summon me, invite me into his private chambers that looked more like a lair, and offer me a drink. "Is this about the accident? I have told you all I know."

"It is not." Admiral Zoran took a sip of his drink, his eyes staying on mine over the rim of his glass.

I hesitantly took a drink, the liquid stinging my open lip. The sharp bite of the liquor mixed with the metallic tang of blood as I swallowed, but the heat slid down my throat and hit my gut with force. I took another sip to chase the first one, and the pain throbbing through my body became dull.

Admiral Zoran waved a hand toward the sofas, and I sat on one side while he sat on the other. The light from the fire cast his face in shadows, making the Drexian appear fierce and stern.

I wanted to snap at him not to toy with me, but even my high-born instincts made me hold my tongue. The admiral was from just as elite a clan as mine. He was no one to be challenged. Even my father had deferred to him, and my father deferred to few. "Is this about my father?"

Zoran swished his drink in the glass, the green liquid catching the firelight as it swirled. "In a way. Your father was not here because of the accident. I did not summon him."

This startled me. Even my father did not have contacts high enough to have heard about the accident without being informed by someone on the inside. "Then why was he here?"

"You asked him to help you. You asked for a connection."

I'd almost forgotten that I had asked him to connect me to former High Commander Kax. He had never responded to my request, and I had assumed that he'd dismissed it along with the news that I'd been inducted into the Blades. "He came to connect me with Kax?"

The admiral's lips pulled down. "He did not. He made the trip to tell you that he did not support your involvement in the human's rescue."

This hit me like a slap to the face. "He came all this way to tell me no?"

"Am I to assume that he did not discuss this with you?"

I gazed into the bottom of my glass and managed to move my head from side to side. "He was too preoccupied with the disgrace I have brought onto my clan."

Zoran grunted. "He told me, although I expect he thought he would find a more sympathetic ear than he did. Maybe he had not heard that I took a human bride."

Or maybe he did not care and savored the opportunity to insult a Drexian of higher military rank, I thought. I had heard my father talk dismissively of humans too many times to think he would respect even the admiral's choice of mate.

"So, he will not help." I tossed back the rest of my drink, gasping as it scorched my throat.

"No." Zoran studied me carefully as I started to stand. "But I will."

This stopped me. "You know the former High Commander?"

"Not personally, but I am very close with someone who does." He looked toward the door as Tivek walked in. "You did not think I chose my adjunct strictly because of his charming personality, did you?"

I glanced from Tivek to Zoran, utterly confused that a low-born assistant would have contacts with a high-born officer who was working undercover for Drexian intelligence.

"I have already reached out to Kax, and he is happy to help in any way he can." Tivek joined the admiral on the sofa, sitting beside him like they were old friends. "He is currently en route to the academy."

"You are to be commended for offering to use your connections—even through your father—to help the missing pilot." Zoran lifted his glass to me. "You are a very different cadet than you were when you arrived, even if you do still tend to get into fights."

"Thank you, Admiral," I croaked, sure the alien booze was causing me to hallucinate, and also sure that I was fine with that.

CHAPTER
FORTY-EIGHT

Jess

T he holographic image flickered off as the lights came on. I blinked a few times as cadets stood around me and gathered their things.

"Don't forget," Fiona called out from behind the lectern. "The battle of the schools is in two days. The best thing you can do to prepare is study the terrain around the academy and prepare your packs for any situation. And don't forget that the Restless Sea is still a type of terrain."

"If we prepare for anything, we won't be able to lift our packs," a Drexian cadet grumbled.

Fiona tossed her hair off her shoulder. "A big, strapping Drexian like you should be able to carry anything, shouldn't you?"

The guy, who was big and burly, stammered something unintelligible as he stumbled toward the door. It never failed to amuse me how Fiona managed to maintain her badass image while still whipping out her feminine wiles to catch the Drexians off guard.

I stood slowly and moved toward the end of the curved row of seats as Fiona moved to intercept me.

"You okay?" She scoured my face intently. "You seemed distracted in class."

My cheeks warmed, and I felt just as awkward as that Drexian must have felt. "It wasn't your lecture, I promise."

Fiona smiled warmly. "I know that. My talk on ancient Persian battle strategy is gold, and normally, you'd be fully into it."

I returned her smile, grateful that she could joke about it. "Sorry. I guess I'm just having an off day." More like I couldn't stop thinking about Torq and how stupid I'd been to trust him, but I wasn't about to admit that to an instructor, even a human one. "I'll be back to normal tomorrow."

She put a hand on my arm. "It isn't the battle of the schools, is it? I promise, that will be nothing like the maze."

"No, although I wouldn't mind if the Drexians could chill out on all the trials and battles and competitions."

Fiona leaned closer to me. "It's all the testosterone. It muddles their brains and makes them want to turn everything into a competition."

I laughed at this, which made her grin widen. After spending days beating myself up, it felt good to laugh and forget about Torq.

"Fiona!"

We both swiveled to see Ariana barrel through the door and dance around the departing cadets as she made her way to the front of the classroom. She was practically bouncing on her toes when she reached us and her eyes were sparkling.

"Did you hear?"

"If you're this excited, obviously not." Fiona grabbed her hands. "What's going on? Don't tell me you're having Volt's baby?"

Ariana barked out a laugh. "Very funny. Not yet, I mean, not for a while, oh, I don't know what I mean, but that isn't it."

Fiona laughed at her friend. "We will definitely be unpacking that later, but what's up?"

"You know how Torq thought he could connect us to the Drexian who'd actually rescued a human from the Kronock space?"

Fiona's eyes lit up. "Yes and yes."

"Well, that Drexian is on his way to the academy."

My jaw dropped. Torq had come through with his promise? A part of me had thought that he might be overstating his connections, but it looked like he'd done it. Not that this changed anything. I still hated the cadet with the intensity of a thousand suns, but it was nice to know that he'd done what he said he would. It was nice to know that not everything he said was a lie.

"So, we're going to get firsthand knowledge about how to pull off a rescue in enemy territory?" Fiona started bouncing on the balls of her feet. "And all without Vyk's help?"

Ariana laughed and shook her head. "It means we're one step closer to rescuing Sasha."

Fiona pulled her into a fierce hug then grabbed me and pulled me in, as well. "I told you there was nothing we couldn't solve if we worked together." She released us both and rubbed her hands together. "This calls for a celebration. Drinks in my room?"

Ariana shared a knowing look with me. "Does this mean drinks, or drinks and cards? I need to know how much money I'm going to lose."

Fiona gave her a wicked grin. "Tonight, I'll spare your pockets. Just drinks."

"Only a few though." Ariana leveled a finger at her. "The cadets need to be on their game for the battle of the schools."

"Should we invite the guys?" Fiona asked. "Between Kann and Torq both reaching out to their contacts, it seems we have one or both to thank."

"Don't forget Vyk," Ariana said. "He's also helping us."

"No," I said so loudly both women shot me startled looks. "Nothing ruins a good girls' night like testosterone, right?"

Fiona nodded. "She makes an excellent point. Girls only."

I released a breath. I could not bear to see Torq this soon. Not when even the thought of him still made my chest twist in pain. I forced myself to smile at Ariana, but her expression was shrewd. She knew better than anyone what it was like to carry on a secret relationship. The big difference was that her guy hadn't been a liar. Her guy hadn't ruined everything for her.

CHAPTER
FORTY-NINE

Torq

"You don't look so bad anymore." Kort scrutinized my healing wounds from across the table.

The cadet dining hall was bustling, but we sat alone at the end of a long, wooden table. Since our misdeeds had been revealed—and our punishment that affected all Blades—we'd spent most meals alone, or with other first-years who'd been with us on the fateful night. I'd grown accustomed to the scathing looks and hostile grunts from other Blades, just as the pain from my injuries had faded over the days.

What hadn't faded was the pain from what I'd inflicted on Jess. I despised myself for the cruel words I'd said to send her away, but I'd hoped the guilt would recede. It hadn't. Every time I caught a glimpse of her, it was like a stab to my gut. Even worse? She wouldn't spare me as much as a glance.

Her pale-haired friend didn't bother to hide her hatred of

me, though. She was generous with her glares and eyes narrowed into slits. I almost feared her more than I feared the vengeful Dom.

I met Kort's gaze over our plates of grilled bread and fried gonji eggs. "Thanks."

"Not that it matters what you look like, as long as you're healed enough to compete in the battle."

It felt like I'd sleepwalked my way through the last classes of the term, but the days had passed regardless, and the battle of the schools was upon us. I took a bite of my now-cooled bread and tried to feign enthusiasm for the final competition of the year that started the next day. "What does it matter how healed I am, since we have a delayed start?"

Kort's gaze hardened. "We are still Blades, are we not? We still rush bravely into the most hopeless battles and defend our people from the fiercest foes."

I straightened, as I realized that I was allowing myself to forget that I was still a Blade; I was still Drexian. "You are right."

Kort gave me a sharp nod. "The Blades have won many times. Maybe it is a kindness to the other schools that we will be delayed."

I couldn't help smiling at my friend. He had never lost his optimism, even when the other Blades had ostracized us. Of course, he hadn't discovered that his brother was a disgraced killer, or that another cadet was bent on getting revenge on him for it. He hadn't been forced to give up the one bright spot in his life to keep her safe. He hadn't broken the one truly good thing that had happened to him.

A pair of Blades stomped by us, scowling and muttering curses as they passed.

"I do not think our Blade brothers agree with you."

"They will not feel the same way when we lead our school

to victory." Kort took a sip from his goblet. "That is why we must win, and why it is good that you are healed."

I had told Kort that my bloodied face and bruised body were courtesy of Dom, but I hadn't told him why. I had no reason to protect my brother, but there was something in me that could not admit that my clan had brushed a murder aside so easily. He would not judge me, but I still could not voice the truth. Not when I'd been raised to believe in the superiority of my clan. Not when everything I'd been told was based on lies and dishonor.

I took a swig from my own goblet and let the cold fruity drink slide down my throat. "Do you have a plan for achieving this win, considering the rest of our school wants nothing to do with us?"

"The way I figure it, it is an advantage that the other Blades will not include us." He lowered himself closer to the table as he dropped his voice. "That way when we go off on our own, they will not notice."

"We still know little about the battle," I reminded him.

"We know that it takes place outside of the academy walls and usually traverses the terrain surrounding the school. We know that we will be given clues that lead us to the eventual destination. We also know that the entire school does not need to reach the end together. Only one cadet is enough."

I shook my head, my faith in his confidence fading. "But we will start after the other schools. We will discover the clues at the same time as the other Blades. I see no advantage."

Kort twitched one shoulder, as if none of my points mattered. "We are Blades. We are the bravest and the strongest."

I did not feel very brave or strong anymore, but I would not tell my friend. "I am glad I am on your team, brother."

He clinked the side of his metal goblet against mine, drained his, and then stood. "I need more. You?"

I shook my head and watched him walk away to refill his drink. Before his seat was cool, Dom slid into it.

I bristled. "What do you want?"

He made tsk-ing sounds in the back of his throat. "Is that the way you talk to a fellow Blade."

"It's the way I talk to a killer of a fellow Blade."

The corner of his eye twitched as he clenched his jaw. "Zenen was never meant to die. Not that you will care about him for much longer."

I wanted to ask what that meant, but I could not let him see that he had rattled me, or that he had any way to hurt me. As long as he did not know about Jess, I had no need to worry. At least, that was what I told myself as he pushed the chair back from the table, the legs scraping loudly on the stone.

"Good luck in the battle, Torq of House Swoll."

So much menace dripped from his voice that, for the first time, I dreaded the battle more than I had dreaded the trials. And those had almost killed me.

CHAPTER
FIFTY

Jess

I smoothed my hands down the front of my uniform pants and took a deep breath as I swept my gaze around my room to make sure I wasn't forgetting anything. I shouldn't be nervous. The battle of the schools wasn't anything like the trials. It wouldn't be used to determine our placement at the academy, or if we could remain. It wasn't even supposed to be deadly.

One of our Drexian Strategy instructors had called it a friendly competition to foster school pride and identity, although I had my doubts as to how friendly anything at the military academy truly was, especially after seeing how the Blades had been treating their first-years. If I hadn't wanted to kick Torq in the balls myself, I would have felt bad for how he and his fellow first-years were being ostracized by the rest of the school. Then again, a cadet had died, and the entire School of Battle was being punished for it.

Since the only conversations I'd had with Torq after the incident hadn't touched on what had actually happened, I only knew what was whispered in the halls or across dining tables. I only knew that the first-years had attempted to climb the forbidden tower, and one of their group had fallen to his death. It was deemed an accident, but even accidents carried punishment at the Drexian Academy.

I scooped my pack from the foot of my bed and hooked it over one shoulder. Fiona hadn't been able to give us any hints about the route or challenges involved in the battle, but she'd given us a list of things that might be helpful. I eyed the curved blade, wishing that wasn't something I would need, but then slid it into the holster around my waist.

A thump on my door told me it was time. I pressed my hand to the side panel and stepped out when it opened, joining Morgan as she bounced from foot to foot. Her pale hair was pulled up into a high ponytail which swished from side to side as she moved.

"Ready? Britta already left with a couple of Irons. We don't want to be late."

"Ready," I told her, even as my pulse fluttered. "Why are you so excited about this?"

"It's a chance for the Assassins to work together. It's what we do best." She threw an arm around me as we walked toward the stairs. "We're going to crush it."

Morgan's enthusiasm was contagious, and by the time we'd reached the main hall, her exuberant chatter about what she thought might be in the competition had become infectious. I was now as excited as my friend.

The large main hall, with its sweeping staircase that curved up and around several levels, was filled with cadets. Even on the busiest days between classes, I hadn't seen it so packed and buzzing with so much energy. Unlike the anxious charge that had permeated the air around the maze, this energy wasn't laced with fear.

I exhaled again as I swept my gaze around the hulking Drexian cadets who all carried packs on their backs and blades on their waists. As fierce as they looked, even the Drexians who had been through battles of the schools before didn't seem apprehensive. Maybe this would be a friendly competition, after all. Maybe this would be fun.

Just as I had decided that this was going to be a good time, I felt someone's gaze on me. I rubbed the back of my neck where the hairs had prickled as I peered around, finally catching Torq standing off to one side. He was pretending to look over my head at the cadets filling the staircase, but I knew it was him.

I narrowed my eyes at him, trying to shoot him a death glare. Why was he looking at me? He'd made it perfectly clear that he was done with me. That meant he wasn't allowed to stare at me or make me feel awkward. Done was done.

"I don't know why he's even here," Morgan said as she followed my gaze to Torq. "It's not like the Blades will be starting with the rest of us."

I shrugged and tried to pretend I didn't care, which was starting to become the truth. After days of nursing my bruised ego and wondering how I could have been so wrong about him, the pain had faded, and looking at him now only provoked a faint twinge of regret. "Who knows and who cares, right?"

Morgan beamed at me. "That's fucking right. Who cares about the Blades. They don't stand a chance this year."

Some other Assassins who'd gathered around us nodded

and grinned. It would be an easier battle without the Blades, and fair or not, we were all going to enjoy the advantage.

"You shouldn't hang your blade like that."

I jerked at the deep voice behind me, whirling around to see a tall Drexian grinning at me. His black hair was a little long around his neck and his eyes were a shade of gold that you didn't see in humans. I blinked at him a few times, wondering if he was talking to me. "What?"

He pointed to where I'd hung my blade off my waist. "You should turn the curve of the blade to face down and move it farther back." He reached forward, pausing before touching me. "Do you mind if I show you?"

I couldn't find the words to tell him yes, but I was able to move my head up and down. He gingerly twisted my holster and then removed my blade and hooked it back on facing the opposite direction. Even though his fingers didn't touch my skin, I could feel his heat through the fabric of my clothes.

"That will be safer and make it easier to grab."

"Thanks." My voice cracked as I finally spoke. "Are you an Assassin?"

He gave me a crooked smile without taking his gaze from mine. "Unfortunately, no. We are not on the same side today."

"Oh." I smiled back, my heart tripping in my chest. At least I hadn't been so caught up with Torq that I'd managed to overlook a Drexian this hot and charming in my own school. "Then thanks again, and good luck."

His smile softened. "You too." He jerked a thumb behind him. "I'd better go."

I usually would have let him walk away, but I didn't want to let being burned by one guy scar me for life. I wasn't ready to get back on the horse, but it didn't hurt to look at them. "What's your name?"

The Drexian paused and bowed his head slightly. "I'm Dom."

"Nice to meet you, Dom. I'm Jessica, but everyone calls me Jess."

The black pupils inside the gold of his eyes flared. "Oh, I know who you are, Jess."

I laughed. "I guess everyone knows who the human cadets are, since there aren't many of us."

"You are hard not to notice, human or not." Then he held my gaze for a long beat, before backing away and melting into the crowd.

I had to remind myself to breathe as I turned back to Morgan. Maybe rebounding from Torq wouldn't be so hard after all.

CHAPTER
FIFTY-ONE

Torq

What was Dom doing, talking to Jess? Waves of panic swept over me, sending cold chills across my skin, and making me shudder. He couldn't know anything about her, could he?

I gave my head a determined shake, as if to brush away any thoughts that he might know about us. It was impossible. I'd made a point to stay far from her. I hadn't spoken to her, I hadn't arranged to bump into her, I hadn't looked at her. Well, I'd tried not to look at her. Sometimes it was impossible. My eyes searched her out even when I knew it was wrong, even when I knew I couldn't allow myself the indulgence.

I glared at the back of his head as he dared to touch her, blood pounding furiously in my ears as I watched his hand go to her waist and adjust her blade. The thought of him touching her, looking at her, smiling at her made me almost forget my promises. I wanted to storm through the crowd, pull him away from her, and throw him to the ground. I wanted to feel the crunch of his bones as my fists pounded them. I wanted to hear him beg me to stop. I wanted to punish him for daring to touch what was mine.

But she isn't yours. Not anymore. You gave her up.

My heart dropped like a black stone in the churning sea. As much as she felt like she was still mine, she wasn't. She couldn't be. Not if I wanted to keep her safe. She couldn't be as long as Dom was still determined to extract his vengeance by punishing me.

I tracked him as he backed away from her, but I snatched my gaze away once he turned. He couldn't see me watching. He couldn't see that I cared.

"You're here early." Kort sidled up to me as the crowd swelled. "I didn't think you would arrive until later."

I was relieved that my friend had arrived to distract me. "I wanted to be ready. There is nothing else to do today but the battle."

"True." Kort cast his gaze across the cadets, his expression rueful. "I have been telling myself that the battle is good practice, even if we don't win."

"I thought you were sure we would win, even with the late start. I thought you had a plan to come out on top and win back the respect of our school."

Kort let out a long breath. "I have not been completely successful in devising a plan. It is why I'm not an Assassin."

I put a hand on his shoulder. "But they do not have your strength."

He grinned. "Also true. But I must acknowledge that the other schools are filled with capable warriors. It would be foolish to underestimate them, even with my Blade confidence."

"Part of strength is understanding your opponents' assets."

Kort rocked back on his heels and flashed me a wicked grin. "I still think we can win."

Before I could tell him that his confidence gave me confidence, there was a murmur in the crowd as everyone shifted to look to the top of the staircase. Admiral Zoran had materialized with his serious adjunct by his side. My heart tripped with anticipation, even though I knew we would not be starting the battle yet.

"Welcome to the battle of the schools," Admiral Zoran boomed, his voice deep and resonant as it filled the spacious hall. "Each year, the four schools, who are newly infused with fresh cadets from the trials, engage in a competition. This is not a test like the maze. There are no deadly challenges. There is not independent glory. It is a test of how well your school can work together to achieve the goals."

He took a breath and let his gaze roam across the eager, upturned faces. "This year, since the maze was fraught with treachery, we have decided to make the battle one of endurance, instead of speed or danger. You will not finish this battle in one day." His gaze landed on me for a beat. "And any handicaps will quickly disappear."

A low rumble of curiosity passed through the cadets.

"My advice is to work with your school and not for yourself. It will take everyone to succeed."

Then he stepped aside and four Drexian instructors stepped up, one from each of the schools. They each held a black envelope high in the air.

The Irons instructor, a Drexian with a grizzled beard and shrewd, blue eyes, cleared his throat. "Your task is inside these envelopes. Each school has the same task and the same goal. I suggest you take a moment to understand the challenge before you rush to complete it."

The Wings instructor was one I did not know, but like the Iron, the lines on his face told me he had seniority. "You will be given your envelope in your school. One cadet must serve as the leader for your school and will take possession of the information held within."

More murmuring. I eyed the Blades instructor, a broad-shouldered, but weathered Drexian I had seen observing our class in the sparring ring. He lowered his arm and stepped back while the other Drexians started to part the crowd and walk down the stairs.

Cadets began to peel off and stride toward the archways that held their insignia carved in the stone overhead. I remained standing with Kort by my side, his body almost vibrating with excitement.

"We do not have to wait long," I reminded him. "And it sounds like this is a challenge that does not benefit from speed."

"How can anything not benefit from speed?" Kort frowned, but quickly shook off his dark mood. "But the Master did say that handicaps would not be a factor. He must have meant us."

"You were right. We have as much of a chance as any of the schools."

Kort folded his arms as we watched the hall empty and cadets stream under the archways leading to their schools. I allowed myself the briefest glance at Jess as she and Morgan hurried toward Strategy. The fact that she would be surrounded by loyal friends gave me some comfort. I caught myself smiling and quickly snapped my head away from her—and right to Dom.

He stood under the Blades arch with his back pressed to the wall and his feet crossed in front of him. He was also smiling, and I knew he'd been watching me. He'd caught me glancing at Jess, and he looked so pleased that I could almost believe that his soul wasn't twisted and mangled by revenge.

But I knew better. I'd watched him kill a Drexian. I'd seen the glint of hate in his eyes as he'd told me that he was going to take what I loved. Fear iced my veins as I suspected that he'd discovered it. He'd discovered the one thing I cared about above all else.

I curled my hands into fists. Dom might be determined to hurt me and anyone he thought I cared for, but I would kill him before he could get close to Jess. I would break him into pieces before I let him touch her again.

CHAPTER
FIFTY-TWO

Jess

I was glad to be away from the crowded main hall and back in the familiar corridor of the School of Strategy, with dim light from the wall sconces flickering across the curved, obsidian ceiling. Upper-class Assassins surrounded the instructor holding the black envelope, with one tall, imposing Drexian cadet taking possession of it and giving the teacher a salute by thumping one fist across his chest.

"Once I have read the challenge, we will divise a strategy," he announced.

"As if the Assassins would approach a task any other way," Morgan whispered, so that only I could hear her.

Even though this wasn't the trials and there wasn't as much on the line, my palms were clammy, and my heart thumped unevenly. That might have been from the Drexian who'd approached me in the hall and adjusted my blade, but I didn't want to think my head could be turned so easily and so soon after...

I shook off thoughts of Torq. I didn't owe him any waiting period. He'd dumped me. I could go out and bang the first guy I saw, not that I would. It had taken me over twenty-two years to find one guy I was willing to sleep with, although I sincerely hoped it wouldn't take that long to find a second.

I refocused my attention on the upper-class Assassin as he opened the envelope and pulled out a stiff white card. His brow wrinkled as he read it, and we all held our breath waiting to hear what it said.

He finally blew out a breath. "We don't have to go into the Restless Sea this time."

More of the upperclassmen let out noticeable sighs of relief, which told me that past battles had been waged in the turbulent sea, and that they hadn't been fun.

"What do we have to do, Fyn?" A gravelly voice asked from the back of our cluster of cadets. "Put us out of our misery."

The cadet holding the envelope, who must have been called Fyn, glanced up and grinned. "We have to find one of four ebony stones from the Black Mountains that have been placed within the Gilded Peaks. Each stone has one of the school emblems carved on it. We must return with our stone to win the battle."

I felt all the air rush from me. We had to find a rock among an entire mountain range of rocks? That made the prospect of a needle in a haystack seem like fair odds. Dark muttering around me told me that I wasn't the only one who felt this way.

Morgan pursed her lips and scrunched them to one side. "Now we know why they said the battle would take more than a day. It could take years to search those mountains."

Fyn cleared his throat pointedly. "The rocks are sizable and have not been hidden underneath any other objects, although they might be inside caves or crevices."

That was somewhat better, although I imagined that the high range of peaks had plenty of both. I rubbed my arms briskly, as if imagining the cold air at the top of the ice-capped mountains. I'd always despised cold weather. It had been one of the many reasons why I'd gladly left the Midwest behind. I would have been happy to never have to don a winter coat again, but now it looked like I'd be going to a place colder than any I'd been before.

"How are you at high altitude?" Morgan asked.

"I try not to be." I made a face. "I prefer plenty of oxygen, thank you very much."

"Then let's hope we find this stone somewhere near the bottom of the mountains."

Somehow I suspected that would be too easy for the Drexian Academy.

"There are more clues to lead us to our stone," Fyn continued. "I will pass the paper around so everyone can memorize the information, then we will divide up into teams. It doesn't make sense to stay as one large group when there is so much terrain to cover."

I took a step closer to Morgan. I did not want to be separated from the only other human cadet in our school, especially since Fiona wasn't allowed to be part of the competition. It wasn't that I didn't trust the Drexian Assassins. I did. I just didn't know them well, and I got the feeling they still weren't sure about us. We were still first-years, and we were new to their planet. I didn't blame them for having doubts about us.

"Do we divide up by class?" a Drexian I recognized from our initiation asked.

Fyn considered this but then shook his head. "I do not

want first-years getting lost in the Gilded Peaks. Each team should have one from each class."

I bit my lip to keep from groaning out loud. That meant that Morgan and I would not be on the same team.

"*Grek*," my friend said under her breath. "They're splitting us up."

"It's probably the best strategy to balance experience," I had to admit. "Even if I hate it."

Fyn handed the paper to the Drexian closest to him as he moved through our group and started assigning cadets to groups. It seemed he knew what class every cadet was in because he didn't ask when he reached me and Morgan. He pointed her to one group of three and me to another.

"See you soon." She winked at me and reached for my hand, giving it a quick, tight squeeze before moving off to join her new team.

I gave her a final look before turning and joining the three Drexian males who were clustered together with their heads down. For a moment, I wondered if this was a team huddle but then I realized they'd been handed the paper with the additional clues. I pushed myself between the two smaller guys, although smaller was a relative term since they were both well over six feet tall.

The tallest Drexian grunted when he noticed me. "You were part of the group that got through the trials with Lieutenant Volten."

"And Lieutenant Bowman," I added, making sure the human instructor got credit for her bravery.

He eyed me for a beat as the other two cadets watched him, as if waiting for him to approve my presence on their team. Then he nodded and handed me the paper. "Welcome to your first battle of the schools, Cadet. I hope you came prepared to win."

There was challenge in his gaze, but I took the paper and met his gaze. "I always do."

Then I peered at the scrolling words on the page and tried not to reveal my relief.

THE ASSASSIN's dagger and mask reside
On ebony stone both long and wide.
Tucked within the heart of the Peaks
Away from the ice but also the heat.
The stream will guide you to a divide
Then chase the tracks to find the prize.

I LOOKED up at my teammates, thrilled that our stone was away from the snow-covered peaks. That meant I wouldn't be scaling ice or climbing to a high altitude.

Then one of the cadets huffed out a laugh. "Stream doesn't seem like the right word."

I knew little about the Gilded Peaks, but the look on his face made me worry.

The fourth-year and our de facto leader shook his head, leveling his gaze at me. "Be sure not to fall in. Once the rapids take you under, there is little chance of pulling you out."

Rapids? That didn't sound like a stream at all.

CHAPTER
FIFTY-THREE

Torq

"Where is he?" I spun around as I surveyed the assembled Blades in our school atrium, which also served as an armory. Weapons hung on the walls of the circular space, the gleaming, steel blades and ancient, bronze shields glinting in the light from the overhead skylight. The eternal flame that burned in the middle of the room was blue as it danced in the high, stone brazier.

We'd gathered around the senior Blade instructor who held the black envelope, but I couldn't focus on him or the clues he was about to reveal. Not when Dom was missing.

"Who?" Kort cut his gaze to me briefly, before returning his attention to the elder Blade.

"Dom." I said the name quietly, as if saying it too loudly

might summon him. I both wanted to be rid of him and to keep him in my sights. "He isn't here."

Kort flicked his gaze to one side and then the other, finally bobbing one shoulder. "I would think you would be glad he is not here, since he still holds a grudge from the climbing wall."

I hadn't told my friend that Dom's hatred of me had nothing to do with my strategy on the wall. It had nothing to do with me, at all. If I confessed that, I would be confessing to my brother being a craven killer, and I wasn't sure if I could admit that yet. There was little love lost between me and my older brother, but the thought that he would kill another Drexian over nothing more than status made bile churn in my gut and shame scorch my cheeks.

"He is probably late," Kort suggested, even though Drexian warriors who had made it into the academy did not run late. Dom was missing for a reason, and I dreaded what that reason might be.

The Blades surged forward, as the envelope was handed to a fourth-year with his black hair tied up in a top-knot. He ripped it open and tossed the black envelope to the floor, his eyes scanning the white card inside.

"Four ebony stones from the Black Mountains that have been placed within the Gilded Peaks. Each stone has one of the school emblems carved on it. We have to return with our stone to win the battle."

"At least it isn't a water challenge," I muttered, remembering our holo-chamber practice where we ended up water-logged and exhausted.

Kort grinned at me. "I will take the mountains over the sea any day." Then he furrowed his brow. "But how do we find a rock among giant rocks?"

The fourth-year waved the card in the air to quiet the rumble of conversation that had burst forth once the challenge had been revealed. "The rocks are large and have not been hidden underneath any other objects, but they can be inside caves or crevices."

"So, we have to scour the Gilded Peaks for a black rock with the Blades emblem carved on it." Kort rubbed his hands together. "It could have been worse."

I nodded, even though I was barely focusing on the task. I could only think that Dom wasn't with his fellow cadets from Battle because he'd already left. He was tracking Jess because he'd decided she was the best way to inflict damage on me. I did not know how he'd come to this conclusion when I'd been so careful, but my gut told me I was right. My instinct told me that Jess was in danger.

The fourth year had started to go into the details about our stone, but I'd tuned him out. If Dom had left, that meant he had a head start on me. It meant he was already in pursuit of Jess. I could not wait until the Blades decided a plan of action. I needed to find Jess before Dom.

"I will catch up with you," I told Kort, as I started to back away. "I forgot something in my quarters."

His eyes widened. "Catch up? We might be halfway up the mountain. Didn't you hear our clue? The Blade stone is covered in ice, which means we have a long trek ahead of us."

I wondered if this was yet another way for the Blades to be punished, but I also did not know if we were the only school with a stone at the highest part of the mountain range. Even if we were, I could not say that some of us did not deserve it.

"Then there is more time for me to rejoin you." I managed to smile at my friend. "Do not worry."

Kort did not look so sure, but he finally got pulled back into the burgeoning discussion about the trek to the ice and what supplies we should take from the school. As my fellow Blades moved to the walls to select weapons, I slipped from the hall and hurried down the corridor.

By the time I reached the main hall, I was almost running. I hadn't spotted Dom, but if he'd left with the other schools then he would not be in the building. I doubted he cared much about being penalized for leaving ahead of the delay imposed upon the Blades. Not if he was planning to violate more serious rules by hurting another cadet, a human cadet, a female.

I hoped I was wrong. If he did what I suspected he was planning, Dom would never be forgiven by Drexian society. He would be cast from the academy, cast from his clan, cast from the planet.

My gaze caught on the back of an Assassin rushing under the archway leading to their school. I fell in step but kept enough distance that I wouldn't be noticed as the Drexian joined a small group and they made for the exit. I could only hope that following them would lead me closer to Jess. I could only say a prayer to the ancient gods that I could save her.

CHAPTER
FIFTY-FOUR

Jess

I pulled the collar of my jacket tighter around my throat as I followed my team along the gulch that ran close to the academy and led into the Gilded Peaks. The air bit at my skin, the wisps of wind snapping and snarling as it blew off the Restless Sea and barreled toward the rising mountains. Only the faintest hints of light slipped through the gray clouds that seemed to be an ever-present shroud over the Drexian homeworld and did nothing to take the edge off the ominous feel of the academy. I snuck a glance at my gloved hands, wiggling the fingers that were still stiff from rappelling down the rocks to reach the water, but I curled them into fists and kept moving.

Our team had started closer to the school, while the others had begun farther along the stream that wasn't so much of a stream. There was no point in multiple teams all taking the same route, and since we weren't positive what divide the riddle indicated, each team had started at a different point along the water. From maps of the mountain range, we knew that the stream forked many times, especially as it went deeper into the hills, but the first divide was not far from the maze.

"You still there, first-year?" The eldest Drexian in our group, Kannt, shot a brief look over his shoulder at me.

I wanted to ask him where else I would be, but I didn't want to antagonize him. Even if he did radiate Drexian superiority, I needed to keep cool and be a team player. "Still here."

He grunted, and I wondered if he wished he hadn't gotten stuck with a human female. Maybe me still being there wasn't the answer he hoped to hear. I ignored the doubts bubbling in my brain. It didn't matter what the Drexians thought of me. I knew I could do anything they could. I knew I was just as smart, just as shrewd, just as capable.

Tipping my head up, I noted the sheer rock wall we'd descended so we could walk the entire length of the gulch. The bridge leading to the maze was suspended at the far end and beyond that was the mouth that spilled into the sea. Turning my attention back to the stream, I followed the carefully chosen steps of the Drexians leading the way, being careful not to veer too close to the water that rushed over smooth stones and churned in whirling eddies. It might seem like a burbling brook from above, but it was far from that once you were close.

Ahead, the water broke into two branches, with one leading to the left and one to the right. There was an island of land in the middle, and then the forks wound in different directions.

Kannt stopped, his head swiveling from one side to the other. "The water divides here but only briefly. I cannot imagine this is the divide from the verse, but the second divide could prove promising."

I tended to agree with him, but maybe that was the trick. It seemed too easy to have the stone hidden so close to the school, but it could also be a clever strategy. Hide the prize so close that it could be easily overlooked in the quest to divine the more challenging spot.

"We should search for tracks," I said, my voice louder than I'd intended. "Due diligence."

Kannt released another grunt and cut his gaze to the third-year. "Take the first-year and search the left fork."

I bit my lip, even though I was dying to remind him that I had a name. I couldn't be too bitter, though, since I didn't know the second-year or third-year as anything other than that. If this was intended to foster school unity, I had my doubts. The upperclassman seemed just like every older student in every school I'd ever encountered, and the last thing they wanted to do was be subjected to newbies.

The third-year didn't bother to beckon me as he headed for the narrowest part of the stream. I followed, threading my way carefully across slick rocks that poked above the water until we were on the other side and trudging along the bank of the forked stream. He kept his head down—searching for tracks, I had to assume—and I did the same.

Leaves crunched under our feet, but I saw no indication of a track to follow. One of my feet was plunged into a puddle of mud beneath an unassuming pile of yellowed leaves, and I cursed as I pulled it out. The mud sucked the sole of my boot, reluctant to release its grip, and coating the black leather with brown sludge.

"Just fucking great," I muttered, as some of the mud seeped through the laces and into my socks.

"Keep up," my teammate said, without looking back "There are some broken branches up ahead. We need to see if they lead to anything."

I stamped my muddy foot on dry ground to release some of the wet mud before I hurried ahead to catch up. The tall, surly Drexian had crossed back over the stream where it narrowed again, and had entered the forest on the other side.

My boots squelched as I jogged and jumped across the water, landing with a satisfying thud on the other side. I surveyed the ground around me, but there was nothing but dry land and faint boot prints from my fellow Assassin. My boots would make more noticeable tracks, which was not something that made me proud.

I pushed through thick foliage that hung from the trees as I entered a crowded copse close to the mountains. The diffused light from overhead vanished as I stepped farther into the forest, and my senses went on high alert. I breathed in a loamy scent that reminded me of the woods back home, but I pushed aside any lingering nostalgia. This would be a place I would hide something, so I narrowed my eyes as I hunted for tracks.

I'd slowed my pace to do a thorough search, and after walking past a few trees, I lost the trail of the third-year Assassin. The ground was covered in patchy grass but the outline of his boot prints was not there. I paused and swung my head in a circle, peering through the trees that rose high and formed a canopy of branches overhead. Where had he gone?

I cursed myself for not learning his name when we'd started, because now I couldn't even call for him without sounding like an idiot. I strode deeper, hoping I'd catch a flash of his dark uniform, but there was nothing but foliage and the chirping of insects. When I turned again, my hair caught on a branch and tangled in the gnarled wood.

I yanked at it, releasing my hair from its clip and sending it falling over my face.

"Hello?" I finally called as I blew hair from my eyes, hoping he'd hear me.

No luck and no response. Then a thought settled over me. Was I being hazed? Was part of the battle of the schools to initiate new cadets and teach them a few lessons?

I hadn't heard any rumors of hazing during the battle, but that didn't mean the cadets I'd been teamed with weren't doing it on their own. Or maybe the third-year thought ditching me was funny or it was part of the adventure. Whatever the reason, I had a sinking feeling that I was on my own.

Then a branch snapped behind me, and hands gripped my shoulders from behind.

CHAPTER
FIFTY-FIVE

.

Torq

I kept my distance from the four Assassins as they tramped across the bridge leading to the maze. I had to wait until they'd almost skirted the gulch to hurry across the bridge and sidestep between the black stone wall of the maze and the sheer drop below.

Do not look down, I told myself. Do not look down.

The Assassins were so busy studying the ground that they didn't notice me shadowing them, but I couldn't hold that against them. There would be no reason to think anyone would be following them. Each school had its own stone to find, so there was no point in sending scouts to follow the other schools. Unless sabotage was your purpose.

That gave me pause. Would the Assassins be sending teams out to find the other stones? Had the other schools decided to find the stone for the School of Battle before our cadets were even allowed to search? I almost laughed to myself. It was obvious that I'd spent a lot of time with Jess. I was starting to think like an Assassin.

Even as the foursome started to tramp along the stream that led into the mountains, I was brimming with impatience. How could I know that this group would lead me to Jess? I couldn't. I did not even know their mission, or why they were searching so close to the academy, when the Blades had been preparing to climb high to the ice-capped peaks.

I flattened myself to the back of a tree trunk when the Strategy cadets stopped before following the stream to the left and away from the Gilded Peaks. I closed my eyes and breathed slowly.

This was foolish. I had no better chance of finding Jess by following the cadets than I did if I just ran into the mountains. She had a significant head start on me, and I was sure Dom did, too, which made my gut clench. I instinctively touched a hand to the handle of my blade, the chill of the steel comforting.

There was not a doubt in my mind what I would do to the Blade if he hurt Jess. I would not hesitate to cut him down. I would not even take a breath before slicing him open.

"Come on, you remember what the riddle said." The Assassin's words drifted to me on the cool breeze.

I stiffened, holding my breath to hear what else he might say.

"The stream will guide you to a divide. This is a divide in the stream."

"But where are the tracks?" Another cadet asked, his voice deeper and easier to hear. "It said to chase the tracks to find the prize. I see nothing that looks like tracks."

"Then we need to keep going."

"I say we take the path that leads away from the moun-

LOYALTY

tains for a while. It is the least obvious choice, which makes it a good possibility."

The other cadets made noises of agreement, and I guessed that the last speaker had been the eldest. I snuck a peek around the tree to watch them head off along the far side of the stream. That path might be the least obvious choice, but the Drexians who hid the stones might not have been Assassins and prone to devising the most complicated solution. In fact, I was willing to bet that the instructors made it a point for members of opposing schools to hide the schools' stones.

I eyed the side of the stream that led into the woods abutting the mountains. My gut told me that the rest of the Assassin teams would have searched there, so I ran to the narrowest place in the stream and leaped across.

Voices that did not belong to the Assassin team I'd been following made me dart my gaze to the right. A large group of what I thought were Wings ran laughing toward the mountains without a glance toward the stream. Luckily, I was only steps from the woods, and I ran toward the cover of the trees before any of the cadets thought to look to the side.

As I was enveloped by the trees, I realized that I hadn't looked at the Wings with longing. There had been no part of me that mourned the school I'd been told was my birthright. There was no regret.

Despite my current disgrace and position on the outskirts of the Blades, there was no school that fit me better. I was a Blade.

"A Blade hunting down another Blade," I said to myself, my words swallowed by the quiet of the forest.

I was only hunting him to save Jess, and Jess was innocent in all of it. She had nothing to do with my brother's crime, and the only reason she would pay any price for his cruelty was me. I had pulled her into my sordid clan disgrace with my desire. I

271

had to have her. I had to be around her. I had been unable to resist her. And now she would be punished for my sins.

Not if I could stop it.

I took determined steps forward, finally catching sight of a muddy footprint on the grass. I'd been so busy barreling forward that I hadn't thought to look for tracks. I shook my head at my impetuous nature. "Typical Blade."

I knelt and eyed the footprint. It was smaller than a Drexian's, which meant there was a good chance it was hers. But there was only one, which told me that she was walking around with a single muddy boot. I continued forward, keeping my gaze to the ground and trailing the muddy outline until it vanished in the grass.

Grek grek grek. I stopped and scoured the woods around me. There was no sight of her, and there was actually no proof that the single boot print was hers. I could be following another human entirely.

The thought sent a wave of despair through me. Did I truly think I could find one cadet in the vast range of mountains? Did I honestly believe that I could track her down before Dom?

I sank down and let my knees touch the grass, closing my eyes and breathing in the loamy scent of the forest. I allowed the sounds of creatures scuttling across dried leaves and leaping from branch-to-branch wash over me, as I searched out the rhythmic thump of boots hitting the ground or crackling branches. If there were cadets near me in the woods, I couldn't hear them.

I opened my eyes, determined to retrace my steps and take another path toward the mountains. Then my gaze lit on something on the ground, something that did not belong with the grass and leaves and moss. My heart pounded and my mouth went dry, as I picked up the hair clip I'd seen Jess wear so many times.

I straightened and closed my fist around the clip, the metal digging into my flesh. She had been right where I was standing. I had not been wrong. I was on the right path. I was going to find her.

I started to run.

CHAPTER
FIFTY-SIX

Jess

The hands on my shoulders made me jump and spin around quickly, fully expecting to find my teammate behind me. It wasn't him.

I took a few steps back when I recognized the Drexian cadet grinning at me. He was the one who'd helped me with my blade earlier. "I know you. You're a Blade. Your name is...Dom."

He inclined his head at me, almost as if bowing and as if he hadn't just scared me half to death. "Correct on both accounts. Good memory, Assassin."

I swept my gaze around the woods, but there was no one else. "What are you doing here? Are the Blades even allowed to be searching yet?"

"We are, but I got separated from my group." He slid his gaze to both sides. "It seems like you did, too."

"My team is nearby." For some reason, I didn't think I should tell him that I didn't know exactly where they were, although the cadet seemed friendly enough.

He held up his hands. "I know this is a competition, and we are supposed to be opponents, but I do not think I should leave you alone in here. Why don't I help you find your team?"

That seemed reasonable, and I couldn't think of a reason why I shouldn't accompany him. He was right about one thing. I did not want to be in the forest by myself. "That works. Like I said, they're nearby and probably looking for me."

He nodded, and we fell in step beside each other with him taking a slight lead. "Are the other members of your team also humans?"

I shook my head. "They spilt us up. One human per team. I guess they don't want to handicap any one team with all of us." I could hear the bitterness dripping from my voice and wondered if I sounded like a whiny bitch.

He glanced at me. "Truly?"

"I don't know if that's why, but they did split us up."

I waited for him to say something obnoxious and cocky about humans.

He made a low sound of disapproval in the back of his throat. "You might be smaller in size than my people, but you are just as capable and clever. Any Drexian who underestimates you is a fool."

This was a surprise. "I couldn't agree more."

The leaves crunched under our boots as we continued trudging through dense trees without any sign of other cadets. I was starting to think that my fellow Assassins might not actually be looking for me.

"Tell me what it is like to be a human at the Drexian Academy," Dom said, as he held a prickly vine to one side for me to walk beneath. "I imagine it must have been a shock when you arrived."

No one had asked me this. I thought back to stepping off the transport and peering up at the black stone buildings that loomed overhead. "It's pretty different from schools on Earth, even our military academies. I think these might be the oldest buildings I've ever seen."

He paused and wrinkled his brow. "Earth does not have ancient buildings?"

"We do, but not where I'm from. I grew up in a pretty new country, so we don't have castles that are hundreds of years old."

"The Drexian Academy is thousands of years old."

I shook my head at that. "It's incredible. I can't imagine a building being around for that long. In my town, if something was fifty years old it was a historic relic."

"Your town must be very modern."

I snorted a laugh at this. My midwestern hometown was about as far from modern as possible. "Not exactly. I come from a rural town—farming, trucks, everything old and falling apart."

"You are not high-born?"

I stifled another snort. "We don't exactly have high-borns and low-borns in the U.S., but we do have rich and poor. I was born poor, but I busted my ass so I wouldn't stay poor."

"You can change your status?"

I nodded. "If you work hard enough, but it's not easy and the odds are stacked against you."

"The odds are also against you if you are not a high-born Drexian." I heard bitterness in his voice.

"I take it you aren't from a fancy clan?"

His twisted expression morphed into a weak smile. "My clan is far from fancy, as you put it."

I stopped and glanced around us. Had we walked this way before or were all the trees starting to look identical because we'd been walking for so long? "We must be getting close to the mountains."

Dom leveled a finger at light slatting through the trees ahead. "That should be it."

I felt a measure of relief and then felt guilty that I'd had a moment of doubt about Dom. For a second, I'd been sure he was leading me in circles.

"So, what is it like coming to the academy as a Drexian?" I asked to break the silence as we strode toward the thinning trees. "I'm guessing you grew up hearing about it."

"It is an honor to be accepted into the academy. Not everyone gets in. Only those who have demonstrated exceptional talent and aptitude. Or those who come from elite clans."

"It's the same where I'm from. Rich kids have an advantage —the best schools, tutors, test prep, more tutors, coaches. Sometimes I'm surprised I made it so far without any clue what I was doing."

"You must be the best. Otherwise, you would not have been chosen for the academy. Very few humans made the cut to be the first to integrate the school."

This made my chest swell. He was right. There were very few of us from Earth, and even fewer women. I loved being one of the ones breaking glass ceilings for others to follow. It made me feel like I was making it easier for someone like me who might not think she had a chance.

We stepped from the trees and the ground gave way to rock as we walked onto a high ledge. Water spilled down from overhead into a pool and then continued to the stream below. So, this was where the stream originated—at least one part of it.

"We are very much alike, you and I." Dom put a hand on

my arm and turned to me. "We both have come from nothing and arrived at the academy, destined for greatness."

"I guess we are similar."

"I am surprised you are so friendly with high-born Drexians who are nothing like you are." His gaze narrowed, scrutinizing my face. "He will never understand you."

Instantly, I knew who he meant, but I could not let him know that. How did he know about Torq? My pulse quickened. Had Torq told his Blade brothers about me? He'd promised he wouldn't, but now I wasn't so sure his promises meant much. "Who will never understand me?"

Dom's lips curved into a small smile. "You wish to be coy? You think no one sees the way he looks at you?"

I remained silent, unwilling to confirm what he obviously knew. Aside from the initial surprise when he'd startled me from behind, I hadn't felt uneasy around Dom—until now.

"Torq from House Swoll will always be a privileged Drexian who knows nothing of struggle." He grabbed one of my hands. "He is not like us. He is not like you."

He was right. Torq was very different from me, and he would never understand where I came from or what it had cost me to come so far. But our difference didn't matter anymore. He had cast me aside, maybe because we were so different and would never understand each other. We would never truly be a part of the others' world.

"He might look at me, but that means nothing." My heart stuttered as I pulled my hand from his. This was true. Torq and I were nothing to each other now. "Torq is not a part of my life."

Dom's gaze drifted to my mouth, his eyes darkening. "I am pleased to hear that." He closed the distance between us and curled an arm around my waist, yanking me so that I was flush against him. "I would hate to have to fight him for you."

My heart raced, but it was with fear, not desire. Dom might be handsome and muscular, but he did not make my heart patter with anticipation. There was something cold and calculating about the way he eyed me, and there was no warmth in the way he held me, only dominance and control.

I pressed my hands to his chest and pushed hard, trying to keep him from kissing me. He pulled at me more urgently, making panic claw at my throat. Then a dark growl rumbled through the air, and we both froze.

CHAPTER
FIFTY-SEVEN

Torq

I bent over and put my hands on my knees, bracing myself while I sucked in a breath. The air was cold and burned my throat, but the trees from the forest shielded me from the worst of the wind. I swept my gaze from one side to the other, searching for more clues that Jess had passed this way, but there was nothing as evident as her hair clip, which I held tightly in my palm.

The metal biting into my flesh was a solid reminder that I would find her, so I straightened and started forward again. Ahead, the trees became sparser, and light crept in, so I moved faster toward that. Jess would have walked toward the light. She would have been moving higher to chase the water. At least that's what the other Assassins had been doing.

I tried not to panic that I hadn't found her yet or that her hair clip had been lying on the ground. I did not want to think what it might mean. Why would her clip have come out and why would she have left it behind? Was there a struggle? Did Dom find her and knock her out?

I shook my head roughly, refusing to accept that. Jess was fine, and I was going to find her. And then what? Did I tell her I was following her because I was sure she was being stalked by a Blade determined to inflict pain on me? Would she believe that? Did she have any reason to believe anything I said?

I emerged from the woods and blinked a few times as light streamed down from a break in the clouds. Water poured down from the start of the mountain range, pooled in a shallow basin and then spilled from that down to the start of the stream that cut through the land toward the Restless Sea.

My gaze went from the waterfall to the two figures standing near the overhang. My heart leapt as I realized I'd found Jess; then it crashed when I saw who was standing with her.

My hackles instantly rose when I saw how close he stood to her. Then he moved even closer and curled an arm around her waist, yanking her body flush to him. I tasted bile in the back of my throat as I watched him hold her, touch her.

"I would hate to have to fight him for you," Dom said, his voice dampened by the sound of the water.

He meant me. They were talking about me. Fury pulsed through me, even though I had no right to be angry. I had been the one to send Jess away. I'd been the one to tell her I did not want her. But I had done it to protect her. I'd done it to protect her from *him*.

Dom's words echoed in my head. I will take what you love.

He did not intend to hurt me by harming Jess. He wanted to hurt me by taking her for himself. I should have been heartened by that. At least she wasn't in danger. He wasn't trying to kill her. Then rage pulsed through me. He was trying to kiss her. Not because he desired her or loved her, but because he wanted to make me suffer.

Jess pressed her hands to his chest and pushed him. She was trying to stop him. She did not want him or his kiss. I was not so arrogant anymore to believe that this meant she loved me, but I did know that she did not want him.

A growl rubbed from my chest, unbidden and uncontrollable. They both stiffened.

"Release her," I ordered, my hands in hard fists by my side.

Dom twisted his head, smiled at me, but did not release Jess. "You are interrupting."

I locked eyes with Jess and saw fear in them as she pushed harder against him. "If you do not let her go, I will make you."

"Are you challenging me?" His arms slackened. "Shall we fight over her?"

"I will fight you to release her, but she is not an object to be fought over."

Without glancing at Jess, Dom dropped his arms, and she stumbled back and away from him. He did not pause to barrel toward me, his eyes blazing with hatred. "You are all wrong for her. She knows that now."

I dodged his first punch, spinning to the side and beyond his reach. "She does not want you."

He huffed out a breath and charged me again. "Not yet, but she will. I will enjoy watching you suffer as I make her mine."

The Drexian was delusional, but that made him dangerous. "Leave her alone. Your issue is with me." I dove to one side as he lunged forward. "Actually, it is with my brother, but I am the next best thing, right?"

His face was red as he swung around, panting. His fury was tiring him. "I have been fantasizing for so long about making your brother pay for killing my brother. Imagine my surprise when you showed up at the academy. I could hurt him by hurting you."

"You do not know my family," I muttered as I crouched in a defensive stance to await his next attack. "My brother would not care if I died."

Dom's brow furrowed, but he shook his head as if to rid himself of any truth that might alter his quest for vengeance. "Your brother has gone into hiding like the coward he is. You will have to suffice."

I was vaguely aware that Jess had not run off. She was watching us, which meant that she was still not safe, although now I did not fear that Dom would kill her, and I was fairly certain she was in no danger of losing her heart to him. That did not mean I couldn't lose my life to him if he decided that it would be easier and simpler to kill me, after all.

I flicked my gaze to her and caught her worried expression. Even though I had been sure she despised me, she was concerned for me, which made me happier than I should have been in the middle of a fight. Her look of concern quickly shifted into shock, her mouth opening as if she was preparing to scream. That was when Dom plowed into me from the side.

I went down hard, my cheek hitting the rock and pain exploding across my face. His weight was on me, but I managed to elbow him in the ribs and maneuver myself onto my back. He quickly straddled me and started to strike my ribs and face. I put my hands over my face to block the blows, but I could not stop all of them. High-pitched screaming was buffeted by the rushing blood in my ear.

Jess's head appeared behind his, and she flung her arms around his neck. Her eyes were wild, and she was screaming. That's when it hit me that she was trying to pull him off me. She was trying to save me.

Dom's mouth gaped and his eyes widened, and he reared

back and clawed at the slender arms crossing his throat. I took that opening to push him off me and scramble to my feet.

Jess clung to his back, her feet dangling as he spun around and hit at her arm to loosen it. When she saw that I'd gotten up, she released her grip, but the momentum of Dom's twisting sent her sprawling backward. She landed unevenly on her feet and as she tried to right herself, she danced closer to the edge of the overhang. Her eyes went wide as she lost her balance and realized that she was falling.

With a roar, and without thinking, I dove for Jess. We both went over the side. My body hit hers hard, and I wrapped my arms around her as the wind rushed around us, and we plunged from the high rock to the churning water below. I used every bit of momentum to spin her so that my body was beneath hers just before we hit.

The impact sent more pain arrowing through me, but it was the freezing water that snatched my breath from me and made everything go dark.

CHAPTER
FIFTY-EIGHT

Jess

I didn't know what was more shocking, Torq showing up and threatening Dom, or learning as they grappled that Dom held a serious grudge against Torq for something Torq's brother had done. I stared at the two Drexians lunging for each other with a new sense of clarity. As charming as Dom had seemed, his act had been just that. It hadn't been real.

I'd sensed something insincere and manipulative when he'd held me. As much of an ass as Torq was—and I did still believe he was a prize-A asshole—he had never felt wrong to me. Dom had felt wrong. His touch had made me jittery, not excited, and when he'd held me I only wanted to get as far away from him as possible.

It wasn't that he was unattractive. He was as big, broad, and gorgeous as all the Drexians. But he wasn't Torq.

I moved out of the way of the fight, hoping they would land

a few blows and pack it in. But then Torq caught my eye and I couldn't stop myself from holding his gaze. For a beat, the waterfall and mountains behind us disappeared. I no longer felt the cold air or heard the rushing water. There was only the two of us.

Then I spotted Dom running at Torq. I started to scream but I was too late. Dom flattened Torq and started to punch his face and body. Panic surged in me. I couldn't stand by while Torq was beaten to death. I swiveled my gaze to see if there was any sign of other cadets, but there was no one. Only me.

I ran and jumped on Dom's back, wrapping my arms around his neck and pulling back on his windpipe. If I could distract him enough for Torq to get up and defend himself, that would be enough. Dom grabbed at my arms to loosen them, which meant that he was no longer hitting Torq. Before I could release my grip, Dom bucked up and dislodged me with such force that I flew back. I managed to land on my feet, but the momentum sent me stumbling farther, until I could feel myself teetering on the edge of the rock overhang.

I held my breath as time seemed to stand still and I wasn't moving or falling. Torq saw what was happening and was diving for me, but he would not reach me in time to pull me back. Then I realized that he wasn't trying to pull me back. He meant to go over with me.

I squeezed my eyes shut as his body impacted mine, and all the air rushed from my lungs. Then time sped up as we plummeted over the edge and toward the water, the wind whipping and the sound of the water making it impossible to hear the thundering of my heart. Torq was wrapped around me, but even his large body couldn't protect me from the shock of the freezing water as we landed in the pool and went under.

The cold arrested my breath, which was good since I was submerged in the water, but as I broke the surface I gasped for air. My lungs screamed and my chest hitched, as I kicked to keep myself afloat. I coughed a few times and spit out a mouthful of icy water before realizing that Torq hadn't come up with me.

"You have got to be fucking kidding me," I said, as I swept my gaze across the pool being fed by the waterfall, but there was no sign of him.

I sucked in a breath and dove under, kicking hard to push myself down and keeping my eyes open. I spotted him a few feet below, but he wasn't moving, and didn't look conscious. I cursed more in my head as I swam to him, got underneath him, and put one arm across his chest. Then I kicked as hard as I could to the top. He was so heavy that my lungs were on fire and my legs were thrashing furiously trying to get us both up.

When we broke the surface, I drew in a greedy breath, but I was aware that Torq wasn't breathing. My legs were rubber as I kicked us to the side and managed to crawl out and then drag half of his body from the pool.

He was on his back, but he wasn't breathing. *Shit shit shit.* I tipped his head back, opened his mouth, and started breathing hard puffs of air into him. Then I paused and pumped my hands on his chest. "Come on, you cocky, Drexian asshole. Don't you dare die on me."

Then I blew into his mouth again. When I pulled back to do more chest compressions, he heaved up a mouthful of water and started coughing.

"Thank you for not being dead," I said, as I helped him roll onto his side, and I gave him a few hard whacks on his back. "I did not need that today."

"You are welcome." He managed between coughs.

His serious response made me grin, but then I realized that I needed to thank him for something more important. "And thanks for going over with me. You didn't have to do that."

"Yes, I did." Water streamed down his face as he blinked at me. "You might not have survived hitting the water, but I knew I could."

"Sweet, yet still cocky." I shook my head. I guess some things never changed. "Why were you there in the first place? Were you following me?"

"Yes."

Okay, I guess he wasn't going to hide it. "Why were you following me? This is supposed to be a competition of the schools. Why are two Blades, who aren't even supposed to be competing yet, out here getting in brawls with each other?"

"I only decided to look for you when I could not find Dom. I suspected he was going after you, so I came to save you."

"Save me from Dom, the guy who was trying to kiss me?"

I swept his sopping hair back from his eyes. "I did not think he would try to kiss you. I believed he wanted to kill you."

I stared at him without speaking for a few moments. "You aren't making any sense. Why would a complete stranger want to kill me?"

"You heard what he said. He is holding me accountable for a horrible thing my brother did when he was at the academy, which means he wants to hurt me."

"And you thought that meant he was following me out here to kill me?" I shuddered. "That's pretty dark, even for a Drexian."

"Now I understand that he planned to hurt me not by killing you, but by taking you as his." He glowered at me. "Which I might like even less."

"Thanks, I think." I blew out a breath. "In case you weren't aware, I still have a say in who I'm with, and I had no intention of being his. He didn't feel right."

"Did I feel right?" Torq husked, reminding me that we were so close that our warm breath was mingling in the frigid air.

I scowled at him. "As if that matters now, and not that it's any of your business anymore."

He pulled back slightly and nodded, then his gaze drifted to the lower half of his body still submerged in the pool. "That is why I am so cold."

I'd been so preoccupied with the fact that he wasn't breathing that I'd forgotten that I'd only dragged him partially from the water.

"Sorry. You're pretty heavy, so I could only pull you out halfway." I stood and helped him move the rest of the way onto the muddy bank. When we were both standing, Torq listed to one side, and I caught him before he hit the ground. "Whoa. You still don't look too good."

I peered up at the sky and noticed that the sun was fading, as was the light. Soon, it would be dusk, and I didn't think I could get him back to the academy before then. Even if I did know the way back, or if I felt confident to make the trek with a battered and weak Drexian. "We need to find a place to stay for the night."

Torq gave me a questioning look then bobbed his head in agreement. "I think my leg wound might have reopened in the fall."

Well, that wasn't good. We needed a place for him to rest and one that Dom wouldn't be able to find. He might not want to kill me, but from what I'd seen, he was happy to end Torq.

I swung my head around, my gaze snagging on a stone ledge that ran along the back of the waterfall and to an opening beyond the cascade of water. "I think I found us the perfect hiding spot."

CHAPTER
FIFTY-NINE

Torq

I let Jess lead me by the hand to the stone ledge that ran behind the waterfall, flattening my back to the wall to keep from being drenched as we sidestepped our way under the water. Cold spray stung my face, but it was more refreshing than bracing, and I was grateful to be alive to feel it. I was alive because Jess had saved me, even though she had every reason to never speak to me again.

She is too good for you.

Despite what I'd been told my entire life. Despite being made to believe that I was superior based on my clan. Despite the lies I'd been fed, I knew that I did not deserve Jess. She was too smart, too kind, too beautiful, and now I knew that she was more forgiving than I deserved.

My heart seized as I watched her walking carefully in front of me, her hair slick and wet down her back and her soaking uniform clinging to her body and making it impossible to ignore her curves. It did not matter what I had told her or what I had convinced myself about giving her up. I still desired her, craved her, loved her so much it hurt.

"Yes!" Her cheer was muffled by the pounding water cascading in front of us, but I could see her face light up when the rock wall opened up to reveal a hidden cave tucked behind the waterfall. "I knew it."

I did not release her hand as she continued the last few steps of the ledge and into the cave. The warmth of her flesh was keeping me steady even as my legs wobbled and my lungs ached. After being submerged under the freezing water, every breath was painful. I might be a Blade, but I was not immune to injury or illness, and I feared that the blows from Dom and the fall from the cliff had only compounded my earlier wounds.

"We should be safe here." Jess stopped and surveyed the shallow cave.

It was tall enough for both of us to stand, but it wasn't deep and didn't appear to have any passages leading from within. Light filtered in through the water and illuminated the iridescent-green moss clinging to the stone ceiling and spackling the walls. I inhaled the humid air, both grateful that it was a touch warmer within the open-mouthed cave and aware that the temperature would drop once the sun sank beneath the peaks.

"You're shivering."

I glanced at her, aware that she was assessing me with shrewd eyes. "I am fine."

She made a sound in the back of her throat dismissing my claim. "You're too cold. You need to get out of that wet uniform."

I managed to summon a cocky grin. "Are you trying to undress me, Cadet?"

She shot me a withering look that told me that she had not forgotten what had happened between us or that I had rejected her. "I'm trying to return the favor and save you. Nothing more."

"I did not mean—"

"You made it clear that we were over. I'm fine with that. I've moved on. That doesn't mean I want you to die." Her expression relaxed. "Not anymore, at least."

I guessed that was all I could ask for, considering what I had said and done. It was too much to expect her to forget my words, even if she chose to forgive me. "I will take it."

She gave me a curt nod and waved at my dripping uniform. "Now take that off, unless you want to die of hypothermia."

As I peeled the fabric from my skin, clenching my teeth to keep them from chattering, Jess explored the crevices of the cave. The light didn't reach the deepest parts, so she poked around in the shadows as I shed first my boots, blade, and pants and then my shirt.

When I stood in nothing but snug, black underwear that clung to my upper thighs, she turned back with an armful of pelts and furs. She opened her mouth, took in the sight of me, and swallowed hard.

"I guess you aren't *that* cold," she said softly, shaking her head and looking away abruptly. "I don't know how old these are, and I'm not going to lie to you and tell you they smell fresh, but they will keep us warm."

I took one of the furs from the pile she held and wrapped it eagerly around my shoulders. "This cave has been here for a long time, and I doubt we are the first to find it."

Jess snuck a glance at me as she unfurled a fur on the rock

floor. "You think academy cadets stocked this place with animal pelts?"

"I think this was used before the castle was an academy, and before it was inhabited by cadets." I swept my gaze around the cave, noting marks carved into the walls and peeking from beneath the shimmery moss. "Ancient Drexians were a warrior species. I grew up hearing of battles for the castle that is now the academy and how clans swarmed the Gilded Peaks and attacked from the Restless Sea. The clans that prevailed became the elite clans that now rule the empire, but it was hard fought and not easily won."

She continued to spread the pelts and furs on the cold stone, overlapping them to create more of a cushion. "So, you've always been badasses with a penchant for violence?"

"Does that not describe every species that remains dominant? Earth also has a violent history with the victors retaining control of the territory and resources."

She straightened and held my gaze. "You might have a point."

Now that I was not covered in wet fabric, my shivering had slowed, but my body ached, and my breathing was labored.

"You should lie down," Jess ordered, pointing to the pile of furs. "Hopefully, our clothes will be dry by first light, and we can return to the academy, but for now, we need to rest and warm up."

I followed her command, if only because my knees were weak, and my leg throbbed where it had previously healed. Once I was sitting, I looked up at her. "What about you?"

She frowned at me then started undressing in a huff. "The only reason I'm doing this is because I'm fucking cold and you're too weak to try anything."

I wanted to protest that I would never be too weak to be aroused by the sight of her shedding her clothes, but I wisely stayed silent. When she was only in a black bra and panties, she dropped onto the furs and pulled one over herself.

Then she cut a stern gaze over her shoulder at me. "If you even think of trying anything, I don't care how injured you are, I will punch you in the throat. Got it?"

I blinked a few times, startled by the sharpness of her words but also oddly turned on by them. I had always thought I liked females to be submissive, but this fierce side of Jess fired something primal inside me. I pushed it down with a stern reminder to myself that I had no right to her anymore. I also might not have enough energy to survive an attack from her, even if she was only a small female. I feared any throat punch from her would contain all her fury at me. It would be vicious. "Got it."

She pushed another fur toward me. "Try not to freeze to death before morning."

I took the fur and covered myself, releasing a deep sigh. So much for saving her and professing my love. This was far from how I'd imagined our reunion going, although we were both alive. That was something.

But where was the Drexian who had wanted to make me suffer? I had a sinking feeling his thirst for revenge had not been sated.

I stared up at the ceiling as dusk darkened the stone above me. He would be back for more.

CHAPTER
SIXTY

Jess

T he light streaming in through the waterfall faded, and I watched the colors refracted onto the stone floor melt into shadows. When it was completely dark, I tugged the fur tighter around my shoulders and tried to fall asleep.

Why did Torq have to be so hot, and why did he have to lie right behind me with barely any clothes on? The second he'd stripped down to his boxer briefs, I'd regretted telling him to take off his wet clothes. The cold water had seemed to have little effect on his significant bulge, and I hated that all I could think about was how good he'd felt inside me.

That is over, I scolded myself. Done. Finished. We were never ever getting back together.

Torq rolled over, his body brushing closer to mine and sending unwanted shivers of pleasure through me. Who was I kidding? It was impossible to lie next to him and not feel the heat pulsing from his practically naked body and not want to press myself against him. It was impossible not to want to go back in time and forget all the pain that made me so afraid to roll over and face him.

I squeezed my eyes tighter in a vain attempt to block out his presence and the powerful pull he exerted over me. I might know that he was a bad idea, that he would hurt me, that he *had* hurt me. But my body hadn't seemed to have gotten the message.

My heart raced and heat pooled restlessly in my core, as I squeezed my legs together to keep them from involuntarily popping open. What was wrong with me? I was a smart, successful, accomplished officer in the Earth Planetary Forces, and I was an Assassin. I was skilled at spotting patterns, which meant I knew what Torq's past behaviors meant.

He couldn't be trusted. Not with my body, and certainly not with my heart. He might have come looking for me because he was afraid Dom wanted to hurt me, but that didn't mean he wasn't just as capable of hurting me. Maybe more so because Dom didn't affect me like Torq did.

I could hear him breathing behind me, and as curt as I'd been with him, I was glad that he was no longer shivering or hitching in uneven breaths. He would be fine. We both would.

We would be able to leave when the sun rose and return to the academy. For the first time since I'd gotten lost in the woods, I wondered how the battle of the schools was unfolding. Had my team searched for me? Were the other Assassin teams still roaming the mountains, or had a victor been declared?

I found it hard to care as much about a competition that brought nothing but bragging rights to the school, but that might have been because I had not grown up hearing about the winners of each year's battle. Maybe it was like the Army Navy football game, which made usually sane people go a little nuts.

I imagined that life at the academy would not change much. One school would be declared the winner at a celebratory banquet, then cadets would leave for a break before the second year started. My gut twisted into a knot. For me, life at the academy would continue without Torq. After this, there would be little reason to interact with him. I might pass him in the corridors, but I would get a polite glance or head nod at most.

Even though he had saved me, and I had saved him, things had not changed. He could never be with someone like me, and I could never forget how he'd cast me aside. The pain was too sharp, too fresh. It was too soon.

I huffed out an impatient breath, irritated at myself for being weak. Why did I have to punish myself? Why couldn't I be the one to take what I wanted and then cast it aside? Why did I have to accept what he'd said without a fight?

I was a strong, independent woman who had beaten all the odds to make it to the Drexian Academy. I couldn't let one cocky cadet knock me off my game or set the rules. Not anymore.

I rolled over and pushed Torq onto his back, straddling him and resting my hands on his bare chest. Without light, I couldn't see his reaction, but I could feel it.

He jerked awake and put his hands on top of mine. "Jess?"

"You don't have to do anything, and you don't have to talk." I leaned down and found his mouth, brushing my lips across him. "Actually, I'd prefer if you don't."

"What are you—?"

I silenced his question with a kiss, capturing his mouth as I rocked my body into his. I had to say, I liked being on top and calling the shots. Not that I didn't like being underneath him and submitting to him, but I felt a rush of power as I felt his cock thickening beneath me.

I tore my lips from his and ran my fingers down the hard curves of his muscles. There was something forbidden and naughty about being in total blackness and having to feel my way around his body. I couldn't see if he was startled or shocked. I could only feel the rapid rise and fall of his chest and the urgent hardness of his cock.

"Do you still want me?"

"Jess." He groaned my name. "You know I do, but I thought you told me—"

"I know what I said." I couldn't allow myself to overthink myself into a sensible decision, which would mean stopping. "But this is just tonight. It means nothing but I want you to fuck me. No strings. No nothing. We pretend like it never happened. Do you think you can do that, Cadet?"

Torq mumbled a desperate yes as he sat up and wrapped his arms around my back, unclasping my bra with impressive speed. He pulled it off me and cupped my breasts in his hands, bringing first one and then the other to his mouth. I arched my back and let my head fall as he sucked on my tight nipples, until I was moaning and scraping my fingers through his hair.

Then I remembered that I was in charge. This was my game and my rules. I gave him a hard shove to push him back and shimmied down until I could grasp his cock with one hand, my fingers curling around the broad base but not touching. I lifted myself and used one hand to pull my panties to the side as I slid his thick crown between my slickness.

"*Grekking* hell, you're soaked for me." Torq's words were gritted out, and their desperation sent a thrill through me. He was at my mercy.

"Tell me what you want," I said as I hovered above him, his cock notched at my entrance. "Beg for it."

A tortured growl emanated from Torq and echoed off the stone around us. "You want to know what I want, little Assassin?"

My heart sped out of control as desire rocked me. I could barely keep myself upright as his hands gripped my hips and his rough fingers squeezed my flesh.

"I want you to take all of me like the good girl you are. I want you to ride my cock until you scream my name," his voice was a velvet purr that both terrified and thrilled me. "I want to stretch that aching little cunt of yours until I ruin you for anyone else. I want to fuck you so hard that you never forget you belong to me."

Then I sank down on his cock, taking him deep and forgetting all the reasons he was wrong for me.

CHAPTER
SIXTY-ONE

Torq

My eyes rolled into the back of my head as she took me, and I grasped her hips to hold her down. I had missed the feeling of her tight heat and the euphoric sensation of being inside her. It was almost too much, and I was grateful to the dark. If I had to see her naked body straddling me, her perfect breasts with their pebbled beige tips, and her parted lips as she gasped for breath, I might not have been able to control myself.

"So tight and perfect," I rasped. "Now ride me, Jess."

She pressed her hands to my chest and shifted so that her feet were planted on either side of me. Then she lifted herself and began to bounce up and down, riding my cock just like I'd told her to.

I bit my bottom lip to keep from roaring as she fucked me mercilessly. In the dark and in this cave, she had lost any inhibitions or hesitation. She was not the tentative cadet who had never spread her legs before. She was not the cadet I'd sent away.

I moved one hand down to where our bodies met. "Sit on my cock and open your legs wider for me."

She obeyed, and I parted her with my fingers then used the pad of my thumb to rub her slick nub as she rocked her hips restlessly, her breath becoming more ragged.

"That's it, bad girl. Come for me."

When her body started to spasm, and her muscles clenched around my cock, she screamed my name.

It was all I could do not to explode with her, but I gritted my teeth and slid my hands to her hips. "Turn to face the other way and keep riding my cock."

She obeyed without a word, rotating without my cock slipping out. I wished I could see her sweet ass as she started to move it up and down, but I grabbed it with both hands as she rode me backward. "That's it. Just like that."

"You like it like this?"

"There is no way that I don't love to fuck you." I gave one ass cheek a gentle slap, and she moaned. "But I did not know you liked to be such a bad girl."

"Isn't this what you wanted?" She teased, tipping her ass higher as she moved herself up and down my shaft.

"You are what I want." I sat up and held her hips as I shifted her forward, moving onto my knees and forcing her onto all fours while keeping my cock inside her. She twisted as if trying to get away or regain her position on top, but I grabbed a handful of her hair and tugged it back. "You with your legs spread for me doing exactly what I tell you," I whispered, as I thrust hard, "your pretty moans as you take me so deep, like a good little toy I can play with all night long." I dragged myself out and drove it into her again. "You were made to take my cock, Jess, so I think you should take it in my bed every night until you beg me for mercy."

Her desperate sounds as I took her from behind made me lose the last shreds of my control. I released her hair and clutched one hip while I pushed her head down and hammered into her. My body detonated, and I exploded, holding myself in her as pleasure pulsed through me in relentless waves.

I slumped over her back and nipped her ear. "You are mine, Jess. You always will be."

Her body trembled beneath mine as she drew in ragged breaths. "Only for tonight and only here."

I wanted to argue with her and tell her that what we had was not something to be thrown away, but I had no right. I had been the one to push her away first, even if I had done it to protect her. She collapsed onto the furs, and I followed her, cocooning my body around her back. "It does not need to end here."

Her laughter bounced off the stone of the cave. "You want to go back to the academy and tell all your Blade buddies that you're with a human cadet? You want to tell your father?"

The confidence I had felt while I was inside her dimmed at her mention of my father. What would he do if he discovered that I was involved with Jess? She was nothing like the mate he expected me to take, and there was nothing her name would do to add to the glory of our clan.

But did I care what he thought? Did I care what any of them thought? I had come to the academy to become a great Drexian warrior. I had already joined a school not of my father's choosing, made Blade friends he would not approve of, and survived the trials with the help of humans. I was already going against everything I had been taught. Why would choosing Jess be any different?

"That's what I thought." Jess rolled away from me and tugged one of the furs over her. "Why don't we just enjoy this for what it was? Tomorrow we can pretend it never happened and go back to our normal lives without each other."

I did not respond to that. I could not. She was right. Our lives did not easily fit together. I flopped onto my back and blinked up into the blackness. If we did not fit, why did she feel so right? Why did I only feel whole when I was with her? And why did it feel impossible to admit that?

CHAPTER
SIXTY-TWO

Jess

L ight teased my eyelids as I snuggled deeper within the covers. I didn't want to wake up even though I knew my alarm would wake me soon. I wanted to spend one more minute in bed, one more minute with the hard body curled around my back and keeping me warm. A heavy arm was wrapped around my waist, and my own hand rested on top, our fingers lightly interlaced.

I fluttered my eyes open as the first tendrils of confusion drifted through my brain. Where was I? I wasn't in my bed in the academy. I slept there alone. I wasn't in Torq's bed, because I had never stayed late in his quarters for fear I'd be caught. Then I blinked a few times as the cave and waterfall came into focus, and it all came rushing back to me.

Memories of the night before flooded my brain and sent heat to scorch my cheeks. What had I been thinking? What had gotten into me? I was not the type of girl to throw myself at a guy, and I was not the type to try every sexual position I'd heard of in one go.

It was the darkness, I told myself. It was dark and we had been alone and cold. That's right. I'd been cold, and Torq had certainly warmed me up.

I glanced at my hand holding his and bit back a groan. There was no way I could coyote my way out of this, even if I did have the teeth to chew my own arm off to avoid waking him. My clothes were spread out on the rocks nearby, and they looked dry. At least drier than they had been the night before. That meant we could get dressed, walk back to the academy and pretend none of this had ever happened.

I untwined my hand from his and started to carefully lift his arm so I could slip from under it. Torq stirred behind me, and I went still. Then he pulled me tighter to him and nuzzled his head in my neck.

"Good morning," he mumbled.

"Morning," I said, sounding impossibly bright.

He made sleepy, waking sounds as he started to move his body, but he made no moves to release me. He didn't nervously jerk his arm away or apologize for grabbing me in the middle of the night. He seemed to be completely unaffected by waking up spooning me. How was he so relaxed and cool about this?

Because he's a guy, I reminded myself. Sex is sex, and there is no way he has a single regret about what we did.

As if to reinforce this, he kissed my neck. "Last night was fun."

"Mmhmm." I made a noncommittal noise, wondering how he could be so chill when I was freaking out. Hooking up with him after I'd been working so hard to get over him had been a colossal mistake, but here he was humming like it was any other morning and we always woke up in bed together. "We should probably get dressed and head back to the academy. Our schools might be missing us."

Torq cleared his throat. "Right. I had almost forgotten about the battle of the schools and the fact that our fellow cadets are probably swarming the mountains searching for the stones."

This was my cue to wiggle from his grasp. "I don't think either of us want to be found like this."

I stood and shed the fur that had been draped over me, leaving Torq still lying on the pile of pelts. I padded over to my pants and picked them up, squeezing the fabric to find it almost entirely dry. Then I realized I was only wearing panties. Where was my bra?

"I would not mind if you stayed like you are for a little while longer."

I swiveled my head to find him watching me intently. I crossed my hands over my bare breasts as I scanned the cave for the bra that Torq had taken off me the night before. When I spotted it, I hurried over and picked it up and slipped it on quickly. This was more evidence that I had lost my mind in the dark.

"You are sure we have to leave?" Torq sat up and swung his head lazily from side to side. "This cave is very private."

I let out a clipped laugh. "I don't think it would take too long for others to find us." Even as I tugged on my pants, I worried that other cadets would stumble upon us. The entrance to the cave might be behind the waterfall, but part of the cave's mouth was visible from the pool. That was how I'd seen it. If Assassins were looking for me, they wouldn't miss it.

"Too bad." Torq sighed and stood, stretching his arms overhead so that his hands brushed the ceiling.

I fumbled getting one leg into my pants because the sight of his muscles rippling as he stretched was a serious distraction. Even the academy tattoo on his arm sent a thrill through me. Then I huffed and snatched my uniform shirt from the floor, irritated that he could be so unconcerned about all of it. Just as I was about to tell him off for being such a cocky, infuriating ass, my gaze snagged on something tucked in the back of the cave where it narrowed.

My heart tripped in my chest as I squinted to see it better. It was black like the rest of the stone in the cave, but it wasn't rough and dull. It was polished and glossy. And were there markings on it?

Dropping to my hands and knees, I crawled to the low nook and reached for the stone. As soon as my fingers closed around it, I knew. I pulled it out and crawled out, straightening and peering at the stone with the Assassins emblem carved into the ebony surface.

"Is that what I think it is?"

I swung to see Torq grinning at me. He didn't appear to be angry or jealous that I'd found my school's stone. If it was possible, he seemed pleased.

I couldn't stop myself from grinning and holding it up. "I found the Assassin stone."

"You didn't happen to see one with two blades on it back there, did you?"

I laughed, but this time it was genuine. "Sorry."

He waved it away. "It would not be here. Our stone is somewhere cold, and do not tell me that isn't further punishment for our school."

I was reminded about the accident at the forbidden tower and the death of the first-year Blade. "I never did get to tell you how sorry I am that one of your friends died."

His expression sobered. "Thank you. He did not deserve it."

Before I could stop myself, I blurted out, "I was terrified when I thought it had been you."

He stepped closer, his gaze intense. "It was supposed to be me."

"What do you...?" My question faded as louder voices came to us through the water. Someone was out there. Someone had found us.

Then I looked at Torq in nothing but his underwear, and panic arrowed through me. This did not look good.

CHAPTER
SIXTY-THREE

Torq

J ess's face was stricken as the voices grew louder. She looked pointedly at me, and I glanced down. *Grekking* hell. How had I forgotten that I wasn't dressed? This was what Jess did to me. She made it impossible for me to think or reason. She even made it difficult to breathe.

I rushed to my clothes lying on the floor and dressed as quickly as I could, yanking on my pants and shoving my feet into my boots. I jammed my arms into my shirt, realizing that the fabric was still slightly damp and that it smelled murky. I ignored this as I buttoned it and tucked it hastily into my pants, knowing that I still looked like I'd gotten in a brawl and fallen down a waterfall.

Jess was lacing up her boots when someone called into the cave. "Hello!"

She locked eyes with me and an understanding passed

between us. We would never speak of what had happened. We would never tell anyone about our night in the cave. It would remain between us always. I gave her a sharp nod.

"In here!" Jess yelled back as she started walking from the cave along the narrow ledge.

I followed her, choosing my footholds carefully. I was soon shielding my eyes from the outside light that seemed bright even though it was barely peeking through the omnipresent thick, gray cloud cover. Droplets of water sprayed up from the cascade pouring from overhead and speckled our boots as we made our way from under the waterfall.

"Grek!" A Drexian on the bank of the pool ran a hand through his hair when he spotted Jess. "We have been searching for you all night."

"Hi, Fyn." Jess continued across the ledge until she reached the ground, and I walked behind her. "Good to see you."

There were two more Drexians with the tall one, and all of their eyes widened when they saw me.

"What are you doing with this Blade cadet?" Fyn asked, his body tensing as if he might need to defend the honor of his fellow Assassin.

I gave a small wave but waited for Jess to explain.

"Torq tried to save me when I fell off the overhang." She pointed to the rock ledge high above us. "We both ended up falling into the pool and getting drenched. It was almost dark, so we found shelter so he could recover from almost drowning."

Her explanation did nothing to change their shocked expressions. They all slid their gazes to me again.

"Your fellow Assassin is a strong swimmer. She pulled me out and resuscitated me."

They still said nothing, so Jess held up the stone. "Look what I found while he was recovering."

That got a reaction.

"Is that the Assassin stone?" The tallest Drexian strode toward us, his eyes glittering.

Jess bobbed her head up and down. "It was in a cave near the stream. Actually, it was in a cave under the stream."

The other Assassin cadets gathered around Jess, patting her on the shoulders and eyeing the stone, which was still in her hands.

Fyn, who was also clearly the team's leader, cleared his throat. "We should get this back to the academy."

"No other school has returned with their stone yet?" Jess asked.

One of the underclass Assassins twitched one shoulder. "We don't know. We have been out here looking for you. But they would sound the horn if the battle was over, wouldn't they?"

"There's a horn?" Jess gaped at them.

Fyn bestowed a small smile on her. "It is rarely used, but you will know it when you hear it. You can hear it all the way across the Gilded Peaks and halfway across the Restless Sea."

"We did not hear it," I said, which drew everyone's attention to me. The air outside the cave was cooler, even though it was daytime, and I was very aware of the dampness of the fabric against my skin. I fought the urge to rub my arms briskly for warmth.

"You are Torq." Fyn said this as a statement, not a question. "House Swoll."

I could tell from his bearing and the way he addressed me that he was also a high-born. "I am."

"He is a Blade," one of the other cadets reminded him, as if I was not standing right in front of them.

Fyn flicked his gaze to the cadet and then to me. "You have our gratitude for saving our fellow Assassin, but you probably wish to rejoin your team in searching for your stone."

I glanced at the Assassin stone. "I do not know if there is any point."

Fyn grunted at this, acknowledging that I was right, but I could also tell that he did not want to return to the academy with a Blade first-year in tow.

I allowed myself to look at Jess, wondering if she would take the side of the Assassins. But I would not know the answer. A deep booming voice broke the tense silence.

"Torq!"

I spun to see Kort crashing through the trees on the opposite side of the pool. His blade was out, and his uniform was dirty. He looked like he'd been through as much as I had.

When he registered the group of Assassins around me, Kort cocked his head. "Did you switch sides, brother?"

"He did not," Fyn answered before I could. "Your Blade rendered assistance to our cadet, and we were offering our thanks before he rejoined your school in the hunt."

Kort's shoulders relaxed, and he beamed at me. "Come on then. I hung back to look for you, but the rest of us are high in the peaks."

I dreaded the thought of going higher into the cold mountains in a damp uniform. I might have recovered from nearly drowning, and the blows I'd sustained from Dom did not ache, but I did not want to join a hunt that was pointless.

I jerked my head toward the Assassin stone in Jess's hands. "The battle has been won, but not by us."

Kort's jaw dropped, and he ran down to where the pool became a stream and leaped from stone to stone until he'd reached our side. "She found it? The Assassins have won?"

"Unless another school returns their stone sooner." Fyn

cast a stern look over his team of cadets. "We should not waste any more time returning to the academy."

"Go." I stepped back, putting distance between me and Jess.

Fyn gave me a curt tip of his head, as he turned and waved his cadets forward. Jess gave me a final glance as the quartet of Assassins started to move toward the academy. For the briefest of moments, I wondered if she might choose to stay behind, if she might choose to stay with me. But then I remembered that she had been the one to insist that the night had meant nothing, and we had both reached an unspoken agreement that we would not speak of it. Jess shot me a small smile then turned and strode away without looking back.

Kort put an arm around my shoulders. "Don't look so depressed. There are other battles ahead of us."

Then both our attention was pulled from the retreating Assassins and to the Drexian ship that was descending through the atmosphere. My breath caught in my throat as I recognized the distinctive emblem of flames on the hull.

Inferno Force.

CHAPTER
SIXTY-FOUR

Volten

I stood on the cracked stones of the shipyard as the glossy, black ship hovered above the ground before landing and causing the ground to tremble. The Inferno Force ship was only a transport, but it was still larger than the fighters that were lined up outside the academy.

I coughed from the dust the engines kicked up and the powerful scent of fuel, as the ship's ramp started to lower. The admiral had briefed me on the former High Commander he was expecting, but I had not thought he would arrive in an Inferno Force vessel. As far as I knew, Kax had not been Inferno Force, even though his brother Dorn had.

The ramp touched down with a jolt and the ship powered down, the engine rumbling before finally going quiet. Then a Drexian was striding down, his long, black hair flapping behind him. This was definitely not how I had imagined the former High Commander.

I thumped a hand across my chest in salute when he reached me. "High Command—"

"I'm not him," the Drexian cut me off before I could finish speaking. He jerked a thumb behind him. "The spy is back there."

I eyed the Drexian with dark scruff covering his cheeks. "Then you are...?"

"Jaxon."

Now I remembered Kann talking about him. "The Inferno Force pilot who escaped from the Kronock."

A half-grin teased his mouth as his gaze snagged on the Wings insignia on my uniform. "You a pilot?"

"I am, but I am also friends with Lieutenant Kann, who served with—"

"Kann! Where is he?" He swiveled his gaze as if Kann might be hiding behind one of the fighter jets. "I haven't seen that Drexian since he convinced me to be his wing man one night at a bar and we ended up in an epic brawl."

That sounded like Kann. "He's inside preparing for the banquet to close the battle of the schools."

"I'm sure there will be time to catch up. First we need to share our information about the Kronock."

Jaxon and I both turned as another Drexian walked down the ramp. Now this warrior looked every bit like a former High Commander and intelligence officer. His brown hair was cut short, his face was clean-shaven, and his uniform was pristine.

"Kax is right." Jaxon twisted his back as if stretching from a long ride. "Business first, then we play." He slapped my shoulder. "I am sure academy pilots still know how to have a good time, right?"

I did not want to correct him and tell him that my idea of a good time was crawling into bed with Ariana after a good dinner. "Of course, we do."

"I know that Admiral Zoran was expecting me alone, but after Kann and Vyk reached out to Jaxon, he contacted me and offered to act as my pilot for the journey," Kax explained as we walked toward the academy. "We both believe it is better you have as much information as possible before going into Kronock space."

"If my wife Samaira could have been here, she would have, but she gave me leave to tell you everything we both know about the Kronock prison moon we liberated."

Chills went through me. "Prison moon?"

"We don't think they have any more of them," Jaxon said. "At least, our intelligence hasn't shown evidence of any new ones."

The three of us strode beneath the archway with the school emblems carved into the ebony stone, and I steered the Drexians toward the Stacks. It would be quiet there since the entire school would be in the dining hall celebrating.

"That's correct," Kax said, taking long strides beside me. "The Kronock Empire is fractured, so they do not seem to be operating their system of prison moons or labs devoted to genetic testing, but that doesn't mean it isn't capable of great destruction or cruelty."

"Is there a way to phrase that so that you do not panic my fiancé?"

Kax and Jaxon both paused when we had reached the tall arched doors leading into the Stacks. Kax put a hand on my shoulder. "The pilot who is being held is your fiancé's sister?"

"She is. Ariana is also a pilot, and it is all I can do to keep her from stealing a plane and leaving on a renegade search mission right now."

Jaxon grinned at me. "Sounds like a human female to me."

"I will do my best not to panic her," Kax told me.

Jaxon snorted out a laugh and gave me a slap on the back. "Good luck to you, brother. Just like all of us with human mates, you will need it."

CHAPTER
SIXTY-FIVE

Jess

My grip around the Assassin stone was firm as we entered the academy through one of the tower entrances and trudged along suspended stone bridges and down twisting stairs to reach the main hall. The air hummed with energy, but it wasn't the nervous energy that I'd felt the morning the battle had started. It was both triumphant and weary.

I recognized some of the Iron cadets rubbing their hands together as if trying to warm them and a handful of wounded Wings limping past us. How many of the teams had returned because of injury or exhaustion?

Fyn motioned for me to walk ahead of him to the four school instructors waiting at the base of the large staircase. I zeroed in on the Assassin instructor, pausing in front of him and extending my arms to reveal the stone.

His face brightened. "You found it. Well done, Assassins."

I wanted to ask if we'd won but that seemed crass, although something told me the Drexians didn't consider competition and wanting to win a rude thing. I squared my shoulders and channeled my inner cocky Drexian, telling myself to act like Torq when he was his most obnoxious. "Are we the first school to return their stone?"

"You are the second."

A breath whooshed from me as if I'd been deflated. "The second?"

"The Irons outsmarted us all." Morgan walked up to me, looking almost as disheveled as me. A leaf was stuck in her blonde hair, and dirt smudged one cheek. "I think it was Drexian techno magic."

Fiona laughed as she came up behind Morgan. "The Irons were not allowed to use their devices, but they did manage to orchestrate their search mission like a well-devised engineering project."

"How fast did they find their stone?" I'd recovered from the initial disappointment and was now just glad to be back in the academy and that much closer to a hot shower and food.

"Our guys only brought it in an hour or so before you," Britta said as she joined us. Her hair was pulled up into a high ponytail and the silvery strands glinted in the light.

That made me feel better. Even if we'd run full speed back to the academy—which no one on my Assassin team had wanted to do, even though we did break into a jog at times—we would not have beaten them. I was proud that we'd found the stone—that I'd found the stone—and that we had been the second team to return it successfully.

Morgan took a moment to look me up and down. Then she leaned closer and took a whiff. "Why do you smell like mildew?"

"I took an unexpected dip in a pool at the base of a waterfall, and my clothes got soaked."

Her brows popped up. "That started out intriguing and then took a turn."

"That pretty much sums it up." I didn't want to go into details with everyone standing with us, so I changed the subject. "What happened to you?"

"I might have been the cadet voted to climb a tree to get a better view." She gave a mournful glance at her dirty uniform. "It was easier going up than coming down."

I sensed eyes on me and turned to see Torq walk in with his friend. There were no other Blades with them, which told me they had not rejoined their team. For the first time since we'd emerged from the cave, I wondered where Dom had gone. Had he come back to the academy, or had he tried to join a search team and pretend like nothing had happened?

But what had happened? He'd tried to kiss me, but he hadn't tried to hurt me like Torq was convinced he would. Should I tell someone, or should I let Torq deal with it?

As if he knew I was thinking about him, Torq pivoted his head to meet my gaze. I felt a jolt as his eyes locked on mine and all the sensations of the night before rushed back to me— the heat of his mouth, the power of his hands as he gripped my hips, the rigidity of his cock as I sank onto him. My face flamed with heat, and I jerked my gaze away.

Morgan's smile was wry as she leaned close to me. "You are holding back on me. I know something else happened out there, but don't worry. I'm patient. You can tell me later over some Palaxian wine."

"Whatever happened means nothing," I told her. "Nothing has changed."

She patted my arm. "You keep telling yourself that, and maybe one day you'll believe it."

I opened my mouth to protest but I clamped it shut. She was right. Who was I fooling? Not my friend and not even myself, if I were being honest. As much as I'd wanted to be able to have meaningless sex and forget about it, I couldn't. My body ached for him, my skin craved his touch, my lips missed the way his claimed mine.

I gave my head a rough shake and swiveled so that I couldn't see Torq. I did not need any more reminders that I couldn't rid myself of the Drexian, and that he had burned himself into my soul. I just needed to keep my distance and try to forget him—again.

"Because that worked so well the first time," I mumbled under my breath.

Britta glanced at me. "What worked well?"

"Nothing," I said quickly. "Just thinking about strategies for next year's battle of the schools."

"I'm just glad it's over and no one died." Morgan looped an arm around my waist and leaned against me. "I'll take this over the trials any day."

"We don't know that no one died." Reina said as she bustled up and shot a furtive look over her shoulder. I sensed she might be telling us something that wasn't common knowledge. "One of the Blade cadets apparently set out across the Restless Sea."

Morgan jerked upright, as if jolted with electricity. "Why would he do that? The stones were all hidden in the mountains, weren't they?"

Reina shook her head slowly and her upswept blue hair tipped from side to side. "One cadet on the sea is suicide."

"That might have been the point," Fiona said in a low voice, with another glance at the Blade instructors huddled in a tight circle.

I had a sinking feeling that I knew what had happened to Dom.

CHAPTER
SIXTY-SIX

Torq

"What do you mean one of our cadets went into the sea?" Kort swiveled his head from Kann to the admiral, who'd silently joined our group of Blades gathered near the entrance to our school.

I had been stunned by the revelation, and it was the only thing that could have drawn my attention from Jess as I'd entered the academy and seen her with her fellow Assassins. I had thought that I could slip back into our previous arrangement of avoiding each other, but the night in the cave had shattered that. I could think of little else but how she felt, tasted, sounded, and I could not continue to pretend that she was nothing to me.

That is, until the lead Blade instructor told us in hushed tones that Dom had been seen returning to the academy and then rushing out again toward the sea. Then I had been unable to think of anything else but the fate of the Drexian who had been in such pain and caused so much pain.

"How do we know he took to the water?" I asked. The last time I had seen the cadet had been at the top of the rock overhang. Had he truly tramped through the forest and then decided to throw himself at the mercy of the stormy sea?

"He was spotted by an instructor from one of the towers." Kann folded his arms tightly across his chest. "He was seen taking a small craft from the stream into the sea."

Kort glanced at me with a look of horror. Taking a boat into the pounding surf that crashed again the cliffs was madness. It meant that Dom had a death wish.

"Has he been seen since?" Kort asked the admiral.

Admiral Zoran gave the smallest of shakes with his head. "By the time the instructor was able to raise the alarm and report the cadet's actions, the watercraft was no longer visible."

I swallowed the lump that had lodged in my throat. I should tell them what I knew. I should tell them why a Blade would do something so reckless and suicidal. But that would mean revealing my brother's crime and my suspicions about Dom's part in the death of Zenen. I would need to reveal the fight on the circuit and the scuffle over Jess. I would have to reveal my relationship with Jess and why I was so convinced that Dom meant her harm. I would need to reveal everything.

I pressed my lips together. It did not matter now. The Drexian had taken the easy way out. He had run from the possibility of being caught or maybe he had run because he realized that he could not get the revenge he so craved. Had he decided that punishing innocents for the crimes of others would not give him relief? Or had his hunger for vengeance simply driven him mad?

The reason did not matter. He was gone, most likely crushed by the waves, or pulled under by the unforgiving current. That meant that I did not need to fear for Jess or watch my back for his next attack.

A deep breath escaped my lips as relief suffused me. Jess was safe. Dom could not get to me through her.

Kort cut a glance at me before huffing out a frustrated breath. "We must do something to find him. He is a Blade."

Again, I stayed quiet. He was a Blade, but he had also been a tormentor. Blades were supposed to protect and defend and be loyal. Dom had lost his way from the ideals of our school, no doubt by grief and pain. Part of me felt sympathy for him for losing his brother to Drexians who would never be punished. But he had not gotten justice by going after me. He had only brought more pain upon himself and his family.

Thinking of his family getting the news that they had lost another son to the academy made my gut clench. Despite the fact that I had not caused his brother's death, my brother had set all of this into motion. My clan was responsible. "We should find him. His family deserves that."

Kort gave me a grateful look for joining his side. "I volunteer to lead a search party of Blades."

Admiral Zoran frowned. "You will need Blades who are good on the water. Not every Drexian knows how to swim, although that is an issue I plan to rectify now that I am Academy Master."

"I know an Iron who is an accomplished sailor." Kann glanced around the hall. "He grew up on the shore of the other side of the Restless Sea."

Zoran eyed us, his expression severe. Finally, he grunted something that sounded like a yes and pinned Kann with a sharp look. "Assemble your party, but I do not wish to lose any more Blades today."

Kann squared his shoulders as soon as the admiral had spun on his heel and left us. "I volunteer."

I opened my mouth to volunteer. It seemed right that I should go considering how much of the cadet's actions were because of me. But my offer was preempted by Lieutenant Volten striding up to our group.

"Volt," Kann greeted his friend with a tight smile. "We are assembling a search party to look for our cadet who went missing on the Restless Sea."

The Wings instructor furrowed his brow, but he did not ask why a Blade would have gone into the sea when the competition had ranged across the Gilded Peaks. "Do you wish me to fly a low altitude search grid for you?"

Kann thumped his friend on the side of his arm. "Could you?"

"Of course." Volt tipped his head at his friend. "Consider it done. But first, I need to take Torq with me."

Kort jerked his head to me. "But he was going to join the rescue."

"He can join you after he speaks with the Drexian who has just arrived." Volten took a step back and waited for me to follow. "Former High Commander Kax is waiting." He pivoted to Kann. "And your fellow Inferno Force warrior Jaxon."

CHAPTER
SIXTY-SEVEN

Torq

The chatter of voices and booming cheers as cadets returned from the hunt in the Gilded Peaks faded as Volten led me away from the cavernous main hall. We did not head toward the School of Flight or the Academy Master's office, which made me wonder where this Drexian warrior who had been so hard to track down was being kept.

When Volten paused outside the heavy doors leading to the Stacks, it hit me that I had not set foot in the place for the entire term. Blades had little use for old parchments or ancient tomes, and the Stacks had always been the domain of the Assassins and Irons. For a moment, I wondered if Jess would be inside. She had been helping Ariana in the search for her sister. Would Kax wish to speak with her and her friend Morgan about their progress?

I steeled myself for the possibility of seeing Jess, telling myself that I could not reveal my feelings, even though it was impossible to keep from gazing at her. My heart raced and my chest constricted, as the Wings instructor pushed hard on the doors to open them.

Walking into the Stacks, I breathed in the scent of dust and aged paper, old leather and candle wax. Even though real candles had not burned in the wrought iron chandeliers hanging overhead for decades, the scent remained. It was a scent I had smelled on Jess when she had come to me from a study session in the Stacks. I might have been the only Blade to be aroused by the aroma of ancient books and melted candles.

We walked through a maze of tall bookshelves jammed with well-worn volumes, until we reached a corner in the back with a wooden table and brass-shaded lamps running the length of it. I released a breath of dismay and relief when I saw that Jess was not among those sitting around the table.

I had expected to see Ariana, and even her friend Fiona, but I stiffened at the sight of Commander Vyk. What was he doing here? I knew he was Inferno Force, but from my understanding, Kax was not. His brother Dorn had been an Inferno Force commander, but Kax had served on the High Command until he left to undertake missions for Drexian intelligence.

All heads turned to us as we approached, and the only two Drexians I did not know stood. The one with short hair spoke first. "Torq of House Swoll? "

The Drexian was tall with sandy-brown hair cropped short and eyes such a vivid shade of green that they seemed to shine. He did not wear an academy uniform or even a Drexian military uniform. The ship that had delivered him was emblazoned with an Inferno Force emblem, but he did not wear any such identifier on his simple black clothes, although it was clear who he was. I thumped a fist across my chest in salute. "High Commander Kax."

He gave me an easy smile. "Not High Commander anymore. Call me Kax."

I relaxed. "Call me Torq."

The other Drexian looked every bit like he was Inferno Force, with long black hair, scruff on his cheeks, and his black sleeves rolled up far enough on his arms to show glimpses of dark tattoos. "I am Jaxon, of Inferno Force."

Kax inclined his head. "I understand you have been working with the Lieutenants to locate the missing pilot."

As much as I liked the sound of that, I could not claim it. "I only attempted to use my father to find you, even though he refused my request. There are others who have been working diligently to find Sasha. They should be here."

Kax studied me for a beat. "You are sure you are from House Swoll?"

I wanted to tell him that if he had met me during the first term or even earlier in the second, he might not have asked that. He would have seen the arrogance and pride that I had shared with my clan for so long. He would have known that I was House Swoll without asking. "I am."

He nodded. "The academy has a way of changing cadets." He flicked a glance at Volten. "I did hear that you were courageous in the trials, and you teamed up with a group of female cadets."

"That is true." I thought of Jess and my heart seized. "I would not have made it through without them."

Jaxon grunted. "I know something about working with strong human females."

"We worked as a team," Ariana said. "Everyone contributed to everyone else's survival."

Commander Vyk shifted slightly in his seat, and I wondered again why he was at the meeting. He had been part of the reason that the trials had been so deadly, and I still held resentment that he had been working to purge the academy of the humans, especially now that I understood the value and intelligence of them.

"I am glad to hear it." Kax pivoted to the table. "It will take teamwork to pull off this mission."

"But you went into Kronock territory to rescue a woman by yourself," Vyk said. "I was part of the team called in by your brother to find you when you did not return."

"Which is why this mission will not be a solo one." Kax leaned down and spread his arms on either side of an unfurled star chart I had not noticed on the table. "Not everyone can call in a favor with Inferno Force like my brother." He shot Vyk a grin. "Thank you for coming after me, though."

Vyk sat up straighter. "Any Inferno Force warrior would walk through fire for your brother."

"A hundred times," Jaxon added, gaining him a resolute nod from Vyk.

"Now we need to walk through fire to retrieve our pilot." Kax met Ariana's eyes. "Your sister fought alongside us in the battle for Earth. Not only does she deserve our loyalty, but we also cannot risk the Kronock using her to their advantage."

"Sasha would never give the enemy information," Ariana said quickly. "She would die first."

"It is not information the Kronock desire." Kax drummed his fingers on the table. "They desire a technological and biological advantage over other species."

"Biological?"

Kax made a low, disapproving sound in the back of his throat. "The Kronock have been known to take DNA from other species and use it to modify their own. We do not want your sister to be used for this."

Ariana's face paled, and Volten walked behind her chair

and rested his hands on her shoulders. "We will not let that happen."

"No, we won't." Kax curled one hand into a fist. "We need to have our team ready to go as soon as possible. I have given the information your Assassins have sourced to some Inferno Force friends, and they will do a deep dive into Kronock communications to find where Sasha is being held."

Jaxon cleared his throat as Kax looked at him. "After that, Inferno Force will execute reconnaissance missions to determine her exact location before a full extraction team can be deployed. I am a bit of an expert of that, as is Kax. Once we have found the target, I assume you all wish to be involved in the rescue?"

"Absolutely," Ariana said as Fiona nodded.

"Are you all prepared to go at a moment's notice?" Jaxon asked.

Everyone agreed, but as his words sank in, I looked around the group, not quite believing what I had heard. "You wish me to be part of the team?"

"It wasn't Volt who insisted, although he vouched for your bravery." Ariana held my gaze, and I suspected she had taken some convincing after her experience with me during the first term.

"Who, then?" I hoped my father had not pulled strings or used influence to gain me a place I did not deserve, although I got the feeling he would be using none of his influence to aid me anytime soon.

"One of the Assassins who has been working with us." Fiona leaned back in her chair with a knowing grin. "Jess insists that you will be an asset to any attack team, and that your Kronock is excellent."

My heart tripped in my chest as I tried to compute this information. Should I be honored that Jess had recommended me for a deadly mission, or should I be worried that she was trying to get rid of me? It was true that my Kronock was very good, all thanks to her, but was I ready for this?

Then I reminded myself that I was a Blade, and no one crossed us.

Jaxon twisted his head and winked at me. "We needed another Blade brother. Welcome to the team."

CHAPTER
SIXTY-EIGHT

Jess

T touched a hand to my hair as I stepped into the banquet hall, wishing I'd had time to do more than towel it dry and run my fingers through it. I'd spent too much time in the shower but standing under the hot water had unwound the knots in my shoulders and rid me of the slightly murky, mildew smell that had clung to my clothes and hair. It had also done a good job of purging me of the unwanted feelings of loss that had been haunting me since I walked away from Torq.

It was the right decision. It was the only decision.

I'd told myself this so many times as the water had pounded on my back that it had become my new mantra. As much fun as I'd had with Torq, and as free as I'd felt, it had been an illusion made possible by the secluded cave and the dark. It hadn't been real. It couldn't be. He was a Drexian who was expecting to align himself with someone just like him, and I was a human cadet who cared more about her career than about being anyone's mate.

"It was fun while it lasted," I told myself now, as I surveyed the growing crowd gathering around long tables and congratulating each other for returning from the hunt for the stones.

"Talking about thinking we won the battle?" Morgan nudged me as she joined me at the entrance.

I managed to smile at her as I marveled at how well she'd cleaned up. The leaves were gone from her blonde hair, and you never would have known that she'd climbed trees and come down them the hard way. "You know it."

"I don't really care that the Irons won. Apparently, it's been a while since their school has been victorious, so I'm happy for Britta."

I glanced around, catching sight of our friend's distinctive silvery-blonde hair, as she stood with a cluster of big Drexian Irons. They did look ecstatic, which took away a bit of the sting from not getting our stone back to the academy first.

"We should be glad you found our stone." Morgan dropped her voice, even though with the chatter surrounding us, I doubted anyone could hear. "The Wings didn't find theirs."

I spotted some Wing cadets near the front of the room. "But they're back?"

"They sounded the horn to bring all the cadets back. No point in searching if there's no chance of winning."

I hadn't heard the horn since I'd been standing under the shower, but that explained why I saw cadets from all the schools dressed in clean clothes and ready for the celebration. This banquet wasn't as euphoric as the one we'd had after joining our schools, but there wasn't the pall of cadets who hadn't survived the maze or been chosen for a school. Then I remembered Dom.

"Do you know if they found the cadet who went into the sea?"

"The Blade?" Morgan made a face as we walked farther into the long room. "I know they sent out a search party to look for him, but it might be more like a body recovery at this point."

I shivered at the thought of going into the rough sea. "They don't know why he went in? No one talked to him? He didn't say anything to anyone before leaving?"

Morgan eyed me. "Why so many questions? Did you know the cadet?"

"Not really." It was a long story, which I planned to tell Morgan, but the banquet was not the place. "I'm just curious."

She nodded as if this made sense. "I can find out." She swiveled her head around. "Where is Fiona? She might know."

"She's meeting with the Drexian who arrived with Inferno Force. I saw her and Lieutenant Bowman talking with him outside the Stacks."

We both turned to see Fyn, who inclined his head at me. "Good work on the hunt, cadet. In case I forgot to tell you."

"Thanks." I tried to focus on the upperclassman, but my brain was stuck on Ariana and Fiona meeting with a mystery Drexian. It must be about the search for Sasha. I shot a glance at Morgan, who seemed just as intrigued. I snapped my fingers. "Shoot. I just remembered something I need to grab back in my room. I'll be back in two seconds."

Fyn nodded, turning his attention to Morgan and asking her a question about her battle team. She cut me a scathing look, and I knew I'd pay for ditching her later, but I had to see if the women were still with the Drexian. I had to know if there had been progress on the search for Ariana's sister.

I hurried from the hall and headed for the Stacks, tipping my head to a few passing cadets. When I'd reached the corridor, I slowed. No one stood outside. Had they gone inside? Just as I put my hands on the door to push it open, an arm jerked me into the shadows from behind.

CHAPTER
SIXTY-NINE

Torq

Where was Jess? I swept my gaze over the crowded banquet hall as I pushed my way through the throngs celebrating the end of the battle of the schools. Everyone had returned from searching the Gilded Peaks, either successful or not, and had changed into clean uniforms for the dinner.

Along with not seeing Jess, I noticed that the Blade search party had not returned, which meant that Kort and Kann were not present. I cast a quick glance at some of the other first-year Blades who were sitting at the end of a long table and pouring Drexian wine into pewter goblets. I could sit with them, but after meeting with Kax and the others involved in rescuing the missing human pilot, I wished to talk about that—and I wanted to talk about it with Jess.

She had been one of the ones to help Ariana from the beginning. I could tell her about the mission and my part in it without worry because she was involved. She would understand. I frowned as I tried to find pockets of Assassins, but she was not with any of them.

I know she had returned to the academy. I had seen her walk away from me with her team, and I had seen her with that team when I'd entered the main hall. So where was she?

"They are still on the water."

I snapped my head to the gravelly voice, startled that it was Commander Vyk who had walked up to me. I did not think the academy's security chief had spoken five words to me before today.

"That is who you are looking for, is it not?"

I nodded without speaking, still shocked that the Drexian with the silvery hair and beard, the one who had been partly responsible for the disaster of the trials, the one who had been open is his distaste for humans at the academy, was engaging me in conversation like we were friends. Even if I trusted him, I would not have told him the truth. And I did not trust him.

I knew that he had tried to stop the High Commanders before the trial, and I knew that he had taken a great risk trying to warn others about their plan. That did not mean I had gotten over his complicity in the difficulty of the maze, or his thinly veiled contempt for human cadets. I might have agreed with him at one point, but that was before I'd gotten to know the humans. That was before I had fallen for Jess.

"You do not like me." Vyk said this without emotion and without question.

I thought about lying and telling him that was not true, but then I remembered the trials and those who were not as lucky as I was to survive. Anger flashed hot as I remembered the decent cadets who had died because some of the old-school

Drexians had an issue with humans. "I did have to fight off more than one of the monsters you were responsible for unleashing into the maze."

A muscle ticked in his jaw. "I regret my part in that. I regret that my desire to keep the academy as it has always been only made it weaker."

"We are not weaker because of human cadets," I snapped, unable to hold my tongue, even if he was my superior and an Inferno Force warrior known for being a brutal fighter. Even if he had been included as part of Sasha's rescue team. "We could all learn a lot from the bravery of the humans coming halfway across the galaxy to an unknown planet and dangerous school. What have we been defending Earth for if we do not believe the humans are worth taking as allies and mates?"

The commander blinked at me, and for a moment, I worried I had gone too far. "You are right. The humans all survived the trials. They were all selected by schools. They have exceeded expectations."

"Are you saying you were wrong about them?"

He folded his arms across his chest. "I still do not believe that females belong on the battlefield, be they human or Drexian."

"But you are willing to join a mission with humans to rescue a female pilot who was fighting against the Kronock?"

His eyebrows pressed together in a scowl. "We must retrieve the female from the enemy. If it was up to me, her sister would not join the mission, but it is not my decision."

The idea that Ariana would sit out on the mission to save Sasha was laughable. I was on the verge of asking him how he had become part of the mission at all, but I spotted a blue tower of hair bobbing through the crowd. Reina! She was close with Jess. Maybe she would know where she was.

I reached for the Vexling's slender arm as she passed. She

blinked her large eyes at me, breaking into a grin when she finally recognized me. "You are the cadet who went through the maze with Ariana and Volten and many of the human females."

"I am." I hated that Commander Vyk was still standing there, but I had to know. "Have you seen one of those humans, Jess?"

If it was possible for her eyes to flare wider, they did. "I was just coming to tell the admiral that I just saw her with the cadet who they're searching for in the Restless Sea. They were walking toward the steps that lead downstairs to the dungeons."

Icy tendrils of fear curled around my heart. "You are sure it was him?"

"I never forget a face. Besides, he was soaking wet. It looked like he'd swum back."

Vyk's gaze sharpened. "The missing cadet is not missing?"

"He was never missing," I said, before pushing past both him and Reina and running for the door. Dom had only faked going into the sea, and now he had Jess.

CHAPTER
SEVENTY

Jess

"I don't understand." My feet fumbled on the stone steps, as Dom led me down the stairs. "I thought you took a boat into the sea."

His wet uniform pressed into my back as he held me close to him with the nose of a blaster jammed into my ribs. "I did, but only to make everyone think I was gone. I was always going to come back for you."

"For me?" I was confused. Had I given this guy the wrong idea at some point? Was this all because I'd talked to him as we'd walked through the forest? "We barely know each other."

His grip on my arm tightened. "That will change. You can be happy with me. I know it."

Okay, now this guy sounded seriously delusional. "Where are we going?"

The sounds of the banquet were long gone and there were

no voices coming from the corridor below as we reached the bottom of the stairs. "We cannot stay here. No one understands. They have it all wrong."

My pulse fluttered. As far as I knew, this was not the way out of the academy. "We're both cadets in the academy. We can't just leave."

He leaned down and his warm breath skimmed my ear. "Who will stop us? The entire school is celebrating. No one knows I am alive, and no one will notice that you are missing until it is too late."

I hated that he might be right. I tried to slow my pace, but the Drexian jerked me forward. "Why take me? You can leave faster without having to drag me along."

He choked out a dark laugh that held no warmth as we moved farther down a dimly lit corridor I'd never encountered before. "You were Torq's. The arrogant high-born risked himself to find you and save you. He would not have bothered to lift a single entitled finger if he did not care for you. But what was his will now be mine. His family stole from me, and now I am stealing from him."

I remembered what he and Torq had fought about, but I still didn't understand what had happened and why Torq needed to pay for it. "Whatever crime his family committed shouldn't be his to pay. It wasn't his fault."

"No?" He poked the blaster harder into my side. "You believe those born into elite clans should be allowed to abuse and kill anyone they want without fear of retribution? Maybe Torq did not kill my brother, but maybe after this other high-born families will think twice before they evade punishment."

I tried not to panic as I processed what the Drexian was rambling about. "Someone killed your brother?"

"He didn't tell you?" He choked out a pained, strangled

laugh. "He is still protecting his brother's honor, not that the Drexian has any."

My mind raced as we walked farther. Torq's brother had killed Dom's brother? That explained the hostility, but it seemed wrong that Dom's rage was focused on Torq, who had done nothing. Not that I dared say that.

I breathed in a dank, loamy scent that reminded me of the underground tunnels that led under the academy, but this was not the way I'd come when Kann had taken us to see the maze, or when Torq had led me to them later. This scent was heavier, and I could swear I detected the coppery tang of blood.

My heart tripped as it hit me that maybe he intended to kill me, instead of take me with him. Maybe he was only telling me he was taking me with him as he dragged me to my death. "Taking me prisoner is just as wrong as what Torq's brother did, and I did nothing to you. I am not high-born. I am like you."

He hesitated and his voice softened. "I will not hurt you. I can make you happy. Happier than you would be with a Drexian like Torq who could never claim you as a mate. I saw you with him and his father. I saw how he treated you. I would never do that."

I had no answer for that, but being reminded of Torq pretending he barely knew me in front of his father made my heart twist. Dom was not delusional about everything. Torq had made his choice about me, but I had also made my decision about him. "I promise you that Torq and I are not together. This will not hurt him the way you think it will."

Dom ignored this, grunting as we moved deeper down the sloping corridor and through a rusty, steel gate that hung loosely on its hinges. Then we were walking on dirt-covered stone with barred cells on either side of us. Was this the dungeons? Part of me had believed that they were made up to scare cadets, but from the smell of decay and urine, it was clear that they were very real. A low growl from somewhere deeper sent fresh waves of fear through me. They were real and they were not empty.

"Release her." The deep voice came from behind us, and it was so calm and steady that it took me a beat to realize who had spoken.

Dom swung around, almost knocking me over as he tried to regain his grip on my arm and press his blaster into my side. Torq stood at the entrance to the dungeons with a curved blade in each hand.

"It is over." His expression was fierce as he stared at Dom. "Everyone knows that you did not drown. You will not escape, and you will not leave the academy."

Dom clenched his teeth so hard I heard them grind. "You would let her die to win?"

"Jess is not going to die. I will not let you harm her." Barely controlled rage hummed through each word, but his eyes were on me. "I will not let you touch her for one more second."

From behind us came the sound of shuffling and scraping, and then iron bars rattled as an enormous creature flung itself onto them with a roar. Dom jerked and glanced behind him, but swiftly regained his composure and gripped me with even more determination.

But the moment of distraction had been enough. Torq had flicked his gaze to the floor quickly and then back up, and when he did it again, I understood. Before Dom had fully focused on Torq again, I elbowed Dom hard and aimed low. He grunted and loosened his grip on my arm, which gave me a chance to duck.

Blaster fire echoed off the low ceiling of the dungeons, and Dom staggered back, releasing me fully and dropping his own weapon. The beast in the cage screeched and swiped a long, furry arm into the passageway. I stumbled away, turning back to watch Dom fall. Commander Vyk emerged from the shadowy depths of one of the first cells still extending his blaster. I didn't know why the security chief was with Torq, or how they'd found us, but I didn't care as Torq rushed forward and swept me into his arms before my knees buckled.

CHAPTER
SEVENTY-ONE

Torq

I didn't let go of Jess until I'd led her from the dungeons, leaving Commander Vyk behind to handle the wounded Dom. I kept my arms wrapped tightly around her as I moved her quickly up the corridor and the stairs, wanting to get her far away from the cadet who'd tried to take her. My heart hammered relentlessly, even though I knew she was safe and could feel that she was unharmed.

I was sure I had lost a year or two off my life as I had run from the banquet hall and toward the dungeons, with Vyk close at my heels. I had not bothered to ask him why he was coming, or why he cared so much. I had been grateful to have the grizzled warrior by my side when we'd reached the underground corridors and had heard Dom recounting my shameful behavior to Jess. The security chief had not hesitated to motion for me to follow while he snuck into a cell with his blaster out, and he had not spoken a word to me after he had taken down the cadet. Maybe he had done it as payment for the sins of the trials. If so, I would take it and consider his debt paid.

Jess was safe and Dom would not threaten her again. That was all that mattered to me.

When we reached the main hall and the bottom of the wide staircase, Jess pulled away from me. "How did you know?"

I brushed a strand of hair from her forehead, grateful to be able to touch her again. "Reina saw you."

Jess released a breath. "I didn't think anyone saw him grab me. I was sure no one was coming."

"I will always come for you." My voice was thick with emotion as I stepped closer to her again, missing the feel of her body pressed against mine.

"Torq."

I stiffened at the all-too-familiar voice booming from above. The voice that had scolded me as a child, the voice that had lectured me when I was older, the voice that warned me now. Jess stepped away from me, her expression shuttering.

I forced myself to look from her to my father as he swept down the stairs, his gaze locked on me. "You have returned to the academy so soon."

"None too soon it seems." His tone was cutting, and he slid a cold glance to Jess. "I came to speak to High Commander Kax. His father was a good friend."

I wanted to correct him and tell him that Kax was no longer High Commander, but I did not. I also wanted to remind him that Kax was not at the academy due to his influence. Instead, I squared my shoulders and reached for Jess. "Father, this is Jess, one of the Assassin cadets."

My father lifted a single brow and inclined his head at her.

"I have seen you before, but my son assured me you were nobody."

I flinched at this, but I proceeded to curl an arm around her waist and tug her to me. "She is not nobody. Far from it. She is all that matters."

Jess inhaled quickly, the sound soft and breathy. I could feel her gaze on me, but I held my father's gaze without looking away.

"You have chosen a human female for bedsport?" His sneer was unmistakable.

"She is not bedsport." My voice was as cold as his. "She is who I have chosen."

My father stepped closer so that he could look down on me. "You would choose a female over your clan?"

I thought about all the pain my clan had brought me, all the shame, all the judgment. I had never been enough for them, but I was enough for my Blade brothers, and I was enough for Jess. "I would."

My father locked his gaze on me for a few heavy beats of silence before snapping them away. "Then I hope you enjoy your life without the protection of me or your clan." Then he spun away and stomped from the academy, his boots echoing as he went.

I could not breathe as I stood holding Jess. Neither of us spoke. I was not sure I believed what had just transpired. Had I truly been exiled from my clan with a few cold words?

"You made the right choice."

I glanced up to see Admiral Zoran standing at the top of the staircase with Kax to one side and Jaxon on the other.

"I would have to agree with the admiral," Kax said. "I would choose my human mate over my clan any day."

Jaxon nodded firmly, touching his fist across his chest to salute me.

I swallowed the tightness in my throat, grateful for the older Drexians' support. If they believed in my choice, it could not be so wrong. If they were behind me, I would not feel so lost.

"Mate?" Jess wiggled away from me. "Whoa. I thought we agreed that we were over. I thought you didn't want to be together."

I shook my head. "I agreed with you about last night because you seemed so determined, but I have changed my mind."

She put her hands on her hips. "You changed your mind? First, you changed your mind about being with me and then you change your mind again?"

I pulled her hands to mine. "I was wrong, Jess. I was foolish and scared, and I thought that I could live without you. I cannot."

Her jaw dropped as she gaped at me. "You're admitting you're wrong? And you're admitting that you were a selfish, arrogant idiot?"

I didn't remember saying that, but I nodded. "All of it, and I regret every moment of hurt I caused you. I only did it to protect you."

"To protect me?" Her eyebrows went so high they almost disappeared beneath the hair flopping over her forehead. "Why the hell would breaking things off protect me?"

"Dom wanted to hurt me because of what my brother did to his, but he told me he did not want to kill me, he wanted to take from me what mattered most. I was terrified that he would discover that was you."

"He went after me anyway." Her voice cracked, and it was a knife through my heart.

"I know, and I am so sorry. I thought if I kept my distance

from you, he would never know. But I guess I could not hide my true feelings."

She peered up at me with glassy eyes. "It's all your fault that Dom followed me into the woods and then took me captive?"

"It is, but that is why I came after you both times. I will always come for you, Jess. I hope you know that now."

Her gaze went to the floor. "I trusted you, and you hurt me."

I felt panic flutter in my chest. I was losing her. I could not lose her. I grasped her hands and lowered myself to my knees. "I regret every moment of pain I caused you, but I thought I was saving you. I thought you would be safer and better off without me. Jess, you are smart and beautiful and you deserve better than a cocky Drexian like me." I sucked in a shaky breath. "I hope you will accept me anyway. I cannot imagine my life without you. Not now. Not ever. I do not want anyone but you, and that will never change."

She swiped at her eyes. "You admit that everything was your fault?"

"Completely."

"And you admit that you have been a word-class jerk?"

"I do."

"And you promise never to piss me off again, or I have permission to murder you in your sleep?"

I squeezed her hands, smiling at her and thinking how much like a Drexian she'd become. "I promise."

She bit her bottom lip as she stared down at me.

"I love you, *cinarra*," I said before she could tell me no. "Let me spend the rest of our days proving it."

She tipped her head back and forth, finally giving me a small smile. "Okay, I guess I love you, too, but as long as you understand that it's against my better judgment."

I stood and yanked her to me and wrapped my arms around her back so she could not escape, lifting her off her feet. "Understood."

"I still think you are a bad boy," she whispered.

"And you are my very bad good girl, "I husked before I crushed my mouth to hers.

CHAPTER
SEVENTY-TWO

Jess

"Where are you taking me?" I put a hand to the blindfold over my eyes, tempted to pull it off.

Torq grabbed my hand before I could peek. "You will see soon. Do you not trust me?"

I sighed. "I trust you." Despite all that had happened between us, I did trust him. When he'd believed I was in danger, he hadn't hesitated. And when he had been given a chance to deny me and save his status, he had chosen me. At least he had the second time, and I was learning that long memories weren't always a good thing when it came to complicated relationships with Drexians.

We had been walking for a while, but we were inside the academy. Was he taking me to his quarters? But why would I need a blindfold for a place I'd been to before? Maybe he was taking me to see the view of the sea or the peaks from a tower. But that would hardly be worthy of a blindfold.

Then the air changed from cool to moist, and my feet crunched on something that was not the hard stone floors of the academy. When had we stepped outside?

Just as I was about to tear off the blindfold, Torq untied it and swept an arm wide.

I inhaled sharply and stared at the inside of the cave under the waterfall. I spun to Torq. "How did you walk me through the woods without me knowing?" Then I realized something was missing. There was no curtain of water behind us, or the sound of it rushing into the pool.

"Because we are not outside. We are in a holo-chamber."

I inhaled the distinct scent of moisture and dirt. "It even smells like the cave."

"That took some refining, but your friend Britta was insistent that we get the smell right."

"Britta did this?" I shook my head in disbelief. "I had no idea. That girl can keep a secret."

Torq beamed. "Do you like it? I wanted to bring you back to a place that had good memories."

Admittedly, I had never had a boyfriend before, but I thought this might be the sweetest gift anyone had ever given me. "It's perfect." I threw my arms around him, and he flinched. I stepped back. "What's wrong?"

He lifted one sleeve of his T-shirt to reveal a freshly tattooed pair of blades on his shoulder.

"You got the Blade insignia on your arm?"

"Jaxon did it for me before he left." He puffed out his chest. "He and Kann said I'm a true Blade now."

"I think you always were."

He nodded. "I've never belonged like this before. It feels pretty great."

"I feel the same way about Assassins and my fellow female cadets." Then a thought hit me. "Wait, did you tell Britta why you wanted to recreate the cave?"

Torq closed the distance between us and circled his hands around my waist. "I have never told anyone about that night. I told your friend that it was a special place, and she told me she did not need to know more than that."

That sounded like my Iron friend. Always the pragmatist, and apparently, also a skilled holo-designer. My gaze snagged on something that hadn't been in the cave before "I don't remember this in the cave."

Torq swiveled his head to follow my gaze and let out a low laugh when he spotted the furs neatly spread out with an ice bucket chilling a bottle of wine and two glasses. "You friend must have suspected my intentions."

I wanted to tell him that most guys had only a handful of intentions and would have fingers left over, so it wasn't a stretch for Britta to imagine that Torq's request for a holo-design might have something to do with seduction. Especially since we'd been inseparable from the moment he'd kissed me in the main hall and Morgan had walked from the banquet hall, seen us, and started cheering.

Not only had the admiral seen it all play out, but Torq had not wanted to keep any more secrets. We'd gotten official approval to date, which wasn't tough since we were in different schools and were both cadets well past the age of consent on either planet. Morgan had given me a hard time about not telling her all the dirt earlier, but she'd gotten over it in about sixty seconds. After she'd threatened to castrate Torq if he ever hurt me again.

"Shall we pour the wine?" I asked, suddenly eager for some liquid courage. The last time we'd been in the cave it had been dark, and I had believed that it was the last time I'd ever be with Torq. I'd let go of all my inhibitions, but now that we were back in the cave, I felt unexpected twinges of shyness.

Torq's mouth curved into a crooked smile, but he released my waist and took my hand to lead me to the furs. I sat while he plucked the bottle from the bucket, drops of icy water dripping from it as he poured the pale-pink liquid into the glasses. Then he eyed the label. "Your friend is not as serious as she appears."

I knew that Britta could be wild and funny, but most of the academy saw her serious, studious side. I picked up my glass. "Why?"

Torq joined me on the blanket, lifted his glass, and clinked it against mine. "Because this is Palaxian Pleasure Tonic."

I took a sip, surprised by how sweet and fruity it was, and by the warmth that instantly spread down to my fingers and bubbled in my chest. "What does Palaxian Pleasure Tonic do?"

He downed the rest of his drink in a single gulp. "Illumination off." The lights flicked off and we were in familiar darkness. I felt the heat of his body as he leaned over and found the back of my head with one hand, tangling his fingers in my hair and nipping my ear before whispering into it. "Why don't I show you?"

CHAPTER
SEVENTY-THREE

Vyk

I stood at my desk, leaning my hands on either side of a report and scowling. The mission into Kronock territory would not be easy. Not since the enemy had obtained some of our technology and had developed even more of their own. Not that there were reports of another, distinct threat from an alien swarm. But it had to be done. The human pilot must be saved.

My top lip curled at the thought of human females. I had hoped that I would never have to encounter them again. I had hoped that spending a career in Inferno Force and battling the galaxy's fiercest foe would have ensured that I stayed far from the blue planet and their mercurial females. I had thought I would be safe from the memories of the female who had rejected me.

Focusing on the report spread in front of me, I tried to

brush aside memories of the tribute bride who had chosen not to accept me as her mate. It had been long ago, and I had been a different Drexian.

I scraped a hand down my short beard, knowing that the silver in it was proof that I was no longer the idealistic, romantic warrior I had once been. I had been so young when I had arrived on the tribute bride space station and met my intended bride, only to be informed that she had chosen not to be with me. She had chosen to live alone on the station with other females who rejected their Drexian mates. She had chosen life as a reject instead of a life with me. Even now, the faint memories stung like a sharp blade sliding stealthily into my heart.

"It is done." I shook my head and banished the lingering thoughts of the past from my mind. They did me no good and stirred up my bitterness. Everyone at the academy already believed me to be bitter and cruel enough.

A pounding on my door made me glance up. Was Tivek summoning me to my meeting with the admiral early? "It is open. Come."

The steel door slid open, but it was not the admiral's adjunct.

"What the hell do you think you're doing?" The human Strategy instructor stormed into my office with her golden hair swinging. She stopped on the other side of my desk and glared at me.

I returned her gaze, trying to control my own heart rate as her blue eyes flashed and made her even more stunning. "I am reviewing a report on—"

"I mean, what are you doing with monsters still in the dungeons? I heard what happened down there when you caught the Blade cadet. I know there is still at least one beast in the dungeons."

I took a breath to steady myself. "One of the beasts survived the maze. We have not been able to return it to its planet yet."

She blinked at me long and slow. "So, you're keeping it stored under an academy filled with cadets after many of them almost died defending themselves against monsters in the maze?"

"For now." I crossed my arms over my chest to keep my hands from doing something I would regret.

Fiona heaved in a breath. "Listen, I know you don't like me. I know you don't like any human. That's fine. I don't care. But if you think I'm going to stand by and let you put any cadets at risk, you can think again."

"I do not dislike you," I managed to say between gritted teeth.

She barked out a laugh. "You don't have to like me but do me the favor of not lying to me. I hate lying."

I clenched my teeth even harder to keep myself from telling her that far from disliking her, I could not stop thinking about her. Since the moment I had met her, the human with the wavy, blonde hair and sharp tongue had occupied my thoughts and tormented my dreams.

I hated that I had fallen for another human who did not want me, and I hated that she insisted on putting herself in danger by coming to the Drexian Academy, and then by volunteering to join the rescue mission into Kronock territory. She was the reason I had joined the effort, and she was the reason I had been poring over reports. I might not be able to have her, but I could not lose her. "I will not lie to you."

Fiona narrowed her gaze at me for a beat. "Everyone else may have forgiven you and decided to trust you, but I don't." She pointed a finger at me as she backed up. "I will be watching you, Commander."

Then she stomped out, leaving me with an erratic pulse and a swelling cock. *Grekking* hell. When would I be rid of my fantasies about the human who despised me?

I raked a hand roughly down my short beard, my fingers scraping both cheeks. "And I will be watching you, Captain."

EPILOGUE

Sasha eyed the prisoner who'd been dumped into the cell next to hers. The light was so dim she could barely make out details of his face, but she could tell that he was big and rippled with muscles covered in dark ink. His lack of shirt helped with that. And he had bumps running the length of his spine, which meant one thing.

"Are you Drexian?"

He stood to face her, dark scruff covering his cheeks as they twitched up into a half grin. His eyes flashed an inhuman shade of gold that reminded her of a wild cat. "Even better, beautiful. I'm Inferno Force."

Sasha knew about Inferno Force. Everyone on Earth knew about the elite Drexian fighters who were rough around the edges and very lethal. What she didn't know was why one was in a Kronock prison with her. "What's a member of Inferno Force doing here?"

The brawny Drexian brushed his arms and ran a hand through his short hair. "Looking for you, sweetheart."

She bristled at him calling her sweetheart, but she was too

intrigued by his claim to tell him that she was no one's sweet-heart. "If this is some attempt to charm me, you can save your breath. This is not some alien cantina, and you're not going to get lucky. In case you haven't noticed, we're locked up."

He chuckled again, the sound low and warm and sending unwanted heat sliding down her spine. "I have noticed, but I'm not here to seduce you." His gaze drifted down her body and then lazily wandered back up. "Not that I would mind that once I get you out."

Sasha tossed her head impatiently. This guy was either the biggest con artist in the universe, or he was delusional. "What are you talking about?"

He walked slowly toward the iron bars between them, his gait loose and relaxed, as if he was on a leisurely prowl. "Is your name Sasha? Sasha Bowman?"

Her heart tripped in her chest, and for the first time since the pilot been thrown into the dank, fetid prison, hope stirred within her. She might have kept herself sane by convincing herself that she would escape and kill every Kronock in her path, but that had been more of a ruse to keep herself from falling into despair. As much as she wanted to convince herself that she could escape or that she would be rescued, that faith had dimmed as the days had passed.

Sasha stared at the Drexian who had said her name, a name she hadn't heard once since she'd ejected from her fighter jet during the battle over Earth. "How do you know who I am?"

He curled his hands around the bars and leaned forward. "I told you, beautiful, I'm here to rescue you."

She gave her head a brusque shake and her long, dark hair swung around her face. Was she going mad? Had she imagined this gorgeous, gruff Drexian so he could tell her exactly what she needed to hear? Had her mind finally snapped and started feeding her delusions? "I'm going crazy. No one knows I'm here. No one is coming for me. You're the result of my desperate imagination. You aren't really here." Her voice cracked as she reached for the bars, the cool metal grounding her as she gripped them. "You aren't real."

She closed her eyes, squeezing them as she felt herself break from the inside out. She'd been holding it all together by channeling her fear into rage, but she could no longer suppress the despair she felt at the prospect of living the rest of her life in captivity. It had already driven her mad. Of course, it had. No one could be left alone in such squalor without cracking.

"At least my brain decided to give me a hot hallucination," she murmured. "I should be grateful for that." She opened her eyes and managed a shaky breath. "You're just my type, too. Big, dark, and a little dangerous looking. If we met in a bar, you would definitely get lucky."

His grin widened. "I'm glad to hear it." He shifted his hands, so they wrapped around hers on the bars. "But I'm not a hallucination, beautiful. I'm as real as you are, and I'm here because I was looking for you."

Sasha gazed at his hands on top of hers. They were warm and calloused, and nothing like any hallucination she'd ever experienced. Her pulse quickened. "You aren't in my mind?"

"I hope to stay in your mind long after I break you out, but I am as real as you are." He squeezed her hands beneath his, and she sucked in a quick breath.

If he was real, then she'd just told her Drexian rescuer that he was her type and that she thought he was hot. She snatched her hands from under his, still not quite able to believe that any of this was actually happening. "How? I've been here for so long. I was sure that I was presumed dead."

He kept his hands on the bars as he leaned into them and let his arms bend so that he hung from them. "You were. It took retrieving an enemy ship and decoding some data for us to realize that the Kronock took prisoners during the battle. Until now, we did not know they possessed the technology to snatch pilots from exploding ships."

Her stomach did an uncomfortable flip as she remembered the violent, chaotic battle, but she forced herself to push those memories aside as more important thoughts surfaced in her mind. "My family? Does my family know I'm alive?"

"They do." He straightened. "Your sister is the one working closely with the Drexian forces to find you. She has a decent number of Drexian Academy cadets working on the mission with her."

Sasha's heart swelled at this, then she cocked her head to one side. "The Drexian Academy?"

"Lieutenant Bowman is one of the newest flight instructors at the academy." He winked through the darkness. "I hear she's a ballbuster."

A laugh escaped Sasha's lips, the first laugh since she'd arrived in the Kronock jail. "Then I taught her well." She narrowed her eyes at the Drexian. "Let's say I believe that you're real, and you're part of the rescue mission headed up by my sister. Why are you alone? Where's the rest of the team?"

He blew out a breath. "I was one of the scouts sent out to narrow down the field of sites where you might be held. Being captured was not part of the initial plan."

Her stomach dropped. If he was in a cell with her, he hadn't been able to return to the Drexians and report about finding her. "So, you're it, and now you're a prisoner too?"

Instead of looking dismayed, the cocky Drexian smiled. "I'm right where I want to be, Sasha." He reached a hand through the bars and stroked his fingers down the side of her face, making heat stir in her core and her skin buzz with desire she had no business feeling. "I promise I will get you out, beautiful. I am looking forward to getting lucky."

~

THANK YOU FOR READING LOYALTY! To read Fiona and Vyk's steamy and stormy age gap, secret romance, be sure to grab LEGEND!

The silver fox Drexian is exactly my type. If only I didn't want to kill him.

Order LEGEND

~

JOIN THE ACADEMY! Want to take the quiz and find out if you're an Assassin, a Blade, an Iron, or a Wing (and get special initiation bonuses)? Go to the quiz> www.tanastone.com/legacy-quiz

~

This book has been edited and proofed, but typos are like little gremlins that like to sneak in when we're not looking. If you spot a typo, please report it to: tana@tanastone.com
Thank you!!

ALSO BY TANA STONE

Warriors of the Drexian Academy:

LEGACY

LOYALTY

LEGEND

OBSESSION

SECRECY

REVENGE

Inferno Force of the Drexian Warriors:

IGNITE (also available on AUDIO)

SCORCH (also available on AUDIO)

BURN (also available on AUDIO)

BLAZE (also available on AUDIO)

FLAME (also available on AUDIO)

COMBUST (also available on AUDIO)

The Tribute Brides of the Drexian Warriors Series:

TAMED (also available in AUDIO)

SEIZED (also available in AUDIO)

EXPOSED (also available in AUDIO)

RANSOMED (also available in AUDIO)

FORBIDDEN (also available in AUDIO)

BOUND (also available in AUDIO)

JINGLED (A Holiday Novella) (also in AUDIO)

CRAVED (also available in AUDIO)

STOLEN (also available in AUDIO)

SCARRED (also available in AUDIO)

The Barbarians of the Sand Planet Series:

BOUNTY (also available in AUDIO)

CAPTIVE (also available in AUDIO)

TORMENT (also available on AUDIO)

TRIBUTE (also available as AUDIO)

SAVAGE (also available in AUDIO)

CLAIM (also available on AUDIO)

CHERISH: A Holiday Baby Short (also available on AUDIO)

PRIZE (also available on AUDIO)

SECRET

RESCUE (appearing first in PETS IN SPACE #8)

ALIEN & MONSTER ONE-SHOTS:

ROGUE (also available in AUDIO)

VIXIN: STRANDED WITH AN ALIEN

SLIPPERY WHEN YETI

CHRISTMAS WITH AN ALIEN

YOOL

DAD BOD ORC

Raider Warlords of the Vandar Series:

POSSESSED (also available in AUDIO)

PLUNDERED (also available in AUDIO)

PILLAGED (also available in AUDIO)

PURSUED (also available in AUDIO)

PUNISHED (also available on AUDIO)

PROVOKED (also available in AUDIO)

PRODIGAL (also available in AUDIO)

PRISONER

PROTECTOR

PRINCE

THE SKY CLAN OF THE TAORI:

SUBMIT (also available in AUDIO)

STALK (also available on AUDIO)

SEDUCE (also available on AUDIO)

SUBDUE

STORM

All the TANA STONE books available as audiobooks!

INFERNO FORCE OF THE DREXIAN WARRIORS:

IGNITE on AUDIBLE

SCORCH on AUDIBLE

BURN on AUDIBLE

BLAZE on AUDIBLE

FLAME on AUDIBLE

RAIDER WARLORDS OF THE VANDAR:

POSSESSED on AUDIBLE

PLUNDERED on AUDIBLE

PILLAGED on AUDIBLE

PURSUED on AUDIBLE

PUNISHED on AUDIBLE

PROVOKED on AUDIBLE

BARBARIANS OF THE SAND PLANET

BOUNTY on AUDIBLE

CAPTIVE on AUDIBLE

TORMENT on AUDIBLE

TRIBUTE on AUDIBLE

SAVAGE on AUDIBLE

CLAIM on AUDIBLE

CHERISH on AUDIBLE

TRIBUTE BRIDES OF THE DREXIAN WARRIORS

TAMED on AUDIBLE

SEIZED on AUDIBLE

EXPOSED on AUDIBLE

RANSOMED on AUDIBLE

FORBIDDEN on AUDIBLE

BOUND on AUDIBLE

JINGLED on AUDIBLE

CRAVED on AUDIBLE

STOLEN on AUDIBLE

SCARRED on AUDIBLE

SKY CLAN OF THE TAORI

SUBMIT on AUDIBLE

STALK on AUDIBLE

SEDUCE on AUDIBLE

About the Author

Tana Stone is the *USA Today* bestselling sci-fi romance author who loves sexy aliens and independent heroines. Her favorite superhero is Thor (with Aquaman a close second because, well, Jason Momoa), her favorite dessert is key lime pie (okay, fine, *all* pie), and she loves Star Wars and Star Trek equally. She still laments the loss of *Firefly*.

She has one husband, two teenagers, two energetic dogs, and three neurotic cats. She sometimes wishes she could teleport to a holographic space station like the one in her tribute brides series (or maybe vacation at the oasis with the sand planet barbarians). :-)

She loves hearing from readers! Email her any questions or comments at tana@tanastone.com.

Want to hang out with Tana in her private Facebook group? Join on all the fun at: https://www.facebook.com/groups/tanastonestributes/